BLOOD ON THE SHORE

Simon McCleave is a best-selling crime novelist. His first book, *The Snowdonia Killings*, was released in January 2020 and soon became an Amazon bestseller, reaching No.1 in the UK Chart and selling over 350,000 copies. His thirteen subsequent novels in the DI Ruth Hunter Snowdonia series have all ranked in the Amazon Top 20 and he has sold over 1.5 million books worldwide. The Snowdonia based DI Ruth Hunter books are now set to be filmed as a major television series. *Blood on the Shore* is the third book in Simon's Anglesey series.

Before he was an author, Simon worked as a script editor at the BBC and a producer at Channel 4 before working as a story analyst in Los Angeles. He then became a script writer, writing on series such as *Silent Witness*, *Murder In Suburbia*, *Teachers*, *The Bill*, *EastEnders* and many more. His Channel 4 film *Out of the Game* was critically acclaimed and described as 'an unflinching portrayal of male friendship' by *Time Out*.

Simon lives in North Wales with his wife and two children.

www.simonmccleave.com

T0006860

Also by Simon McCleave:

THE ANGLESEY CRIME THRILLERS
The Dark Tide
In Too Deep

THE DI RUTH HUNTER CRIME THRILLERS
The Snowdonia Killings
The Harlech Beach Killings
The Dee Valley Killings
The Devil's Cliff Killings
The Berwyn River Killings
The White Forest Killings
The Solace Farm Killings
The Menai Bridge Killings
The Conway Harbour Killings
The River Seine Killings
The Lake Vyrnwy Killings
The Chirk Castle Killings
The Portmeirion Killings
The Llandudno Pier Killings

THE DC RUTH HUNTER MURDER CASES
Diary of a War Crime
The Razor Gang Murder
An Imitation of Darkness
This is London, SE15

To find out more visit **www.simonmccleave.com**

BLOOD
ON THE
SHORE

SIMON McCLEAVE

Published by AVON
A division of HarperCollins*Publishers*
1 London Bridge Street
London SE1 9GF

www.harpercollins.co.uk

HarperCollins*Publishers*
Macken House, 39/40 Mayor Street Upper
Dublin 1, D01 C9W8
Ireland

A Paperback Original 2023

First published in Great Britain by HarperCollins*Publishers* 2023

Copyright © Simon McCleave 2023

A catalogue copy of this book is available from the British Library.

ISBN: 978-0-00-852488-3

Typeset in Sabon LT Std by
Palimpsest Book Production Limited, Falkirk, Stirlingshire

Printed and bound in the UK using
100% Renewable Electricity at CPI Group (UK) Ltd

For Andy, Catherine, Tom and Millie x

ANGLESEY

There is a word in Welsh that has no exact translation into English – Hiraeth. It is best defined as the bond you feel with a place – a mixture of pride, homesickness and a determination to return. Most people that have visited Anglesey leave with an understanding of Hiraeth.

PROLOGUE

Friday, 25 March 2022

Out of the darkness, a sleek car came up the hill and approached a pub in the popular seaside town of Benllech. Located on the eastern coast of Anglesey, Benllech's name was derived from the Welsh word *penllech*, which meant capstone or head of the rock. The beach itself was supposedly haunted by the Steed of Brwyn, a vast black sea-going water horse. It was said to be over thirty feet in height, with a great twelve-foot arched neck and oar-like legs. Once trapped on his back, riders would become horribly entangled in his enormous mane, then be carried out to sea, where they would eventually drown and be taken on to the otherworld.

Zoey looked over from the heated passenger seat to the dark, handsome, middle-aged man driving the car. She had planned to spend the evening with him at the Fox and Grapes pub. They would drink wine and talk about travel or politics. He would tell her more about his time in the Middle East, which she found fascinating. She didn't care that he was older than her. The boys at the sixth form college she had recently attended were total morons. Immature, pathetic, parochial, they were classic examples of Gen Z males who had watched too much online porn and thus expected all women to be large-breasted and submissive. She had lost her virginity to Tom Fowles when she was sixteen at a house party. It had been three minutes of fumbling and disconnected disappointment. She knew she needed to be with an older, more experienced *man*.

As they drove past the turning to the car park, Zoey frowned at him. 'I thought we were going for a drink?'

With a reassuring smile, he reached over and patted her hand. The cuff link in his expensive-looking cobalt-blue shirt glinted for a split second. 'You know what? I thought we could walk along the beach.' He gestured to the clear night sky and the smoky moon. 'Look at that sky, Zoey. It reminds me of when I used to walk on Corniche beach in Abu Dhabi when I worked there. I will take you there one day.'

Zoey felt a little jolt of excitement as she squeezed his hand. He had big, powerful hands – but smooth. Not the hands of a manual-working man. Even though he was good-looking, it was actually his mind and life experience that really attracted her to him. Exotic, colourful and intriguing.

'A walk on the beach sounds good to me,' she replied, trying to sound casual. She certainly had no burning desire to sit in a pub under the scrutiny of locals. She knew what they would be thinking. What was a girl of her age doing with a man old enough to be her father? She was just glad to be out of the home she shared with her mum, Bethan, and her mum's creepy partner, Alun. Zoey's father had run off with his best friend's wife when Zoey was about four and resettled in Devon. She reluctantly saw him once a year, at Christmas. He would give her some kind of gift voucher, an awkward hug and then disappear again for twelve months. It had hurt and angered her when she was younger. Now she just wished she didn't have to go through the motions. An uncomfortable charade of being remotely interested in seeing her father.

Pulling out a melon-flavoured vape, Zoey took a long drag, buzzed down the window and blew the vapour outside. She watched as the wind grabbed the white mist and flung it away with a dramatic twist, like a vanishing ghost. She then caught the scent of the sea through the melon. Thick and salty. It reminded her of childhood days eating ice-creams when her parents were still together. It felt painful to remember the innocent joy before her father had abandoned them. When he eventually died, she promised herself that she wouldn't even attend his funeral.

She glanced around the interior of the car. It was immaculate. It smelled of pine and lemon. That was another advantage of 'seeing' an older man. Teenage boys' personal hygiene and tidiness were appalling. Spotting a packet of menthol chewing gum, she picked it up and waved it. 'Mind if I . . .'

'Help yourself,' he said with a winning smile as they pulled into the empty car park on the seafront.

She popped the chewing gum into her mouth and squeezed it with her back teeth, enjoying the crack of its hard shell and then its soft, chewy centre. If she was going to kiss him, she wanted her breath to be minty. 'I like your car,' she remarked and then immediately wondered if the comment had made her sound young, even infantile.

'Actually, it's my sister's,' he replied as they parked facing the beach. He turned off the ignition with a wry smile. 'Mine's tidy, but not this tidy.'

'Showroom tidy,' Zoey quipped, content that she had said something pithy.

'Exactly,' he laughed. 'Showroom tidy. I like that.'

Glancing up at the enormous dark sky, Zoey had a warm glow inside. She saw that the soft edges of the vanilla moon had now hardened. 'It's beautiful here,' she muttered under her breath, as if talking to herself.

'Yes, it really is,' he said, gazing up. 'Why do you think I brought you here.'

For a second, their eyes met. His soft brown eyes rested on her casually, enveloping her with a twinkle of attraction.

Her pulse quickened with excitement. She wondered what he saw in her. Someone so young and inexperienced in life. She put the thought out of her mind. She didn't care.

Zoey looked out from the car at the deserted beach, which swept away to the left and right, as far as the eye could see. It was a shame they hadn't brought something to drink. She pictured it in her mind: a romantic, moonlit walk on the beach, the roaring wind, swigging from a bottle of red wine, talking and laughing. It felt perfect.

'Come on, let's go,' he suggested brightly as he opened his door.

'Okay.' Zoey nodded as she got out. The wind picked up noisily, biting into her face and ears and swirling her hair. She could just about hear the gentle hissing of the waves whooshing onto the sand in the distance. Shivering, she wrapped her arms around herself.

'Cold?' he asked gently, putting a reassuring hand on her shoulder.

'Yeah.' She nodded. 'I am a bit.'

'Think there's a few hoodies and coats in here.' He gestured to the boot of the car and disappeared around the back. 'I'll see if I can find one to fit you.'

Very chivalrous, she thought as she smiled to herself. *I could get used to this.*

Zoey glanced at her own reflection in the glass of the windscreen. She looked like her mum. They shared the same strong jawline and high cheekbones, the same arch to their eyebrows that most people took for aloofness.

For a moment, she allowed herself to think of how her life might turn out in the next few years. She had so many plans, giddy plans, that swirled in the mists of her exciting future. Where she might live. Manchester, London or even Sydney. She so desperately wanted to travel and see the world. She had saved over a thousand pounds. When she had two thousand, she would be off. She imagined what her friends would be like in the future. Intelligent, creative types. Maybe they'd work in the media or be filmmakers or musicians. That's what she wanted. To work in something creative. Secretly, she wanted to be a writer. Novels, scripts, it didn't matter. A storyteller who would touch people's lives and say something profound about the world they lived in. She would bid Anglesey farewell and not return. It had never been a place of warm, tender memories. It was provincial, insular and suffocating. It might have been the island of her birth but it would never be a place that she would return to once she had left.

The wind seemed to suddenly bring the sound of breaking waves with it – like the abrupt sound of shattering glass. It unnerved her for a moment. She turned to look at the shoreline to the east. Twinkling lights of houses and streetlights as if they had been scattered carelessly. The sea's surface looked silky under the moonlight.

Suddenly a gull cawed overhead, making her jump.

Jesus!

Over to the west, an almost imperceptible spot of light on the horizon. She assumed it was a ship of some sort.

She sensed his presence behind her but didn't turn. Instead she pointed and asked, 'Do you think that's a ship out there, or is it a trick of the light?'

He didn't say anything.

She found herself hoping that he would wrap his arms around her.

Silence.

CRACK!

Suddenly, Zoey felt something smash hard against the back of her skull.

A horrible blackness.

She staggered. A blinding eruption of pain.

Shock. Terror. Bewilderment.

What just happened?

Her balance was off. Trying to gasp for breath, she tasted the metal in her teeth. Her ears rang with a piercing white noise.

What the . . .?

As she regained her footing, she managed to turn around to see that he was now wearing leather gloves and holding a large, metallic mallet with a wooden handle.

Oh my God!

'Bitch!' he hissed through his teeth. His nostrils flared and mouth twisted with utter fury, as though he was possessed.

'What . . . are . . . you doing?' she mumbled in an utter daze, hardly able to speak or get her breath.

His unblinking eyes were now dark and dead.

In that moment, she realised he was going to kill her.

Zoey felt her throat clench and she tried to swallow. The hair on the back of her neck prickled to attention.

Panic.

He swung the mallet again. 'You asked for this, you bitch!'

She managed to jump backwards and the mallet glanced off her shoulder blade, spinning her around.

A searing pain across the top of her back.

Through her blurred vision, she managed to spot that he was slightly off balance. She turned and sprinted for her life.

Please God, don't let him kill me. Please.

The sound of her shoes slapped against the road and then the pavement as she thundered towards the beach.

'Stay there!' His voice roared like a sergeant major's.

Her legs were heavy and unsteady, as if she were drunk.

Throwing herself over the blue metal rails that separated the beach from the roadside, she hit the wet sand on the other side, lost her balance and fell into the sand.

Oh God, Oh God.

Scrambling with everything she had, she struggled to her feet, paralysed with overwhelming terror. Desperate. A sickening fear that throttled her very being.

Run. Just run!

Trying to keep upright, she ran.

She opened her mouth to scream but the thick sea air felt like cotton in her throat.

Crying, panting and sobbing.

Please God . . .

The delicate bones in her ankles felt like they were going to snap as she ploughed on.

She could hear him behind her.

No, no, no . . .

Grunting, panting, muttering under his breath as he ran.

Her heart was thumping, about to explode out of her chest.

She was going to lose control of her bladder.

Oh God, no, no.

A whimper as she sensed that he had nearly caught up with her.

Keep going, Zoey. Don't let him do this to you. Just run.

She turned to look.

His face was distorted by a frenzied mouth. His lips were moving, but no sound emerged from them.

His hand shot out like a whip. He grabbed her hair and yanked her backwards. Fingers gripping her skull like a vice, he slammed her down into the sand.

The wind was crushed out of her.

She tried to suck in air. Unable to breathe.

Out the corner of her eye, the mallet loomed into view.

CRACK!

He smashed it against her temple.

A sickening, blinding wave of pain and stupefying confusion.

She gasped.

Please, no.

'You think you can tease me like that, do you?'

The palm of his other hand crushed her nose so hard that she thought it might snap.

'Nothing to say?' he seethed.

Zoey was fighting to breathe and stay conscious.

She opened her mouth, but she had no breath to form a scream. Pain ripped through her head.

She grabbed at his thick wrist as she blindly kicked out at him.

'No, no, no,' she whispered, shaking her head desperately.

Another scream that was trapped inside by utter panic.

Then tears filled her eyes and slid down her face. A dark, crushing acceptance.

It was over.

This was it.

She had nothing. No fight left.

Was this the moment when some passer-by, who had spotted what was happening from the road, intervened? Came over, yelling, and saved her? Like on those TV dramas that she watched.

Nothing.

Silence.

His gloved hands moved towards her throat.

She refused to look at him. Refused to make any eye-contact. She wouldn't give him the satisfaction of seeing the fear in her eyes. It would be her little victory.

Glancing up at the clear sky, she saw the patterns of stars so many millions of miles away.

It was fitting that the infinite universe was the last thing she saw as her own eternal darkness came.

CHAPTER 1

Beaumaris, Anglesey
Five hours later

Wisps of mist hung motionless above the surface of the sea as if the clouds had dropped from the early morning sky and settled there instead. Up above, the night was giving way to hues of blue as first violet and then apricot shades of light appeared on the horizon to the east of Beaumaris, a small seaside town on the south coast of Anglesey. Beaumaris was the place chosen by Edward I in 1294 for the last of his 'iron ring' of castles, which were constructed to tame the Welsh and finally make the country part of England. It wasn't for another one hundred and fifty years, when the last crowned King of Wales, Owain Glyndwr, fought against English rule, that Wales achieved another period of independence. It might have been six hundred years later, but there were still many on the island that remained suspicious of the 'bloody English'.

The Isle of Anglesey was home to Detective Inspector Laura Hart – who wasn't English but, having spent many years working in Manchester and only recently returned to Wales, sometimes felt like an outsider. She stretched out her arms and took in a long, deep breath of the salty air. Spring was coming but it was still cold. She didn't care. Cold-water swimming before work was her *thing*. Wild swimming. Time to herself. Behind her on the sand, beside a navy-coloured towel and hoodie, sat her beautiful caramel-and-white Bernese mountain dog, Elvis. His chin rested on the sand as he watched her with his big chestnut eyes that always seemed to have a trace of sadness.

There was a sudden shift in the wind or the tide, or both. Laura looked to see if it was the wake of some passing ship out in the strait but there was nothing. The sound of several waves breaking in quick succession, like hard smacks against human skin, unsettled her. And then, just as suddenly, the waves were as before, gently swishing and raking softly across the wet sand.

It had been nearly four years since Laura had returned home to the place of her birth just off the North Wales coast with her children, Rosie, eighteen years old, and Jake, twelve years old. Four years since that horrific day in Manchester that had turned all their lives upside down. The day that her husband Sam had been so cruelly taken away from her. Laura had managed to rebuild her life in a ramshackle house that she had now decorated and fixed, just outside the picturesque town of Beaumaris.

Returning home had been both comforting and challenging. Laura had always been *the one that left the island*. When returning at Christmas, the main question was always, *What's it like over in the big city?* It might have been the twenty-first century but most of her classmates had stayed on the island, married young and then had kids. She knew there was always a smug sense of comeuppance when an islander returned after time away. As if they hadn't been able to hack life on the mainland. Of course, Laura had been through such intense trauma with Sam's death, the overwhelming response had been nothing but supportive and compassionate. But being an islander meant people also remembered you, and often had preconceived ideas as to what kind of person you were, based on vague memories from decades earlier.

Laura looked out at the sea before her. The Menai Strait. A strip of water that separated the island from the Welsh mainland. She remembered when a few years earlier, a local lobster diver had found an old anchor on the seabed. It belonged to a Roman landing craft and dated back to the invasion of Anglesey in AD76. It had sat there untouched for nearly two thousand years.

At this point, the coast of Gwynedd on the Welsh mainland was about three and half miles away. Behind that, the dark, looming contours of the Snowdonia mountain range stood commandingly, like an ancient protective barrier.

Laura glanced down at her goose-fleshed thighs and tingled from the exciting prospect of hitting the icy water any second now. It was a morning ritual.

Come on, Laura, let's do this.

She broke into a hop, skip and run, the balls of her feet padding against the wet sand. Icy water hit her shins, then splashed against her thighs and tummy. She winced. After another long step, the water was now deep enough for her to arch her back and dive in.

Here we go.

WHOOSH.

For a few seconds, she was under the surface of the freezing sea. Silent. Nerve endings tingling like they were on fire. An electrical rush of the senses that was intoxicating and overwhelming.

For a moment, it was a swirling mixture of pain and pleasure.

And then a glorious silence as she drifted under the surface. The sounds of the water were now indistinct, quietly resonating in a frequency dictated by the sea. A shapeless echo.

Breaking up through the surface of the ocean, she gasped, reborn. Tension, anxiety and lethargy had been blasted from her body like coal from a stubborn underground seam.

Wow, gets me every time, she thought, aware that her face now wore a smile of relief.

For whatever reason – and she had no desire to analyse it – these early cold-water swims gave her a perspective and gratitude for life like nothing else. It was as if a light bulb clicked on to show her what she had in her life. Healthy happy kids, nice house, good job and a blossoming relationship with Gareth. Actually, Detective Inspector Gareth Williams, who was in charge of Beaumaris Crime Investigation Department (CID) and therefore her boss. Laura had recently seen a film where the world was only seconds from ending. A character turned to the others and said very calmly, *We really did have everything, didn't we?* When she thought about it, she knew exactly what he meant.

'What are you looking so smug about?' asked a voice behind her, breaking her train of thought.

It was Sam.

She felt a twinge of guilt. Her self-satisfied smile had been a recognition of what she had in her life. A life that he was no longer part of.

Her late husband had been appearing as a figment of her vivid imagination ever since his death. She assumed it was her way of coping with her loss. However, Laura was aware that while she allowed Sam to continue to appear and conversed with him, she wasn't truly letting go of him and moving on with her life.

'I wasn't smirking,' she protested. 'My morning swim makes me happy, that's all. You know that.'

Sam stood and pushed the black hair back off his face. His twinkly blue eyes looked over at her and caught her off-guard. A surging wrench of loss settled deep inside her.

12

'I know you're lying,' he said with a wry smile. 'Cohabiting with DI Dickhead still okay?'

Even though Gareth still had his house in Beaumaris, he had spent increasing amounts of time at Laura's home, much to her daughter Rosie's irritation.

'We're not *cohabiting*,' she replied defensively. It was easier to be angry with Sam than to remember how attractive and humorous he had been.

'If you say so,' Sam teased her with a shrug. 'I know that Rosie is thrilled.' She bristled as she recalled his ability to get under her skin with a carefully worded remark. He could turn stinging sarcasm into an art form.

'A little spiky this morning, aren't we?' she asked, raising an eyebrow.

There were a few seconds of silence.

The wind skimmed off the water's surface and cut into Laura's face.

'You know what today is, don't you?' Sam asked as he swished onto his back in the water and kicked his feet.

Laura shook her head. 'No idea.'

'The 26th March,' Sam explained as if she should know what he was referring to.

Laura frowned. 'Which is . . .?'

Sam stopped floating and shook his head slowly in mock disbelief. 'Twenty-one years since our first official date.'

'Yes, of course.' Laura trawled her memory.

'I'm hurt that you didn't remember.'

'No, you're not,' Laura snorted and then pulled a face as she recalled the evening. 'And you took me to see Coldplay so it's not an evening I particularly want to remember.'

'Not this again.' Sam sighed. 'What the hell is wrong with Coldplay?'

'Everything.'

'You played 'Fix You' at my funeral.'

'You told me that's what you wanted,' she snapped.

'I did. And there wasn't a dry eye in the church.'

Laura wanted to say that she had found the song mawkish and sentimental, but that didn't seem fair.

'Coldplay are a band for people who don't like music,' Laura stated. 'They're the Dire Straits for Generation X.'

'Rubbish,' Sam protested. '*Parachutes* was a great album.'

'But it was downhill from there,' Laura chortled, enjoying winding Sam up. 'Public schoolboys with trite stadium anthems.'

Sam laughed and held up his hands in mock surrender. 'Okay, okay. I give up. You win. I'll never take you to a Coldplay concert again.'

They looked at each other for a few seconds with all the terrible irony of Sam's comment. *No, you won't*, Laura thought, feeling suddenly choked.

'I've got to go,' Laura said, gesturing to the beach.

As she reached her towel and hoodie, she got a sudden flash of the moment that Sam had died. The explosion and a thunderous noise that had split the air. The flashback startled her. She knew that it was part of the PTSD that she had suffered from ever since.

On that day in August 2018, intelligence from a CHIS – a covert human intelligence source, or informant – had revealed that a powerful Manchester drugs gang, the Fallowfield Hill Gang, were using a disused warehouse on the Central Park Trading Estate in West Manchester as a drug factory, manufacturing crack cocaine and heroin. Laura remembered the tension as the armed raid she was on descended into a gun battle. Then to her horror, Laura learned that her husband, Sam, a uniformed police officer, and his patrol partner, Louise McDonald, had been called earlier to a report of suspicious activity at the warehouse and had subsequently been taken hostage. They were inside.

Even though Laura was the top hostage negotiator in the Manchester Met, she just couldn't make any progress in securing Sam and Louise's release. She felt so incredibly guilty and helpless at the time.

Instead, she'd had to watch in total panic as armed units stormed the building to rescue them. However, members of the Fallowfield Hill Gang had rigged explosives and, to Laura's utter horror, the warehouse was blown to pieces. She felt like her insides had been ripped out as she realised that Sam and Louise had been killed instantly in the terrifying explosion. It was the day her life was torn apart. She'd had constant nightmares about it ever since.

Laura swore she'd get to the bottom of why Sam had died that day. She and Pete weren't satisfied with the Independent Office for Police Conduct (IOPC)'s inquiry. DCI Pete Marsons was a close friend of Laura – they'd trained together. He had also been one of Sam's closest friends. Pete had been at Laura's side during the operation on 12 August 2018 in which Sam had died. He'd been a great support to her and the kids ever since.

They thought the IOPC inquiry left too many unanswered questions. How did the gang know the warehouse was going to be raided, for starters? Laura and Pete suspected the gang had someone on the inside in the GMP.

Taking the towel from the sand, Laura rubbed her wet hair.

'You look distracted,' Sam observed, 'which is not surprising.'

'Yeah, it's all hands to the pump.'

Sam gave her a meaningful look. 'Any closer to finding a suspect?'

Laura shook her head. 'I wish.'

Sam locked eyes with her for a moment. 'Make sure Rosie comes straight home and doesn't go anywhere.'

Laura wanted to point out that she was more than capable of keeping Rosie safe. But she didn't want to argue.

'I will,' Laura promised. 'There's a lot of women on the island who are too scared to do anything at the moment.'

'I'm not surprised,' Sam said.

'I've got to go, Sam.'

'Maybe see you later?'

'Maybe.'

'Laura?'

She turned to look at him.

'Be careful.'

'Yeah,' she said as she took her hoodie from the beach.

Laura's visions of him weren't usually so full of warning – but she knew exactly why he had been this time. For the first time in two thousand years, Anglesey had its very own serial killer.

HIM

The early morning blushed flamingo pink across the sky, falling into a deep blue as the sea crept up towards the horizon. A swathe of tawny, rosy light lit up his face as he walked across the dunes high up on Beaumaris beach. The sea breeze seemed even fresher today, if that was possible, and he enjoyed its coldness pressing on his face, pushing him along against his back. But it wasn't the sea or the breeze, or the soft sand beneath his feet that was making him smile today.

In his mind's eye, he saw her face.

Zoey, Zoey, Zoey.

It was that look of utter terror in her eyes that excited him so much.

In the distance, he spotted a woman walking out of the sea. He watched as she dried herself with a towel, pulled on a hoodie and wandered up the dunes with an enormous dog in tow.

Nearby, just where the tide had reached its limit several hours earlier, two black, bloated crows fought over the bloody entrails of a fish carcass. It was probably a bass. They flapped, screeched and pecked at each other. Scavengers. They lacked any dignity, any restraint or finesse as creatures.

He watched the woman again as she walked away from the beach. Something about her reminded him of his mother. His *glorious, glorious* mother, he thought with a dark irony. She had been a bitch. A cold, loathsome, destructive bitch. She had had her uses – genetically. He had got his razor-sharp intellect from her. She was an over-achiever. But the outpouring of negative disappointment and criticism that came to him on a daily basis as a child had been unbearable. Sometimes it had escalated into violence. Hard cuffs around the back of the head. Beatings with a belt buckle. Even days without food. Maybe that was why he was so introverted as a teenager. He had found it almost impossible to make friends, let alone talk to girls. His shyness had been excruciating. He would lie to his mother that he was going to a friend's home and roam the dark streets of their village alone. He could spend hours just watching people in their homes, especially young women. He loved to live undetected in the darkness and the shadows. Sometimes he would trawl through their rubbish bins looking for some kind of trinket to take home with him. He loved to collect tissue paper with lipstick marks, discarded make-up and even used tampons.

By his late teens, he had begun to follow teenage girls while remaining undetected. Wearing black clothes and soundless shoes, he turned his invisible stalking into an art form. But he became aware, as the months went on, that he was getting less and less of a thrill from it. He needed to up the stakes. He needed something more.

And then one night, instead of keeping out of sight, he made his presence known to the girl he was following. She had turned to see him wearing a mask, screamed and ran. He had pursued her for less than thirty seconds before stopping but the sheer delight of having scared her half to death was deliciously addictive.

He was hooked.

CHAPTER 2

Gareth sipped at his coffee before realising that it was now unpalatably cold. He wiped the coffee foam from his top lip and sat back with a deep sigh. His feet were crossed and up on his desk. He ran his hand over his shaved head and then squeezed the back of his neck. The muscles across the top of his shoulders and his back were tight. He couldn't remember a time when the pressure on him and Beaumaris CID had been greater.

Anglesey was an island in shock. It was also an island full of fear. Two young women had been murdered on the island in the past two months. Their deaths had been brutal and violent. Severe blows to the head, strangulation and sexual assault postmortem. Their bodies had then been partially buried on two different beaches to the south of the island with their heads exposed. There was no doubt that it had been the same killer. Two women had also gone missing at the end of 2021, so a few months before, and concern for them was growing. There was nothing suspicious in their lives that could explain why they had vanished. In fact, the only thing they had in common was their age and their appearance: late teens or early twenties, brunette and brown eyes.

Beaumaris CID were leading the investigation and Gareth had been appointed SIO – senior investigating officer. He was now managing a team of over fifteen detectives as well as liaising with the other police stations on the island and North Wales police across on the mainland.

Since a national tabloid had run a story two weeks ago with the headline *Search continues for missing women and The Anglesey Ripper*, the pressure on Gareth to get results had intensified significantly. Most of the major UK newspapers, television and radio had now run stories about the murders and disappearances – and all of them had dubbed the killer 'The Anglesey Ripper'. There had been several comparisons with Peter Sutcliffe's reign of terror in the late 1980s. The Yorkshire Ripper had murdered thirteen women between 1975 and 1980. Gareth knew that every day that went past when they didn't find the killer was another day when there might be another victim. And the thought of that weighed heavily on him.

Glancing down to look at his watch, he saw that he had forgotten to put it on that morning. It was a sign that his mind was elsewhere. He had left Laura's home at 5.30 a.m., returned home, showered and changed into clean clothes. He and Laura had finally got their relationship on an even keel, after a series of false starts. They had also got past the fact that Gareth had slept with his ex-wife Nell six months ago. It was a stupid mistake and he was glad that Laura had forgiven him.

However, there was now another issue. Laura's eighteen-year-old daughter Rosie had made her feelings about their relationship very clear. Despite Laura's reassurances that Gareth could never replace Rosie's father Sam, she had chosen to ignore Gareth's presence in the home in recent weeks. It was making life uncomfortable. He had started to dread walking into a room where Rosie was sitting for fear of the little looks, huffs or what were these days called *micro-aggressions*.

Looking down, Gareth saw that his trousers were a little tight around his stomach. He had always prided himself on keeping himself trim and having a 32-inch waist. Now he was working long hours on the murder cases and splitting his time between Laura's home and his, he was grabbing snacks as he went.

Come on, mate, let's keep it together, he thought, trying to rally himself for the day. In the words of the ex-captain of his least favourite football team, Steven Gerrard, *We go again!*

Swinging his legs from his untidy desk, he stood up. He had slight pins and needles in his left foot and he squeezed his toes until the sensation ceased. He wandered out of his Detective Inspector's office and into the main CID office. It smelled freshly hoovered and cleaned. By the end of the day it would be thick with the smell of coffee and sweat.

A couple of detectives were already in and hard at work. Most of the CID team would be in before eight a.m. and often they would stay beyond ten p.m. unless he told them to get an early night. There was a powerful collective zeal among his officers to find the killer before another innocent woman was murdered. He couldn't have been prouder to call them his team. They deserved – and needed – a break-through in the case.

He walked slowly over to a series of scene boards that stood at the far end of the office. They were covered in writing, photographs, maps and other pieces of evidence. Red pins on a map of Anglesey showed where the women had been found or went missing.

To the right, a photograph of an attractive woman in her early twenties was pinned at the centre. Her bright, smiling face beamed at him out of the dark strands of hair that curled and fell onto her shoulders. Her deep chestnut eyes had a twinkle in them, as if she had just heard a joke. There was a delicate tattoo of a purple flower on the back of her right hand.

Caitlin May Thomas. Born 23 May 2000.

Gareth studied her image for a few seconds. So full of life. So blissfully unaware of the horrific, devastating and untimely way it would end. The hair on his neck stood and prickled, making him shiver for a moment. On a place like Anglesey, it was impossible to keep subjective and removed in an investigation. He didn't want to. Feeling involved kept him sharp and motivated.

Caitlin had been a primary school teacher from Llanddona who still lived with her parents. Gareth knew her uncle, Jim Gover. They'd played cricket together when Gareth was in his twenties. Jim was an incredible spin bowler, and ran a local stable.

On 22 January 2022, Caitlin had told her parents that she was going out for a drink with a friend. They suspected that it was a man but she was old enough for them not to worry or to pry. Someone picked her up at 8.15 p.m. and that was the last time they ever saw her.

At six thirty the following morning, Caitlin's body had been found on Llanddona beach by a man walking his dog. She had been buried in the sand up to her neck so that all that was visible was her head. It had been like the terrible images Gareth had seen of women who had been stoned to death. The very thought of it made him shudder.

Taking two steps to the left, Gareth looked at the second victim. Again, she was in her early twenties, with brunette hair and dark brown eyes. Her skin was olive, almost Mediterranean looking.

Gemma Ramsey. Born 30 May 1999.

The photograph showed Gemma on a night out. She was holding a dark red cocktail with a straw and grinning at

22

the camera. There was an array of bangles and bracelets on her wrists. Gemma had worked in a local pub, the Crown, and lived in a small flat above. She had been saving for a trip to Australia to visit her sister and brother-in-law in Perth.

On 3 March 2022, Gemma had the night off. She told friends she had a date with a man. She had intimated that he was significantly older than her. She never returned to her flat and was found the following morning, buried up to her neck in the sand of Red Wharf Bay.

As Gareth took a step back, he peered closely at the scene boards in front of him. They had made little progress in finding Gemma and Caitlin's killer. No DNA or fingerprints from either of their bodies. No eyewitnesses that had seen the victims with anyone the evenings that they were murdered. Nothing that significantly linked them except their age, appearance and where they lived geographically.

Further down the board were the images of Ellie Gates and Shannon Jones. Both in their early twenties, they had gone missing in early December 2021. They fitted the victim profile but even though nearly four months had elapsed, they still couldn't be found.

For a few seconds, he was swamped by feelings of self-doubt. Was he really up to the task for being the SIO on a huge investigation like this? His boss, irritating career copper Superintendent Warlow – or Partridge, as CID officers called him behind his back, after the incompetent television character – had intimated that the longer the investigation went on, the more likely it was that they would be forced to bring in help from outside i.e. other police forces. That was the drawback of being a CID detective on a small island like Anglesey. The perception that you were a yokel rural copper with no experience of anything other than small time burglary and theft. The misconception made him angry. He knew that he was an excellent officer with over twenty years on the job. He also rated his CID team highly. However, talk of outside help had dented his self-belief, and his faith in his team. What if their lack of experience resulted in another murder? How would any of them deal with that?

'Boss?' said a voice, breaking Gareth from his negative train of thought.

Detective Constable Ben Corden approached. Blond, handsome, with an athletic build, Ben was a bright young copper whom Gareth had taken under his wing.

However, there was a darkness to Ben's expression that immediately made Gareth uneasy.

'How can I help?' Gareth asked.

'We've got another missing girl,' Ben explained. 'Her parents are downstairs.'

Gareth felt his stomach sink at the news.

CHAPTER 3

Gareth and Ben were sitting opposite Alun James and Bethan Garland. Bethan's eighteen-year-old daughter, Zoey, had gone out for a drink the night before but hadn't come back home. They were clearly very frightened.

'Could Zoey be anywhere else?' Gareth asked, looking over at Bethan's anxious face.

'No,' she said quietly. 'I rang her mobile but there was no answer. Then I called a couple of her friends but they haven't heard from her. She told me she'd be back by midnight and she would never stay out.'

Alun looked at them. 'She would have called. She calls her mum if she's gonna be late. Especially at the moment, with everything that's going on.'

'Do you have any idea who she went out with?' Ben asked, looking up from the notebook that he was scribbling in.

'That's the thing,' Bethan said, shaking her head. 'She told me she was going out with one of her friends. I wouldn't have let her go out if I thought she was going to be in any danger. But she said they were going to the pub and then straight home. I heard a car pull up outside, she shouted goodbye and she went.'

'What time was that?' Ben asked.

'Just after eight.'

Gareth looked at her. 'You didn't see who was driving the car?'

'No. I wish I had.' Bethan's eyes had now filled with tears. 'I wish I'd seen her to the door.' Bethan began to sob and Alun put a comforting hand on her shoulder. 'I'm just so scared that something's happened to her.'

'You said that you've checked with her friends?' Ben said.

'Yeah. There's only two or three she would have gone out with but it's not any of them,' Bethan explained. 'I went up to her room to get some washing after she'd gone out. Her room stank of perfume. That's what makes me now think that she was meeting a man.'

'She doesn't usually wear perfume?' Gareth enquired.

'No.' Bethan shook her head. 'Not if she's going out with a friend, no. Her hair straighteners were out too. You know, like she was going out on a date.'

Gareth leaned forward in his seat. 'Does Zoey have a boyfriend?'

'No.' Bethan wiped a tear from her face. She was visibly shaking. 'Not really.'

Gareth raised an eyebrow. 'Not really? Was she seeing someone, even casually?'

Bethan gave a slight shrug. 'I know she'd seen someone a couple of times. But she didn't say much about him.'

'We got the feeling that he might have been older than her,' Alun stated.

Gareth frowned, wondering if that was significant. 'Why was that?'

Bethan looked at him. 'A few weeks ago, we'd warned Zoey about the dangers of getting in a car with young blokes. Boy racers. There was that crash over towards Holyhead. Zoey told me not to worry. She said this bloke, whoever he was, wasn't a boy by any stretch of the imagination.'

26

Alun shifted awkwardly in his seat. 'We told her that she shouldn't be going anywhere at the moment. We said it wasn't safe.'

'How did she respond to that?' Gareth asked.

Bethan took a breath and then said, 'She just laughed and said this bloke wasn't "some weird psycho".'

Ben stopped writing and looked over. 'Did she say anything else?'

Alun nodded with a dark expression. 'She said, "They don't let serial killers work with kids these days."'

Gareth exchanged a look with Ben and saw his own feelings mirrored back at him: a wary excitement at the prospect of their first real lead.

'I take it Zoey isn't at school anymore?' Gareth said. Maybe this man she had started to see was a teacher.

Bethan shook her head. 'No. She left Llangefni Sixth Form College last year.'

'Does she work?'

Alun nodded. 'Yeah. Zoey works on the tills at the local shop. She had a shift this morning from seven a.m., which is why we're so worried. She's never missed a shift since she started working there.'

Gareth nodded, trying not to look too grim as he rounded off the interview and saw the worried parents out, assuring them that they would be doing everything in their power to find Zoey and would be in contact as soon as they heard anything. But the details of Zoey and her disappearance were darkly familiar, and made him fear the worst.

CHAPTER 4

Laura walked over to her coffee machine and considered her options. Melozio, Fortado or Stormio. *What the hell?* They sounded more like Italian footballers than coffees. She wondered what archaeologists in the year 3022 would make of finding all these colourful aluminium pods with meaningless Italian names. That their ancestors were sophisticates who had finally ditched the ghastly drink that is instant coffee? Or that they were idiots who had been duped by George Clooney ads into drinking mediocre coffee from exorbitantly priced machines? Laura didn't actually care. The coffee tasted good to her and it was the perfect start to the day, even if it was overpriced.

The BBC 5Live news was burbling in the background on a digital radio. She had a love-hate relationship with the media at the moment. She knew she needed to keep abreast of the media's perceptions of their ongoing investigation. It was national news. But every time she heard or saw it, she became either angry at the melodrama or inaccuracy of the reporting, or terrified that this was happening on her own doorstep. Rosie was eighteen years old. It made her feel sick to think that she was vulnerable to the monster that was roaming their island.

She heard the word 'Anglesey' mentioned and began to listen to the news report.

'*The Chief Constable of North Wales Police, Andrew Burke, has defended his force's handling of a series of murders and disappearances on the island of Anglesey off the North Wales coast. This came after there had been calls for Burke to resign over the force's handling of the case, which has seen two brutal murders and two disappearances of young women on the island in recent months. Many observers believe that Anglesey has its first ever serial killer, dubbed the Anglesey Ripper . . .*'

Laura snapped the radio off as soon as she heard someone coming down the stairs. She was trying to protect Rosie and Jake from what was going on. There was no doubt that there was a general climate of fear, but she wanted her children to be cautious, not hysterical.

Laura finished Jake's packed lunch, zipped up his lunch bag and then glanced around the kitchen to see what else she needed to do before leaving for work.

Jake walked in. He was bleary-eyed and his hair was sticking up at different angles.

'What have I got?' Jake asked nonchalantly, pointing to his lunch bag.

'Jam sandwich,' Laura replied. Jake had decided that he was going to be vegan about a week ago, so ham and cheese sandwiches were out. 'Is that okay?'

'Cool.'

'And I put a bag of Cheese and Onion crisps in there for you,' Laura explained as she looked around for her car keys.

'I can't eat Cheese and Onion crisps,' Jake huffed. 'I'm vegan.'

Rosie entered and caught their conversation. 'There's no cheese in Cheese and Onion crisps, silly.'

'Of course there is!' Jake snapped.

Laura rolled her eyes. 'Ready salted okay?'

Jake nodded.

Laura spotted that Rosie had a very excited look on her face as she held her phone. 'You okay?' she asked her.

Rosie could hardly contain herself as she beamed and showed her a screenshot on her phone. 'I got an offer from Newcastle Uni.'

'Wow.' Laura's heart filled with pride as she hugged Rosie. 'That's brilliant, darling. What do you need?'

'Two hundred and sixty points,' Rosie explained, still full of excitement as she looked at her phone.

Laura shrugged. 'And that means?'

'One B and two Cs,' Rosie replied.

'And that's okay?'

Rosie rolled her eyes. 'Mum, I'm predicted two As and a B so that's amazing.'

'I'm so proud of you, darling.' Laura smiled. 'Although I'm not sure where you get your brains from.'

Rosie grinned. 'Dad, obviously,' she quipped, teasing her.

'Hey!' Laura pulled a face of mock offence. 'I got eight GCSEs, I'll have you know.'

'We do know.' Rosie groaned and then said, 'I haven't got any tights.'

Laura pointed to the utility room. 'In the dryer.' It wasn't the day to point out that Rosie was nearly nineteen years old and should probably now do her own washing. Laura pointed to Jake's head. 'Go and brush your hair.'

'Why?' Jake protested.

'Because you look like some mad professor who's been electrocuted,' Laura joked.

Jake stomped out of the room, suitably unamused.

'Oh my God!' Rosie cried from the utility room. 'Are you kidding me? That's disgusting.'

'What's wrong?' Laura asked, trying to remain calm. Even

though it sounded as if Rosie had found a dead rat in her clean clothes, she knew it was likely to be far less dramatic.

Walking back into the kitchen, she saw that Rosie held a pair of black adult boxer shorts up with a peg as if they were infected with the bubonic plague. 'These were in my clean clothes.'

Laura shrugged. 'So what? They're clean, aren't they?'

'I don't want some pervert's boxer shorts infesting my clothes,' Rosie growled, dropping them to the floor with a disgusted expression.

'For God's sake, Rosie,' Laura sighed. She didn't have time for this – she was late already. 'Gareth isn't a pervert and if you don't like it, do your own washing.'

Rosie just glared at her and then walked away with her tights.

Laura took a deep breath, grabbed her car keys from the counter and headed out of the kitchen and into the hallway. 'Right, you two, I'm going now. Rosie?'

'What?' Rosie snapped as she headed for the stairs.

'Come here please,' Laura said in a stern tone.

Rosie stopped in the stairs and Laura went over to her. 'You come straight home from school, okay? You don't go to anyone's house, get in anyone's car or walk anywhere. You get on the school bus in the car park and that's it. Do you understand?'

Rosie raised an eyebrow sarcastically. 'Erm, yes. You tell me this nearly every day, Laura.' Laura took a breath, fighting the urge to remind her daughter to call her 'Mum'.

'And you know why, don't you, darling?'

'Yes.' Rosie turned and headed down the hallway again. 'There's a maniac out there.' She disappeared up the stairs.

'Right, I'm off, guys. Don't miss the bus. And I love you,' she called out as she headed for the front door.

She was greeted by a resounding silence.

Laura jogged down the steps and towards her car. Even though Rosie had followed her instructions to go to school and come straight back home for the past few months, she couldn't help but worry.

Her train of thought was broken as her phone pinged with a text message.

Opening the door, Laura settled herself in the driver's seat and then pulled the phone from her pocket and looked at it.

It was from Pete. In the months after Sam's death, Laura and Pete had conducted their own off-the-record investigation into what had really happened. Their suspicion had grown about the commander of the raid on the Brannings Warehouse, Superintendent Ian Butterfield. By tracing the burner phone used to report the disturbance at Brannings early on the morning of the twelfth of August, they discovered the phone call had been made by someone inside Trafford Police Station. It made no sense unless it was a deliberate attempt to ensure Sam and Louise went to the warehouse immediately.

In July, they found a more shocking revelation. Not only did they realise the burner phone belonged to Butterfield, but also that Sam's partner, Louise McDonald, who everyone assumed had perished by his side, was very much alive and well. They had eventually tracked Louise down and spoken to her, but then she had been deliberately run down by a car and killed.

In the September, Superintendent Ian Butterfield had turned up on Laura's doorstep one evening looking utterly broken and very drunk. He had told Laura that he wanted to explain about what had happened to Sam that day. As he burbled incoherently, Butterfield admitted that both he and Louise McDonald were working for the Fallowfield Hill Gang. As Louise had told Laura before she had died, the gang had used a mixture of intimidation, threats and bribery to force them to supply information. That included a warning that their drugs factory at Brannings Warehouse was going to be raided in August 2018. Butterfield claimed that the OCG had bent coppers on the take throughout the city, and all the way to the top of the Greater Manchester Police. Before he could elaborate, Butterfield had left claiming that he was convinced he was being followed. Laura had been alarmed by his paranoid behaviour that day.

Since then, Pete and Laura had continued to do their own private research into the links between the Fallowfield Hill Gang and the GMP but had come up against a wall of silence.

Laura opened the text from Pete with a sense of trepidation.

Hi Laura.

You guys okay? This investigation must be driving you into the ground. I'm guessing it's a bit scary for the kids too? If they or you need a bit of a break or change of scene, you're more than welcome to come stay here for a bit.

Just a quick heads up. I think someone is following me. Well, I know they are. To be honest, they look like coppers to me. Not sure if it's connected to what we're doing. Just thought you might need to be on the lookout. I'll call you later. P xx

CHAPTER 5

Gareth had been summoned to see Superintendent Warlow. He knew that he would have to break the news to him that another girl was missing. It wasn't a conversation that he was particularly looking forward to. No doubt the top brass at North Wales Police were putting Warlow under increasing amounts of pressure to make an arrest. He'd heard the news on BBC 5Live that morning, followed by Chief Constable Andrew Burke giving a statement about the investigation. There had been calls for Burke to resign.

Preparing himself to deal with Warlow's usual bullshit, Gareth knocked on the door and glanced at the metallic nameplate – SUPERINTENDENT RICHARD WARLOW. That was the problem with the police force. The wrong people got into positions of power through meticulously planned careers coupled with skilful corridor politics and back-covering.

'Come in,' Warlow said.

Opening the door, Gareth spotted Warlow sitting over at the small, oval meeting table. He was studying documents on the table in front of him.

'Gareth,' Warlow said, looking over. 'Come and sit down.'

'Sir,' Gareth said, pulling out a chair.

'I need to run something past you,' Warlow said. 'We've been offered a Behavioural Investigative Adviser. He's been working mainly with police forces in the North West but I want to get your thoughts on the idea of bringing him over here.'

BIAs were sometimes called 'Offender Profilers'. They were known to the great British public as criminal profilers and popularised in films, television series and books. The theory was that a criminal's personality and their behavioural and demographic detail could be deduced from crime scene evidence. There was part of Gareth that wondered how accurate or useful this was. In his experience, criminals weren't very predictable in the crimes that they committed. In something as extreme as murder, the crime was often an ill-thought-through response to a highly charged emotional situation. That meant that any work based on habits or traits would be both incorrect and a waste of valuable time. *The Silence of the Lambs* and *Cracker* had a lot to answer for.

'I'm not a fan, sir,' Gareth admitted. Allowing a BIA to work with them in CID was tantamount to admitting that they didn't know what they were doing.

'Really?' Warlow gestured to the paperwork in front of him. 'We've got no suspects to date.'

'Our killer knows what they're doing. No DNA, no finger-prints, no eyewitnesses,' Gareth explained.

'And we've still got two further missing women and there's no progress on the MisPer investigations, is there?' Warlow asked.

Gareth gave Warlow a dark look. 'Actually, sir, as of this morning, it looks like we now have three missing women.'

'Oh God, really?' Warlow muttered under his breath, shifting awkwardly in his seat.

'Zoey Garland, nineteen years old,' Gareth explained. 'Got picked up around eight p.m. last night and never came home. It's completely out of character.'

'Jesus.' Warlow shook his head and then looked at Gareth.

'As you know, I'm under a huge amount of pressure to make some kind of breakthrough in this investigation. Anglesey Police is taking a hammering in the media. Unless you have a significant development in the next forty-eight hours, then I'm going to insist that we bring in outside help.'

Laura stirred her coffee with a thin wooden stirrer on the far side of the canteen at Beaumaris nick. They had recently installed a proper automated coffee machine, which offered everything from an espresso to a flat white. It allowed her to take regular breaks from the CID office and stretch her legs around the station rather than stay put.

Detective Constable Andrea Jones approached her with a curious expression. Laura knew she had been on yet another date the night before and was keen to find out how it had gone. Since Andrea had joined Beaumaris CID in September 2021, she and Laura had grown close. Although she didn't want to admit it, Laura suspected that she might act as a mother figure for Andrea, whose parents had both died when she was very young.

'How was "soldier boy"?' Laura asked with a wry smile. Andrea had been using a dating app but had been on a series of fairly disastrous dates or short relationships with men in their early twenties. Laura had given them amusing monikers – 'teacher boy', 'ginger boy', 'Labradoodle boy' and now 'soldier boy'.

'Horrible,' Andrea groaned as she grabbed a cup, placed it under the machine and hit the latte button.

Laura pulled a face. 'Oh dear. That bad?'

'He described to me in detail why the Warrior Infantry Fighting vehicle is actually superior to the Challenger 2 Battle Tank, even though most people think it's the other way around,' Andrea sighed as she took the cup and placed a plastic lid on it.

'Fascinating stuff.' Laura smirked. 'He has got a point, you know.'

'Funny,' Andrea said, rolling her eyes. 'Then he showed me all his tattoos. I've only got a butterfly tattoo on my hip so I wasn't showing him that. He picked his nose. He drank four pints of what he referred to as "driving lager" and then drove home. Jesus.'

Laura laughed. 'He sounds like a real catch.'

They began to weave their way past tables of mainly uniformed officers, who were eating breakfast and chatting loudly.

'Given what we're investigating, maybe it isn't a bad idea to put meeting men on hold for a while,' Laura suggested. It wasn't the first time she had told Andrea that she needed to be more cautious.

'Hey, I'm not putting my life on hold because some sick psycho is out there,' Andrea growled. 'If I go out, I drive myself. We meet in a public place. I'm very careful.'

'Okay,' Laura said in an unconvinced tone as they went through the doors to the canteen and headed towards the CID office.

'You heard the rumours that Warlow wants to bring in help from the mainland?'

'Great,' Laura moaned. 'That's just what we need.'

Even though she knew Beaumaris CID were stretched and working flat out on the two murders and the two disappearances, she was confident in their ability to run the investigation effectively. Laura had spent nearly twenty years as a copper in the Manchester Met, working on major crimes such as murder and drug gangs, and had been slightly worried that the standard would be lower when she rejoined the police in Anglesey. However, she had found that the detectives she now worked alongside were every bit as sharp, dedicated and hard-working as those in the big city. Even though she knew she might be biased, she thought Gareth was a good CID boss and SIO. Technically, Laura wasn't averse to other officers joining a case if their sole objective was to provide a fresh pair of eyes. But in her experience, those coppers who came in had their own agendas, ruffled feathers and sometimes even hindered an investigation.

Andrea pushed open the doors to CID and saw that the rest of the team were moving chairs in preparation for the morning briefing. Gareth was at the front of the room beside the scene boards.

Gareth turned, scratched his chin and pointed to the scene boards. 'Okay. As some of you know, we do have another missing girl this morning who fits our victim profile. Her name is Zoey Garland. We know that all of our victims went out to meet someone or were picked up. That means they were targeted. The killer isn't attacking random women whom he happens to come across. That means the killer has interacted with all our victims in the past and has formed some kind of relationship with them, however tenuous, where they agree to meet up or be picked up. He is selecting them due to age and colouring. There may also be other criteria that we're not aware of.' Gareth then pointed to the photos of the missing women, Ellie Gates and Shannon Jones. 'Any news from the MisPer Team?'

The Missing Persons Team were separate from CID and were focused on finding Ellie and Shannon. Technically they were 'missing' until a body was found or a court issued a Declaration of Presumed Death, but that usually took seven years.

Andrea shook her head. 'They're still drawing a blank, boss.'

Gareth pointed to the murder victims and the two missing women. 'Is there something that connects these five women? If we can establish what that is, then I think we've got a decent chance of also determining where and how our killer interacted with them. And we might have a lead. Zoey told her mother that the person she was meeting worked with children. So, I want us to look again where all our victims went to school and college. And if there are any other settings where our killer might have met them. A sports team, music lessons or a drama club . . .'

Before Gareth could continue, Ben stood up sharply from his desk and looked over. He was holding his phone in his hand.

'Everything all right, Ben?' Gareth asked him.

Ben gave him a dark look. 'Boss, we've got a body on Benllech beach.'

CHAPTER 6

By the time Laura and Andrea arrived at Benllech beach, it was already a hive of solemn activity. Four marked police cars, lights flashing silently, had been pulled across the seafront to stop traffic. Uniformed officers had already taped off the whole area with blue evidence tape that now fluttered noisily in the wind that came off the sea. A terrible atmosphere of horror and quiet distress seemed to fill the air.

A white SOCO van, with its back doors wide open, had clearly just arrived and SOCO officers were climbing into their white nitrile forensic suits ready to trawl the crime scene.

Getting out of the car, Laura looked over at the sandy beach that stretched away before her. A white forensic tent had already been erected over where the body had been discovered. The details of Zoey's last movements, her age and her physical description – brunette hair, brown eyes – matched the two previous murders plus the two missing women.

Standing over by the tent were the distant figures of Gareth and Declan, who had arrived before them. If the other two murders were anything to go by, she knew what would be inside that tent, which was now bustling with a forensic photographer, a pathologist and other SOCOs. At its centre would be the head of a beautiful young woman, eyes wide open, buried up to her neck in sand. It had been a grotesque, sickening sight on both previous occasions – a horrifying image that had been burned for ever in her memory – and this one would be no different. It was at moments like this that she was glad murder victims never got to witness how they were found.

The breeze that came off the beach was surprisingly warm. Spring was on its way. The sky was blue and cloudless. Somehow it didn't seem right or appropriate on a day like this. An idyllic, sandy beach with purplish stones and scattered strands of dark seaweed. The metal railings, bollards and benches had all been painted a shade of cornflower blue. Even a nearby telescope, where tourists could look out to sea, had been given a lick of paint. A seagull sat on a railing, eyeing them suspiciously.

Glancing to the far right, Laura remembered visiting Benllech beach with her sister, Emma, when they were only about eight or nine years old. Their nain – Welsh for grandmother – had brought them on a blistering hot summer's day and the beach had been busy with holidaymakers. Sitting by an orange windbreak, they had eaten thick fish paste sandwiches and chipsticks. As their nain snoozed under an umbrella, they made intricate sandcastles with some local boys who told them about Birch's cave, suggesting they swim over to it. Their nain overheard them and recounted in a spooky voice how Birch's cave was an old smugglers cave from the 1800s. A man named Joseph Birch had been shot and killed by soldiers while trying to smuggle tea, wine, spirits and lace onto Anglesey. She told them that the lower cavern of the cave was only clear of water for an hour at low tide. It was a perfect place for smugglers to avoid detection. It was said that as the last part of the cavern filled with sea water, a blood-curdling yell could be heard. It was Birch's final sound before he died and disappeared into his watery grave. Ever since she'd heard the tale, Laura had always thought there was something distinctly unsettling, even eerie, about Benllech beach. The dark irony of the nature of her trip there forty years later wasn't lost on her.

'Better get over there,' Andrea said quietly, breaking Laura's train of thought.

Laura nodded as they began to pace across the vast, wet carpet of sand before them. She stepped over the tiny tributaries where lay freshly deposited seaweed that was shiny and leathery. Hiding beneath were brown wracks, kelp with their claw-like holdfasts and jewel-like blue-rayed limpets. Some of the seaweed had a red hue that marked it out as sea lettuce. Laura recognised the common dog whelk, looking like a misshaped spongy white ball, which blew around the tideline. Once the seaweed started to decay, its inhabitants would die and creatures such as sandhoppers, beetles and worms would feast on the rotting seaweed. To her left, she glanced at the herring gulls and crows pecking away at the seaweed, looking for molluscs and fish corpses. She couldn't help reflecting on the contrast between the natural order of nature and the unnatural, shocking perversion of what they were about to witness.

Laura and Andrea approached the young female officer who was in control of the police cordon on the beach.

'DI Laura Hart and DC Andrea Jones, Beaumaris CID,' Laura said as she flashed her warrant card.

'Morning, ma'am,' the constable said quietly.

Laura and Andrea continued their walk towards the forensic tent. Trepidation curdled in Laura's stomach.

Gareth gave her a dark look as she approached. 'I've looked on social media. It's definitely Zoey Garland.'

'Same MO?' Laura asked, already knowing the answer.

Gareth nodded and moved back from the entrance to

the tent so that Laura and Andrea could enter and look for themselves.

Drawing in a deep breath, Laura stepped inside. A SOCO was taking photographs, the flash illuminating the material of the tent for a millisecond. As he moved out of Laura's way, she allowed her eyes to rest on Zoey.

Even though she had seen the other two victims in exactly the same way, she still found her breath catching in her throat at the scene before her.

Zoey Garland's head protruded above the sand, which had then been deliberately patted and rubbed smooth so that it appeared as though her head were simply resting on the sand's surface. Her skin had a grey-white tinge. There were red marks and small lacerations around her neck where she had been strangled – probably manually, thought Laura, as there didn't seem to be any ligature marks. Her eyes were wide open. Around them, the skin was creased as if the intense pain of her death was now etched into her face. A perpetual scream that would never end.

The once-deep chestnut pupils were now a cloudy, opaque void where all signs of life had vanished. Zoey's dark hair was pulled back in a tight ponytail and was scattered with sand. It moved and swung for a moment in a gust of wind, as though Zoey was still alive and answering a question with a slight shake of her head.

For a moment, Laura crouched down on her haunches and gazed into Zoey's eyes. Small portals, where life had so magically sparkled. Behind them now lay death. She wondered what Zoey had seen with those eyes in the horrific last few seconds of her life. It made the hairs on the back of Laura's neck stand up just thinking about it.

She took a deep breath and then looked at Andrea, who was ashen-faced. Even though Laura had a lot more experience of looking at dead bodies than her, these particular ones had made a huge impression on her. She assumed they would have an even more profound effect on Andrea, young as she was.

Laura glanced back at Zoey again. There was something so cruel and mocking about the way the killer had deliberately positioned her in the sand. It was an expression of such absolute power and control. For a second, Laura hated the peering, intrusive eyes of the SOCOs, the photographs, the gloved hands picking tiny fragments from her hair and from her face. She was so exposed out here on the beach like that. It felt humiliating. Laura had a sudden urge to take Zoey away from the prying eyes and clinical examination. Take her somewhere quiet, warm and safe until her parents could come and see her and be with her. Take her somewhere where there was dignity for her as an innocent young woman who had had her life so brutally snatched from her. Laura would never grow used to the cruelty and pain that one human being could inflict upon another.

Laura knew that Zoey's parents would have spent the last few hours clinging to the fading hope that their daughter had just decided to stay out for the night without telling them. She had got drunk or taken drugs and was lying hungover, oblivious to the distress she was causing. Zoey would come back through the front door that morning full of hollow apologies and an embarrassed smile. After a telling off, they would hug her and hold her. They would make her promise that she'd never do anything like that again. But the relief and joy of having her home safe and well would temper any anger or resentment. And they would vow never to let her go out again without knowing exactly where she was going and with whom. Names, addresses and phone numbers. They didn't care if they were being over-protective.

But the horrific reality was that none of that was going to happen this morning.

The devastation of Zoey's murder would change the lives of everyone close to her. Her parents' lives would never be the same again. In Laura's experience, most couples of a murdered child didn't stay together in the long run. The other person was a constant, painful reminder of the loss they'd experienced together. The only way to move on was to find someone new.

Standing up, Laura saw that Andrea had left the tent and was looking out at the sea. As she went outside to join her, Laura felt an uneasy sense that she was somehow abandoning Zoey by leaving her there.

'You okay?' she asked Andrea.

Andrea swept the hair from her face. 'I just don't understand it, do you?'

'No,' Laura admitted. 'I don't suppose it's our job to understand and I'd be worried if we did. We just need to make sure no one else ends up like this again.'

'Yeah, of course.' Andrea nodded. 'I might just go for a little wander back to the car.'

'It's okay to be affected by this stuff. You wouldn't be human if you weren't.' Laura put a comforting hand on her shoulder. 'And the monster who is doing this certainly isn't human.'

As Andrea wandered away, Laura wondered who on an island as small as Anglesey was capable of such appalling, sickening acts.

HIM

It was mid-morning as he sat parked high on a vantage point overlooking Benllech beach. In the distance, a forensic tent was no more than a white dot against the darkening sand as the leaden clouds rolled in from the south and covered the sun. He watched the outlines of various figures scurrying around the beach where he'd left her.

Zoey, Zoey, Zoey.

At this distance, he imagined that somehow the figures were pieces of a board or video game. He had set them in motion in some virtual world that he had created. He was Oz behind the curtain of this horror show. How wonderful it would be to be able to take one of their lives with just the click of a finger. To see a figure drop dead on the beach with just a single thought and know that you had done it. Then he remembered the words of Harry Lime, Orson Welles's character in the film *The Third Man*. He and the male central character, Holly Martins, are looking down from a Ferris wheel at the people below. Lime talks of them as 'just dots' and asks Martins if he would feel any pity if one of those dots 'stopped moving for ever'. Lime probes Martins, asking him how many dots he would allow to disappear for £20,000 each. He knew exactly what Lime was talking about.

Clicking on the car stereo, he glanced down at his phone and found his Rolling Stones playlist. 'Sympathy For The Devil' caught his eye and he clicked play. He was more than aware of the dark irony of the title and the lyrics as he continued to stare out at the beach and the sea beyond. *I was around when Jesus Christ had his moment of doubt and pain . . .* He tapped his gloved fingers on the steering wheel and hummed along to the song. It was a mystery to him that it had been The Beatles and not The Stones who had inspired Charles Manson and his psychopathic family to enter 10050 Cielo Drive and butcher pregnant actress Sharon Tate and four others. The words 'Helter Skelter' were painted in the victims' blood on the walls and fridge, along with words such as 'Pigs', which referenced The Beatles' *White Album*. In Manson's twisted imagination, The Beatles were condoning a violent revolution.

In his opinion, though, it was The Rolling Stones who were the band of darkness. Jagger wrote 'Sympathy For The Devil', the first-person lyrics of which painted the Devil as a charming and sophisticated seducer. He felt that somehow the lyrics were talking to him. They provided a blueprint for his modus operandi. The whole point about darkness and evil was that they were seductive and alluring.

He peered at the beach again, wondering what the detectives were discussing by the tent. '*What kind of maniac is capable of this?*' Maybe they would get one of those criminal profilers that he'd seen so often on television and in films.

Buzzing down the window, he took a long, deep breath as he tried to clear his mind of the horrors.

His eye was drawn to the solid darkness of the hill behind him. Then the song of a single bird, complex, like that of a soaring flute. He saw it sitting on a branch high above where

47

he had parked. Its feathers were a brown and cream colour, like the swirled top of a milky coffee.

Is that a nightingale? he wondered. *Do nightingales live by the sea?*

Then he remembered the Greek myth of a young woman called Philomela. When she was raped and had her tongue cut out by her sister's husband, Tereus, she turned into a nightingale to escape him. Because of the violence of the myth, the song of the nightingale had always been seen as a mournful lament.

He watched the nightingale for a moment, thinking how apt it was that it should be singing while watching over the beach. It was as if the bird was warbling a dark requiem to the lost soul of Zoey.

Suddenly the nightingale flitted away, as if startled by something frightening and invisible.

Glancing down at his watch, he saw that it was time to go. He had to get to work and keep up appearances.

However, his mind had already allowed the sliver of a thought.

When can I kill again?

CHAPTER 7

Andrea stood next to the blue metal railings that separated the pavement from the beach. She felt numb. There was a liquid heaviness in her legs. She tapped the ring on her right hand against the top of the railing so that it made a quiet sound. The shock of what she had just seen reverberated around her whole being. It seemed to be affecting everything. Her hearing seemed to be heightened, her balance off, and her stomach churned.

Even though she had attended the other two murder scenes, she had only glimpsed the two victims from outside the forensic tents.

Andrea took a deep breath, trying to compose herself. Trying to get the image of Zoey's head poking from the sand out of her mind's eye. Every time she blinked, it seemed to be there. Her eyes, wide and pained.

The sound of waves collapsing onto the shore at regular intervals broke in on her thoughts as a welcome relief.

Turning her back to the beach, Andrea caught sight of a navy-coloured Audi A5 parked up on the pavement just where Bay View Road bent round to the right and headed inland. A man who looked to be in his late thirties was standing by the back of the car and intently watching events on the beach. It wasn't that surprising. There were police cars everywhere and the beach was a hive of activity.

However, when the man spotted her looking his way, he began to act strangely, diverting his gaze elsewhere.

What's he up to? Andrea wondered as she began to walk past the police cordon and headed his way. Something about his manner made her uneasy.

With that, the man turned, hurried back to his car and got into the driver's door.

Now that's a really stupid thing to do when you've just made eye-contact with a police officer.

Andrea broke into a run, memorising the car's number plate as soon as she got close enough to make it out: *DW18 FRF.*

The CID team at Beaumaris had already had a discussion about the possibility of the killer hiding in plain sight. There were various examples of killers intentionally involving themselves in their own cases. In 1986, Russell Bishop joined a huge police search for two schoolgirls that had gone missing in Brighton. He even told police officers that his dog was a trained tracker dog. Bishop had in fact strangled the girls and hidden their bodies in nearby woods only hours earlier. In 2002, Ian Huntley, a school caretaker, spoke to journalists and gave an interview to Sky News as it was believed he had been the last person to see two missing schoolgirls alive. Huntley spoke at length about the girls and what they were like. The twisted truth of the story was that Huntley had strangled them in his home and dumped their bodies ten miles away the previous day. Therefore, CID officers on Anglesey were on the lookout for anyone taking an unusual interest in the investigation.

As Andrea arrived, she heard the car engine start.

Are you kidding me?

She went to the window on the driver's door and tapped forcefully on the glass. The man looked up at her as if he'd never seen her before his life and had no idea she was coming over.

Nice try, mate, but I'm not buying any of it.

Buzzing down his window, the man peered up at her. He had a dark, olive complexion, big brown eyes, a shaved head and neat goatee. She thought he was either Middle Eastern or possibly Spanish or Italian. He was wearing a smart navy designer suit. In different circumstances, she would have said that he was attractive. In fact, he reminded her of a Latino gangster she had seen recently in a Netflix series.

'Hi there,' he said in an accent she couldn't place.

'Everything okay, sir?' Andrea asked with a forced smile.

The man blinked his long, dark eyelashes. 'Yes,' he replied, looking confused as if he had no idea why she had come over and knocked on his window.

'Would you mind turning off the engine and getting out of the vehicle, please, sir?' she said.

The man gave her a perplexed smile, shrugged and got out. His manner was fidgety. 'Have I done something wrong, officer?' he asked with in a slow, pedantic tone. She couldn't tell if he was smirking or agitated.

'Do you have any form of identification on you, sir?' she asked.

'Erm, yes,' he replied as he reached into his jacket and pulled out a thick brown leather wallet. 'I have my driver's licence in here somewhere.'

After a few seconds, he handed her his plastic driving licence. *Anthony Giuseppe Conte. DOB – 03.4.1983.*

'Thank you, Mr Conte,' Andrea said, handing the licence back to him. 'Can you tell me what you're doing here?'

'I was planning on driving down this road on my way to work,' Conte explained now with calm confidence. 'But it's been closed off. So, I turned around. I just stopped for a moment to see what was going on.'

She looked at him for a moment. There was definitely something *off* about him but she couldn't say exactly what it was. Just an instinct. 'Can I ask where you were going, Mr Conte?'

'I'm going to my gym,' Conte explained with a tone of self-importance. 'I own a gym and fitness studio just outside Llangefni.'

'Okay. And you can give me the name and address of that business should I need it?' she asked.

'Yes, of course,' he replied confidently. Then he gave her a curious look and asked in a virtual whisper, 'Has there been another murder?'

'I'm afraid I can't discuss that with you,' Andrea replied.

'You see, I used to be in the police force myself,' Conte stated with an air of grandiosity. 'Well, when I say police, it was the Military Police actually. Long time ago, though.'

For some reason, what Conte had told her just didn't ring true. Her instinct was that he was lying but she couldn't see any reason why.

'Right,' Andrea said with a dubious nod. 'Well, I'll let you get on your way, Mr Conte.'

'Thank you, officer. Have a good day.' He nodded, smiled and got back into the car.

She looked inside and spotted a pair of leather gloves on the passenger seat along with a mobile phone and a bottle of water.

The Audi pulled away. Andrea watched it go, wondering whether Anthony Conte had something to do with the murders.

CHAPTER 8

The mood of the CID office at Beaumaris nick was sombre with the news of another murder. Detectives were sitting quietly at their workstations, typing at computers or following up leads on the phone in low voices. It was obvious that morale was low. Despite working long hours and poring over every shred of evidence, there were many in the room who felt somehow responsible for Zoey Garland's death. A feeling that she had died because they hadn't managed to apprehend the killer quickly enough.

Gareth looked out from his office and saw Laura approaching. He scratched at his forehead and scalp. For the first time since he was a teenager, he had eczema. Small, irritable red patches of skin on his hairline, eyebrows and nose. There was no doubt in his mind it was a result of the stress of the investigation. Warlow's threat to bring in outside help hadn't helped his anxiety.

'You look tired,' she said quietly as she came in and put a reassuring arm on his shoulder for a second. No one in the CID office knew that they were having a relationship. They had somehow managed to keep it a secret for about nine months, but didn't know how much longer they would be able to stop people finding out. They knew it would be frowned upon by those in senior management. What he would give for the case to be over and to spend some time with Laura somewhere quiet and romantic.

'If I'm honest,' Gareth said under his breath, 'it's a little overwhelming.'

'Yeah,' Laura said sympathetically. 'I never came up against anything like this in twenty years in Manchester.'

Gareth sat back, let out a sigh and gave her a wry smile. 'And to cap it all, I've lost my lucky pair of boxer shorts somewhere in your house.' He needed a moment of flippant humour to break the despondent mood.

Laura laughed and then looked around to check no one had heard her. 'Things really are getting bad.'

'You're telling me.'

'Hang on.' Laura pulled a face. 'You have a lucky pair of boxer shorts? What are you, fifteen?'

'Yeah, I don't mean like that, I mean . . .' Gareth said, trying to backtrack fast. 'My favourite pair.'

'Nice save there, mister,' she joked.

'Thanks. I thought it was touch and go there for a minute.'

She rolled her eyes. 'Yeah, well, Rosie found them in a pile of her clothes that came out of the dryer, so you can imagine how that went down?'

'Fart in a spacesuit,' Gareth groaned.

'She actually called you a *pervert*.'

Gareth frowned. 'For wearing boxer shorts?'

'That's teenage girl logic for you.' Laura shrugged. 'You're not her dad. And for some reason that seems to have made you the enemy.'

'I'm at a loss as to what to do,' Gareth admitted. He had tried everything he could think of to win Rosie round. Humour, bribery, patience.

'Yeah, it's not ideal,' Laura said.

There was a knock at the open door, which broke Gareth's train of thought.

It was Declan, who was wearing his usual concerned expression. In his early forties, he had dark green eyes and a chubby face that was covered with a gingery-blond beard.

'Boss,' he said. 'I think we've got something.'

'Okay,' Gareth said, getting up from his seat and following Declan and Laura out into the main office. He'd known Declan long enough to know that this was something significant, and he felt a tingle of anticipation.

Declan grabbed a file and showed him. 'I think we've managed to link nearly all the victims.'

Gareth nodded optimistically. 'Okay.'

'We'd looked before at a possible connection between the victims and where they were educated, but have only just been able to narrow it down enough to potentially be of use.' Declan then handed him a photograph of a handsome man in his forties with shoulder-length salt-and-pepper hair and a beard. 'Professor Henry Marsh. He teaches psychology A-level at Llangefni Sixth Form College,' Declan said. 'He is also a private tutor in maths and sciences.'

'What's the connection?' Gareth asked, praying that Professor Marsh was a viable prime suspect.

'Both of our missing women, Ellie Gates and Shannon Jones, our first victim, Caitlin Thomas, *and* Zoey Garland, all attended Llangefni Sixth Form College in the past five years,' Declan said.

Gareth felt his pulse quicken. 'Did this Professor Marsh teach them?'

'We haven't been able to establish that yet,' Declan admitted.

Gareth raised an eyebrow. 'What about the others?'

Ben looked over and gestured to his computer screen. 'Marsh is also a private tutor for a company called tutorsinwales.com.' Gareth walked over to look at the screen. 'So, I went onto

Marsh's profile page. As I scrolled down I found a whole load of recommendations by current or former students that he had tutored.' Ben then pointed to the screen as he read, '*Henry Marsh is a fantastic maths tutor. He was patient, professional and our son Tom has hugely benefited from working with him. I can't recommend him highly enough. Bethan Garland.*'

Laura frowned. 'Zoey's mother?'

Ben nodded. 'Yes.'

'Marsh was a regular visitor to the Garlands' home while he was tutoring their son Tom,' Declan stated. 'And he would have come across Zoey when he visited as well as knowing her from college.'

'What about Gemma Ramsey?' Gareth asked.

Declan shrugged. 'Nothing to link Marsh to Gemma yet.'

'Anything on the PNC?'

'A couple of convictions for petty theft as a teenager,' Declan explained. 'Since then, nothing.'

'Well, I think we've got enough to go and see what Marsh has to say for himself,' Gareth said. 'Have we got an address?'

'Yes, boss,' Declan replied. 'It's on the council tax records and the electoral register.'

Gareth looked at Laura. 'I think you and Andrea should pay Marsh a visit and see what you think.'

Declan looked over at Gareth and frowned. 'You don't want to go yourself, boss?'

'No.' Gareth explained. 'Our killer has a very complicated and uncomfortable relationship with women. I'm guessing that he struggles with any woman in a position of authority. Two female officers arriving on his doorstep might well rattle him. Let's see how he reacts.'

* * *

It was early afternoon by the time Laura and Andrea arrived in the tiny village of Rhosmeirch, which was located a mile and half north of the county town of Llangefni and east of the Llyn Cefni reservoir. They passed a row of nondescript, grey bungalows and a man walking a black Labrador. To the west, the fields stretched away into the distance. A green tractor pulling a silver trailer trundled across the road up ahead and pulled into a farm.

'You're quiet,' Laura said after a while. Andrea was normally a bit of a chatterbox but she had been virtually monosyllabic since they left Beaumaris.

'Sorry,' Andrea said quietly. 'I can't seem to get what I saw this morning out of my mind. I know it goes with the job . . .'

Laura gave her a kind smile. 'If it helps, I've found it difficult too. With all of the victims. And I've seen all sorts of stuff over the years. But it does get easier with time.'

'Thanks,' Andrea muttered as they pulled up outside a smart-looking house, which was the address they had been given for Professor Marsh.

They got out of the car. The air was thick with the pungent smell of the nearby farm.

Laura wrinkled her nose. 'Mmm, fruity.'

Andrea smiled. 'I won't be taking a deep lungful of that.'

As they wandered up the neat garden path, the sun broke through the clouds, slanting along the front of the house, casting elongated rectangles of shadow across the garden, wooden decking and flowerbeds. The lawn to the front and side of the house was clipped and there was a neat hedge of raspberry spiraea bordering the path. Somewhere in the distance a cuckoo called.

Andrea pointed to the gleaming black BMW that sat upon the gravel drive. 'Looks like he's in.'

As they arrived on the doorstep, they could hear jazz blaring loudly from inside.

Laura raised an eyebrow at Andrea at the music, then rapped loudly on the door and took out her warrant card.

A moment later, the door opened and a man in his late forties looked out at them quizzically. 'Hello,' he said in a deep, soft but gravelly voice.

'Professor Henry Marsh?' Laura enquired.

'Yes,' the man replied with a bemused smile that lit up his tanned face. He was disarmingly handsome in a George Clooney kind of way.

'DI Laura Hart and DC Andrea Jones, Beaumaris CID,' Laura explained.

'Oh, right,' Marsh said calmly and then frowned and opened the door fully. 'Do you want to come in?'

Laura nodded. 'Yes, please. We won't take up too much of your time.'

'That's fine.' Marsh shrugged casually and then gestured down the hallway. 'I've just made a pot of coffee, if you'd like one.'

Laura looked at Andrea and then nodded. 'Actually, that would be great.'

Marsh pointed to the living room. 'I'll just turn that down,' he said, clearly referring to the jazz music. He had shoulder-length greying hair, a dark beard, twinkly blue eyes and was over six foot and slim. He wore a thick black cardigan with a shawl collar, jeans and brown suede brogues. If she didn't know better, Laura would have assumed that he was an actor or maybe a film director.

The sun splashed onto the fashionable floral wallpaper in the large hallway. There were tasteful pictures on the wall and the house was warm and smelled of fresh coffee and aftershave.

Andrea gave her a look, widening her eyes.

Oh God, she fancies him.

Before Laura could say anything, Marsh returned and beckoned them to follow him. 'Kitchen's down here.'

The kitchen and dining area were ultra-modern and took up the whole of the back of the house. It was high spec with granite work tops, a huge American-style fridge and the obligatory breakfast bar with chrome stools.

Okay, this is very stylish.

'Grab a pew,' Marsh said, pointing to the long oak table.

Glancing around, Laura couldn't work out if there was a Mrs Marsh. There didn't seem to be the kind of feminine touches you might expect. She peered over at the fridge and walls. Not a photograph in sight.

'I could get used to a kitchen like this,' Andrea said as she pulled her chair under the table.

'I love it,' Marsh said with a winning smile as he pointed to the far wall. 'But it nearly killed me doing it. I extended it out the back.'

Andrea raised an eyebrow. 'You did all the work yourself?'

'Except for the electrics,' Marsh said as he arrived at the table with mugs, a blue-and-white milk jug and a small bowl of sugar. He went and got the pot of coffee and placed it on a mat at the centre of the table.

Laura watched Marsh carefully. Everything about him seemed almost too considered, as though it could be an act.

Sitting down at the end of the table, Marsh gestured. 'Please. Help yourself.'

While Andrea grabbed two mugs and began to pour them coffee, Laura opened the folder she had brought with her.

'We're hoping you can help with our inquiries,' Laura explained as she took out photographs of the three murder victims and the two missing women. 'Can you take a look at these photographs for me please, Professor Marsh?'

'Henry, please,' he said with a self-effacing smile as he fished stylish preppy reading glasses from a pocket in his cardigan. He peered at the women in the photographs for a few seconds before giving Laura a sombre look.

'Can you tell us if you recognise any of these women, please, Henry?' Laura asked casually.

Marsh's face darkened and he nodded slowly. 'Yes, of course I do,' he replied steadily. 'That's why you're here after all, isn't it?'

For a moment, Marsh fixed her with an unsettling gaze before taking off his glasses and giving them a clean with a white handkerchief that he'd taken from a trouser pocket.

Andrea leaned forward and pointed. 'Can you tell us how you know the women in these photos?'

Marsh nodded slowly and began to look upset. 'To be honest, I didn't know them well. I know who some of them are and what's happened to them.' Marsh pursed his lips and he blinked. 'I can't bear to think about how their families must be feeling.' He let out an audible breath and sat back. 'It's just a bit of shock seeing them all.' He then frowned as something occurred to him. 'Oh God, am I suspect in what's happened to them?'

Laura studied Marsh. She just wasn't convinced by his show of emotion and shock.

Andrea shook her head. 'No. We're just trying to gather as much information as we can about all these women, that's all.'

Marsh took a few seconds as he processed this. His face seemed to have changed.

Laura looked at him. He appeared to be gritting his teeth as though he was suppressing something. He coughed as though trying to stifle some kind of outburst.

There is definitely something not quite right about him, she thought.

Andrea pointed at the first photograph in the line. 'How did you know Ellie Gates?'

Marsh's face immediately softened as he put his glasses back on, pushed them up the bridge of his nose and peered thoughtfully at the photograph of Ellie. As with all the victims, Ellie was in her early twenties, with straight, long brunette hair and brown eyes. She had gone missing back in December and hadn't been seen since. The photo showed her sitting in a pub garden, smiling in the sunshine.

'I didn't really know Ellie,' Marsh stated. 'She did start to do A-level psychology at Llangefni Sixth Form College where I work . . .' Marsh then turned to look at them over the top of his glasses. 'Which, of course, you already know. She came to two or three lessons and then decided to switch to Media Studies.'

'Did you ever see her outside of college?' Laura asked.

Marsh pulled an indignant face. 'No, of course not. She was a student at the college I worked at. That would be completely unethical.'

'Did you ever see Ellie after she left Llangefni Sixth Form College?' Andrea asked.

Marsh shook his head. 'No, I didn't.' He then pointed to two other photos. 'The same is true of poor Shannon and Caitlin,' he explained quietly. 'I knew them from around the college, nothing more. I never had any contact with them outside or after they left.'

Laura leaned forward and pointed to another photograph. 'Can you tell us how you know Zoey Garland, please?'

Marsh studied the photograph and then narrowed his eyes. 'I don't understand. Has something happened to Zoey?'

Laura didn't respond. 'Can you tell us how you know Zoey?'

'Oh God,' Marsh looked shocked. 'Please. I've got to know the Garland family very well when I've been tutoring Tom. And Zoey went to my college. What's happened to her? Is she all right?'

Andrea looked at him. 'I'm afraid we can't discuss the details of the case with you, Henry.'

'You wouldn't be showing me a photograph of Zoey if nothing had happened to her,' Marsh said quietly as he put his hand to his mouth for a few seconds. 'That's terrible.'

Laura couldn't work out if his reaction was genuine or some kind of act. Her instinct was that he was play-acting. There was definitely a disconnect between the way he was behaving and reacting on the surface, and what was actually going on beneath.

'What about Gemma Ramsey?' Laura asked bluntly as she pointed to another photograph.

'No, I'm sorry. I don't know her. I've never seen her before.' Marsh shook his head. Taking off his glasses, he looked at them both. 'Listen, I know you're here because I have some kind of connection with nearly all these women. But this is a small island. And if you're a teacher and a tutor, you end up getting to know a large percentage of the people here. I'm sure you know what I'm talking about in your line of work.'

Laura waited for a few seconds before speaking. 'So, you had nothing to do with what happened to these women.'

'No, of course not,' Marsh said sharply.

Laura studied his face, looking for the slightest tell. Then she asked, 'I take it you're from Anglesey?'

'Yes, that's right.'

'And you've remained on the island all your life?' Andrea asked.

'God, no,' Marsh replied. 'I've lived and worked all over the country. I mainly followed my wife and wherever her career took her.'

Glancing at his left hand, Laura asked, 'You're married?'

Marsh held up his left hand and said sadly, 'I was . . . I'm afraid my wife died just over six years ago.'

'I'm sorry to hear that,' Andrea said.

Laura sipped her coffee. That explained the lack of feminine touches around the house. The lack of photos also suggested there weren't any children.

'Just for our records, can you tell us where you were last night between the hours of eight p.m. and eleven p.m.?' Andrea asked.

Marsh thought for a moment and nodded. 'I can, actually. It was a friend of mine's fiftieth birthday bash. At the Bull Hotel in Llangefni. Do you know it?'

'Yes,' Laura replied. 'And you were there all night?'

'Oh, yes,' Marsh said. 'I think I fell out of there about midnight and into a taxi back here.'

'And there are plenty of people that will corroborate that, are there?' Andrea asked.

'Of course,' Marsh replied and then looked at them intently. 'What's happened to those women is horrendous. But I can assure you, I had nothing to do with it. And I'm happy to go through any other dates and tell you my whereabouts. I just don't want you wasting your time when you should be out there looking for whatever psychopath committed these crimes.'

CHAPTER 9

Andrea and Laura made their way along the back roads as they headed towards Beaumaris. They had hardly said a word since leaving Marsh's home as they both processed what he had told them.

As they turned the corner, a single traffic light showed red as there were roadworks. Laura slowed the car to a stop.

Looking in a rear mirror, she spotted a black Range Rover, which had been behind her for the past few miles. After Pete's concerns that he was being followed, she had found herself being extra vigilant. She was sure that it was nothing and that the car would turn off in a few miles. She had enough to be worrying about at the moment.

Glancing to her right, she saw they had stopped beside an old church. Old gravestones, now covered with the pale green of lichen and moss, lay at angles where age had disrupted the soil beneath. It was such a strange thought to know that one day she would be in a place like that. However, the thought of dying had never frightened her. Maybe it was Sam's death that had heightened her awareness of her own mortality. She suspected there was part of her that wanted to believe that when she died, she and Sam would be somehow reunited. Although she wasn't religious, she did believe that there was something beyond death. Not a traditional, trite biblical heaven. Just something otherworldly, benign and peaceful.

A grave closest to the road had a stone-draped urn and obelisk. Further to the right, the land sloped down towards the sea. Behind the ivy-clad church, there were trees in a small valley and the pale façades of a line of houses were caught by sunlight.

'What did you think?' Andrea asked, breaking her train of thought.

Laura took a moment to bring her head back into the present. 'Marsh?'

'Yes.' Andrea nodded. 'I mean, apart from being completely gorgeous.'

Laura rolled her eyes. 'Really?' It didn't sit comfortably with her to hear Andrea make such a flippant comment about someone they had questioned about the murders of young women.

'You didn't?' Andrea asked.

'I'm pretty sure we were there to establish if he had murdered three women,' Laura said sharply.

Andrea bristled. 'Sorry. I was obviously joking.'

There were a few seconds of tense silence.

As the light turned green, Laura pulled away and raised an eyebrow. 'I thought there was something creepy about him actually.'

'Really?' Andrea frowned. 'I thought that he couldn't be less like a serial killer if he tried.'

'Isn't that the point?' Laura said, feeling vaguely annoyed by Andrea's attitude.

Glancing in the rear-view mirror, she saw that the Range Rover was still behind her as they turned right.

'How do you mean?' Andrea asked.

'Harold Shipman was a popular, respected local GP. Happily married with four children,' Laura explained. 'He murdered 250 people. Levi Bellfield was a successful local businessman, married with children. He murdered three teenage girls.'

'Okay, point taken,' Andrea said. 'My instinct was that he was telling the truth, that's all. And you've always told me to trust my instinct.'

'I have.' Realising that she had annoyed Andrea, Laura glanced over. 'Sorry if I've been a bit short this morning. I've got a lot going on.'

'Trouble at the ranch?' Andrea asked.

'Sort of,' Laura admitted. Even though Laura was technically Andrea's boss, they shared pretty much everything – with the exception of her relationship with Gareth, of course. Laura didn't care whether or not it was professional to be that open with Andrea. In her book, to be a good copper you needed to know what was going on in the lives of those you worked closest with. 'Rosie's being a little bit tricky at the moment.'

Andrea laughed. 'She's a teenage girl. Goes with the territory. I was a banshee when I was her age. I went totally off the rails. Got in with some right scumbags. Drinking, drugs and sex.'

Laura remembered that Andrea's parents had been killed in a car crash when she was little and she'd grown up in care. She'd admitted before that it had been difficult. Laura felt a little guilty moaning about Rosie's mini tantrum from that morning. 'Yeah, I guess I should count my blessings.

Looking in the rear-view mirror, Laura spotted that the Range Rover was still behind them.

Are they really following me? And are they coppers?

There was a small convenience store on the left-hand side of the road. It advertised Costa coffee. Laura pulled the car over to the kerb without indicating and gestured to the shop. 'Fancy a coffee?'

Andrea raised an eyebrow. 'I wondered what you were doing there. But yeah, I'd love one.'

Laura checked as the Range Rover went past slowly. She tried to look inside to spot who had possibly been following her but the windows had a slight tint so it was impossible to see anything clearly. Just two shadowy figures in the passenger and driver's seats.

She watched the Range Rover to see if it stopped or turned around. But it continued driving and disappeared out of sight.

'Everything all right, boss?' Andrea asked, giving her a quizzical look.

'Yeah, fine,' Laura replied, now wondering if the car had been following her at all. Reaching for the handle, she smiled at Andrea. 'So, white coffee? Latte if they got it? Is this a sugar type of morning?'

Andrea shook her head. 'No. I'm trying to lose weight.'

Laura pulled a face. 'Don't be so ridiculous.' Then she grinned. 'What about a pastry? Go on.'

Andrea groaned. 'Are you trying to deliberately ruin my diet?'

'Yes,' Laura laughed. 'So, pastry then?'

'Yes,' Andrea said with a smile. 'Please.'

As Laura and Andrea entered Beaumaris nick, the burly-looking duty sergeant looked over from the main desk and signalled to her.

'Ma'am,' he said in a deep North Welsh accent.

Laura glanced at Andrea. 'I'll see you up there.'

As Andrea left, Laura approached the reception desk to see what the custody sergeant wanted to tell her. She wondered why he hadn't just emailed her.

'Everything all right, sarge?' she asked.

He gave her a quizzical look. 'Two detectives from Manchester arrived about ten minutes ago to see you.'

What's that about? she thought. The unscheduled arrival of two CID officers from Manchester made her feel uneasy. The logical thought was that it had something to do with a case she had worked while she was in the Met. However, usually that was something that would have been done on the phone, which is why she felt apprehensive. Did it have anything to do with the Range Rover from earlier? Or was she becoming paranoid?

'I shoved them in Interview Room 2, ma'am,' the custody sergeant informed her as he went over to answer a ringing phone.

'Thanks, sarge,' she said as she turned and headed away towards the row of interview rooms on the ground floor of the station. In her head, she played back various unresolved cases that she had worked while she was a detective in Manchester. Maybe that's all it was. Detectives looking at an old case she had investigated. It happened once in a while.

Arriving at Interview Room 2 she opened the door and spotted a man and woman sitting on the other side of the interview table.

'Hi there,' Laura said with a friendly smile as she approached and held out her hand. 'I'm DI Laura Hart. I believe you've come to see me?'

A man, black, fifties, rotund, in an ill-fitting suit, got up and shook her hand. 'DS Ashley Carmichael.'

To his right stood a diminutive woman in her thirties with bottle-blonde, brittle hair that curved around the sides of her head as if to cocoon her face. She seemed to be hiding behind her glasses and neat clothes. 'DS Heather Watkins.'

As they all sat down, Laura looked over at them. 'So, how can I help?'

Carmichael opened his briefcase and pulled out an orange folder. 'We're taking another look at Louise McDonald's murder,' he explained.

Laura felt her stomach tighten. Louise had been run over and murdered in North Wales. These officers were from Manchester. So, what were *they* doing looking into Louise's death? Even though Louise had been an officer in the Manchester Met, it wasn't their jurisdiction to look into a murder nearly a hundred miles away in a different country.

'Okay,' Laura said cautiously, trying not to show her growing anxiety. 'I'm pretty sure I gave officers from North Wales Police everything they needed six months ago.'

Watkins gave her a forced smile. 'We just wanted to check a few details with you about what happened that night and the circumstances of Louise's death. It's part of a wider investigation we're carrying out.'

A wider investigation? As far as she knew, Louise and Butterfield had both been bribed and intimidated into working for the Fallowfield Hill Gang. However, when Butterfield visited Laura at her home six months ago, a few days after Louise's death, he had made it clear that corruption didn't stop with him and Louise. He insinuated that the OCG had people working for them all the way to the top of the food chain. Was that what Carmichael and Watkins were there to investigate? It wasn't something she could ask them directly. Surely that kind of investigation would come under the remit of the IOPC.

'As you know from my testimony,' Laura said, treading carefully, 'I confronted a known member of the Fallowfield Hill Gang at the hospital where Louise was being treated. My assumption at the time was that he had come to kill her. I assume that your investigation is into that particular OCG?' She knew she was fishing.

Carmichael shifted awkwardly in his seat. 'I'm afraid we're not able to divulge the nature of our investigation. As I said, we're just here to clarify a few things about Louise's death, that's all.'

Laura nodded. It was a nice try but they weren't going to tell her anything. 'Okay, fire away,' she said, trying to sound confident and unflustered.

Watkins took a document from the folder and peered at it. 'In your statement, you told officers that you had spotted Louise McDonald while on a night out in Llandudno?'

'That's right,' Laura lied. The fact was that she and Pete had spent months tracking her down there.

'I assume you were pretty shocked?' Carmichael asked.

'Yeah, you could say that,' Laura replied with a fake sardonic snort. 'She was meant to have died with my husband in a warehouse in August 2018.'

Watkins put the document down and peered over at her. 'And you confronted her?'

'Yes. Of course,' Laura said, her eyes widening. 'She was meant to be dead. I went to her bloody funeral, for God's sake.'

'Can you tell us again what you talked about?' Watkins said.

'As I said in my statement, we didn't get to talk,' Laura said, lying again. 'Louise said that she would tell me everything outside the bar. When we got outside, she ran. I chased her. A car came out of nowhere and hit her. That's it.'

'And you believe that the car hit her deliberately rather than it being any kind of accident?'

'Yes. Definitely. In fact, the car drove at both of us. It's just that I managed to dive out of the way.'

'What about when you visited her in hospital?' Watkins enquired.

'How do you mean?'

Watkins frowned. 'Did Louise say anything to you before she went into a coma?'

'No,' Laura replied. 'I have already explained all this to detectives from North Wales Police and in my witness statement.'

Carmichael fixed her with a quizzical look. 'It seems an incredible coincidence, doesn't it? You happen to bump into Louise in a bar in Llandudno.'

Laura shrugged and nodded. 'Yeah, you're telling me.'

For the next few seconds, Carmichael and Watkins didn't say anything as they pulled more documents from the file.

Laura was trying desperately to calculate how much the detectives knew and how much they were holding back at this stage of the interview.

Carmichael scratched his face and then leaned forward. 'Do you know a Detective Chief Inspector Peter Marsons?'

Oh shit.

'Yes, Pete is an old friend,' Laura explained but her pulse had quickened with the mention of his name. Up until now, no one knew that Pete had been working in the background to find out who was actually responsible for Sam's death. 'And we worked together in Manchester.'

'We understand that DCI Marsons and your late husband were close?' Watkins asked. The question sounded loaded.

'Yes.' Laura nodded, wondering quite where they were going with all this. 'They were best friends.'

Watkins moved a strand of hair from her face and then looked over. 'Did you see DCI Marsons on the night that Louise was run down?'

'Yes. When he arrived at the hospital,' Laura replied. Her pulse was now racing and she took a deep, calming breath.

'But not before that?'

'No.'

'You're sure about that?'

'Yes.' Louise held her breath for a second. Interviews like this were a game of poker. She knew the routine well. Get a suspect to lie and then reveal what you know – never the other way around. If they actually knew that Laura and Pete had been working on tracking down Louise McDonald and

71

had been together that night, now would be the time to play that card. And in the process, prove Laura was lying to them.

'Do you have suspicions that Louise McDonald was somehow responsible for your husband's death?' Watkins enquired.

Wow. Where did that come from?

'Erm . . .' Laura thought for a second. 'I don't know what to think. I assumed at the time that she was mixed up in something criminal. But I never got to ask her.'

'No, you didn't,' Carmichael said in a tone that bordered on suspicious. He then frowned and fixed her with a quizzical look. 'I'm just going to play devil's advocate here for a moment, Laura.'

'Okay,' Laura said, trying to sound unflustered.

'Let's say hypothetically that you and DCI Marsons had managed to track down Louise McDonald months before you ran into her,' Carmichael said.

'Which we didn't,' Laura snapped but her anxiety was growing. Were they really on to what she and Pete had been doing?

'Humour us,' Watkins said dryly.

'You discover that Louise had been working for a Manchester OCG,' Carmichael continued. 'That would lead you to assume that she was responsible for Sam's death in August 2018. After all, Sam and Louise had responded to the 999 call about suspicious behaviour at Brannings Warehouse. You might assume that she had set Sam up?'

'I don't know what you're talking about.' Laura looked at them and frowned. 'I just told you, I didn't know what to assume. I never got to speak to her.'

'Come on, Laura,' Watkins snorted. 'You're an experienced CID detective. The only conclusion you could draw from Louise being alive and well was that she set Sam up for some reason. Maybe he'd discovered that she was working for the Fallowfield Hill Gang. And maybe she led Sam to them that morning.'

That was exactly what Pete and Laura had deduced. But they also knew that the gang's use of corrupt officers didn't stop at Louise.

'I'm not sure where you're going with all this,' Laura said in an annoyed tone.

'Let me put it to you that if you and DCI Marsons had discovered the whereabouts of Louise McDonald, a woman you believed had led your husband and DCI Marsons's best friend to his death,' Carmichael said calmly, 'isn't it a terrible coincidence that she was murdered the very night that you both went to confront her?'

Whoa! Hang on a second! Laura felt very uneasy about what Carmichael was implying.

'Jesus Christ! You think we were involved in her murder?' Laura growled. 'I've told you that I was on my own. I bumped into Louise McDonald by accident. She ran. And someone hit her with a car and killed her.'

There were a few tense seconds of silence.

'Were you following me this morning?' Laura asked.

Carmichael frowned. 'Sorry?'

'Black Range Rover? That wasn't you following me?'

'No, it wasn't.'

Laura gave them a disbelieving look. 'You sure about that?'

'Yes,' Carmichael replied, his tone now stern.

Watkins looked over at her. 'Unfortunately, we believe that our version of events that night is a more plausible explanation.'

'You think that Pete ran down Louise and killed her?' Laura snorted. 'That's ridiculous.'

'Is that what happened?' Watkins asked.

'No!'

Carmichael shrugged. 'Maybe you found Louise and confronted her. And she did run. And you and DCI Marsons pursued her. And maybe something went wrong and Louise was accidentally hit by his vehicle. If that's what happened, then you need to tell us.'

'No, that's not what happened,' Laura hissed. 'I've told you what happened.'

'We're not satisfied with your version of events,' Watkins said.

'That's your problem,' Laura growled. 'Are you going to arrest me, then?'

'No,' Carmichael replied. 'Not yet. We just want you to tell us what actually happened that night.'

Laura shook her head. 'I just did that.'

'Okay,' Watkins said quietly. 'My suggestion is that the next time we speak about this, you bring your federation rep and possibly a solicitor.'

'That's fine,' Laura snapped. 'In fact, that's a very good idea.'

Laura got up from the table and headed for the door.

She felt sick.

CHAPTER 10

Laura and Andrea had been sent over to check on Zoey Garland's postmortem. Laura knew that she had been noticeably quiet on the way. The interview with Watkins and Carmichael had really shaken her. She needed to talk to Pete and get his perspective. If it came to it, she and Pete would have to give full disclosure of everything they had done with regards to investigating Sam's murder up to that point. Their reason for keeping it quiet was that they still didn't know who to trust in the GMP. However, if they were going to be linked in any way to Louise McDonald's murder, it would be time to come clean.

Trying to put those thoughts to one side, Laura pushed through the double doors into the hospital mortuary, followed by Andrea. The air with thick with preserving chemicals and detergents, and the temperature dropped to a ghostly chill. By her calculations, it was the third time she had been to this mortuary. Even though the layout was the same as the ones she'd visited in Manchester – mortuary examination tables, gurneys, aluminium trays, workbenches and an assortment of luminous chemicals – it was very modern. Several of the mortuaries she'd visited in the past, especially the Royal Manchester Infirmary mortuary, dated back to the Victorian era. Even though it was thoroughly modernised, the walls, floors and ceilings were over 150 years old. It seemed to have an eerie, even malevolent atmosphere like no other place she had visited. Laura wondered if it was something to do with the thousands of bodies that had passed through over the years. She was glad to be in this more modern one now.

Looking around, she spotted Chief Forensic Pathologist Professor Lovell. In his fifties, Lovell was dapper and charming. He was on the far side of the mortuary, taking photographs, using a small white plastic ruler to give an indication of scale. Attached to his scrubs was a small microphone, as postmortems were all now digitally recorded.

As Lovell moved away from the metallic gurney, Laura saw the pale, naked corpse of Zoey Garland laid out. Now that all the forensic evidence had been taken from her, Lovell was establishing cause of death, plus anything else that might help the investigation.

Laura approached, her gaze fixed on Zoey's lifeless body. In some ways there was a relief that she was no longer buried in the sand as though she were an exhibit on display in a grotesque horror show. That's how the killer had wanted her to be found. He had manipulated and controlled her in death, but now she was free from that.

Lovell was dressed in pastel-blue scrubs. As he pulled down his surgical mask, Laura could see that he had grown a blond beard in recent months. It suited him.

'It's hard when they're this young,' Lovell commented sadly as he gestured to Zoey. The front of her torso had a large scar where she had been cut open for examination. It had been stitched back up with blue thread.

That's what Laura liked about Lovell. He treated the people he performed postmortems on with the utmost respect. She had encountered other pathologists who were incredibly cold and clinical, treating those in front of them as no more than a slab of meat that needed to be scientifically tested.

'What can you tell us?' Laura asked as they approached. She found herself compelled to look at Zoey's face. Such heart-breaking innocence. There was something about Zoey's murder that had struck an emotional chord with her. Maybe it was her resemblance to Rosie.

Lovell flicked the wall-mounted light box on, backlighting an X-ray of Zoey's skull. Then he pointed to the back of Zoey's head where the hair had been shaved. There was a dark red and black wound and severe bruising. 'There is significant damage just here, which is consistent with a heavy blow to the back of the head. A blunt force trauma. Your killer used something like a hammer or a mallet. There is also a fracture to the side of the skull. This darkened patch directly beneath the fracture is the resulting intracranial haemorrhage.'

'And that's what killed her?' Andrea asked.

'No.' Lovell shook his head. 'It might have done had she lived longer. She would have probably died from a bleed on the brain.' He then pointed to dark marks around the neck and throat. 'However, she died from manual asphyxiation.'

'She was strangled?' Laura asked, to clarify.

'Yes,' Lovell replied quietly. 'It's exactly the same pattern of injury as the other two poor women that I saw in recent months.'

Andrea looked at him. 'So, it's the same killer?'

'Yes.' Lovell nodded. 'You can see the pattern of finger-marks around the windpipe here, which have caused a very particular pattern of bruising. As I said in my previous post-mortem, this is an incredibly personal and brutal way of killing someone. You are looking directly into their eyes as you choke the life from them. It's chilling, when you think about it. Your killer is devoid of all empathy, and is incredibly dangerous.'

Beaumaris CID office was a hive of activity as it had been for months now. Ben was over by the scene boards updating them with photos of possible suspects, maps and other information. Laura sat at her computer trying to work, but she couldn't concentrate. Pete was taking longer than usual to get back to her text. The computer fans whirred loudly as if sharing the panic that was rising inside her.

She leaned forward, stretching out her legs. Her hamstrings felt tight. It had been a while since she'd done any running. For a moment, she thought of the police running club she'd been a member of back in Manchester. She would run a good ten miles on a Wednesday evening. The thought of it now made her wince. She used to wear a blue Nike T-shirt that carried the logo THERE IS NO FINISH LINE. She cringed at the thought of it. It was how she was feeling about her and Pete's investigation into Sam's death.

Andrea turned from where she was sitting and looked over at Laura and Gareth. 'PNC and HOLMES check on Henry Marsh. Just those petty theft charges as a teenager but nothing else is flagged up.'

Gareth shrugged. 'Doesn't mean he didn't do it. I want his alibis checked and double-checked.' Gareth was already aware that most serial killers had a history of theft, vandalism and minor sexual offences such as exposure that often then escalated in their severity. But there were others that had no criminal record until they start to kill. He was taking no chances.

'Boss,' Declan said as he pointed to the monitor that was mounted to the wall. 'You need to take a look at what Ben found.'

There was grainy CCTV on the screen along with a time-code and date: *11.53 p.m. – Friday, 25 March 2022.*

'Traffic sent this over,' Ben explained as Gareth, Laura and Andrea approached to take a look at what he had found.

Ben clicked his mouse and the CCTV footage played. 'So, this is the A5025 which goes south from Benllech beach past Red Wharf Bay.'

On the screen was a dark, empty road. After a couple of seconds, a car came into view and then stopped in a lay-by. A figure got out, went to the boot, pulled out a rubbish bag and then jogged towards some trees.

Ben played the CCTV footage forward and then stopped after about ten minutes as the figure returned to the car without the bag, got in and drove away.

Laura felt her pulse quicken slightly. Given the timing and location, it was incredibly suspicious behaviour.

Then Laura peered at the screen and then over at Ben. 'That looks like a BMW to me.'

Gareth frowned. 'Is that significant?'

'Marsh drives a BMW,' Andrea explained.

Laura went closer to the screen for a better look. If it was the kind of BMW that Marsh drove then it might prove to be a major breakthrough in the case.

'We can get digital forensics to clean it up but can we get a closer look now?' Gareth asked.

Ben went back to his computer. 'I'll give it a go.' He clicked a button and the screen zoomed in.

Laura spotted four silver interlocking circles on the back of the car. 'Bollocks, it's an Audi,' she said with a swoop of disappointment. It wasn't Marsh's car.

'What about the plate?' Gareth asked.

Ben manipulated the image and the plate came into the middle of the screen – *DW18 FRF.*

'Right, get onto the DVLA and see who the registered owner of that car is,' Gareth said with a sense of urgency.

Laura spotted that Andrea was thumbing quickly through her notebook.

'We don't need to,' Andrea called over as she found what she was looking for. 'The car belongs to an Anthony Conte.'

'How do you know that?' Declan asked.

'He was lurking around the crime scene this morning and acting very suspiciously,' Andrea explained. 'When I went over, he ran back to his car. I got him out and checked his driving licence. And I memorised his numberplate, especially after our conversation about our killer hiding in plain sight.'

'Good point.' Gareth looked at her.

Andrea pointed to the screen and asked, 'Can we run the CCTV back a bit?'

Ben nodded. 'No problem.'

As the CCTV played again, Andrea went closer to the screen. 'Stop there.'

Although it was grainy, the figure's face was visible.

'Yeah, that's him,' Andrea said with a nod as she turned to Gareth.

He raised an eyebrow. 'I don't suppose you memorised his address?'

'No, boss,' Andrea replied. 'But he was definitely agitated. He claimed he was trying to cut down Bay View Road and just stopped to see what was going on.'

'Any idea what he does for a living?' Laura asked, wondering if or how Conte might have come into contact with the victims.

'He owns his own gym and fitness studio,' Andrea explained. 'And he's a personal trainer.'

'Maybe that's how he met our victims?' Laura said, thinking out loud.

Ben was already typing into the computer. He looked over. 'Anthony Giuseppe Conte?'

'Yes, that's him,' Andrea stated.

Ben pointed. 'I've got an address in Capel Coch.'

'We need to retrieve that bag that he dumped asap,' Gareth said urgently. 'PNC check?'

Ben nodded. 'I've just run one, boss. Anthony Conte has a string of minor convictions. Auto theft and arson.' Ben gave them a meaningful look. 'He also has convictions for indecent exposure, stalking, coercive behaviour and sexual assault.'

Laura glanced over at Gareth. It was textbook stuff. It sounded like they'd made a significant breakthrough – even if it wasn't Marsh.

CHAPTER 11

Gareth stood on the doorstep of Anthony Conte's three-bedroomed home. It was pouring with rain. He gave an authoritative knock on the door and then squinted through the raindrops at Laura and ran his hand over his scalp. 'The only advantage of being bald: no wet hair.'

Laura rolled her eyes and pointed to her matted hair under her hood. 'Look at me. A drowned rat.'

Gareth raised an eyebrow. 'A sexy drowned rat.'

'Nice try.' Laura smiled. 'You know your nose wrinkles when you lie.'

Their eyes locked for a second and she smiled.

Aware that there had been no movement or sound from inside the house, Gareth stooped down, opened the letter box and peered inside. The hallway was clean and tidy. There were a couple of framed prints on the wall.

'Mr Conte?' he called.

Nothing.

Silence.

At the same time, Laura moved across to a ground-floor window, cupped her hands and peered inside.

'Anything?' Gareth asked, looking over at her.

Laura shook her head. 'Not a peep.'

Gareth glanced at the driveway. The navy Audi was parked on the drive. 'His car is here,' he remarked with a frown.

The hamlet had no shops and was fairly remote, so Conte would have had to drive if he was going anywhere. Did that mean he'd seen them and was now avoiding opening the door?

A sudden noise came from somewhere outside.

It sounded like it had come from the rear of the property.

Gareth exchanged a look with Laura. 'You hear that?'

'Yeah,' Laura replied and then pointed to the side of the house where there was a passageway leading to the back. 'Let's have a look.'

As Gareth and Laura moved down the side of the house, the rain intensified. They came out onto a neat patio and a substantial, well-tended back garden that seemed to stretch for at least 100 yards to the rear of the property.

It was empty.

Huge raindrops drummed rhythmically on the decking and on a large blue and white sun umbrella that was still open over a wicker garden table and chairs.

Out of the corner of his eye, Gareth caught sight of a figure moving. He peered through branches of a huge sycamore tree and saw a man in a black raincoat and hood climbing over the slatted fence in the far right-hand corner of the garden.

The figure glanced back in his direction.

It was him.

Conte!

'Shit! Laura!' Gareth shouted as he sprinted across the lawn and down the garden towards Conte, who had scrambled his way to the top of the fence and dropped down the other side.

'Stop! Police!' he bellowed.

Gareth arrived at the fence, placed a foot on the wet slat and tried to pull himself up. His foot slipped.

'Bloody hell!' he snapped angrily.

He tried again. This time he managed to get a decent grip and hauled himself over and down the other side.

He turned to see that Laura had followed him over.

'Okay?' he asked.

'Yes,' she said, wiping her wet hands on her coat.

A muddy pathway led to the right and down past a field. Conte was sprinting and already well ahead of them. A dark green sign read: PUBLIC FOOTPATH – LLWYBR CYHOEDDUS.

As rainwater filled the shallow potholes, Gareth and Laura gave chase. A fence of steel poles and barbed wire to the left marked out a field where cows were lying in the long grass, oblivious to what was unfolding.

Gareth was running flat out, breathing heavily. Behind him, Laura had got into her stride. Splashing through the deepening puddles, he felt the water flood into his boots and soak his socks. He wiped the rain and sweat from his stinging eyes.

If Conte ran a gym and was a personal trainer, then he was fit. It didn't bode well in a foot race.

As Gareth rounded the corner, he came to a ramshackle farm and outbuildings. It was a dead end, and the thick smell of slurry took him by surprise.

Rusty steel-pipe fencing enclosed the pens where dairy cows were kept at night. A covered stack of hay bales and an enormous feed shed towered over a weathered green and yellow tractor.

Conte was nowhere to be seen.

Shit! Where is he?

Laura arrived beside Gareth and stopped. They both sucked in air as their lungs burned.

'Where the fuck did he go?' Gareth gasped, his pulse thundering. His eyes scanned around, looking for the smallest movement, but the incessant rain made it difficult to see clearly. He used the back of his hand to wipe the water from his eyebrows.

'No idea,' Laura replied as she blew out her cheeks.

'He can't have just vanished,' Gareth growled as he continued to search the undergrowth for Conte's whereabouts.

Then came the distant sound of rustling, and a twig cracked as Conte emerged from the back of the farm. He turned, looked at them and then ran up the slope into the dense forest.

'Over there!' Laura shouted as they broke into a run again.

Great, Gareth thought. *Just what we need: an uphill chase through a forest.*

His legs felt heavy as he slipped and lost his footing on the bank that led up to the forest's edge. His knee skidded on mud, soaking his trousers.

'Bollocks!' he muttered.

They reached the forest.

Gareth stared intently into the darkness created by the tightly knit rows of Welsh oak, pines and birch. The trunks reached nearly 100 feet above their heads.

Conte had disappeared again.

The whole environment had suddenly changed. The air around him smelled of dampness and the decay of fallen leaves. But the rain had also made it fresh and light.

Gareth continued to run and then stopped, listening intently for the sound of movement. The falling rain was masking any sound Conte might be making.

Laura was lagging behind a little.

Gareth came to a clear uphill pathway and broke into a sprint. Then he stopped to see that Laura was struggling in the mud.

Laura waved him away. 'Go after him! I'm fine.'

Gareth turned and ran, ducking and weaving through the branches. He pumped his fists as soon as he got a clear run.

He was gaining on Conte, who had now slowed down. Maybe he was tiring?

For a moment, he lost sight of Conte. His eyes zipped right and left across the greenery.

Where the hell did he go?

A sudden noise of twigs snapping brought his attention hard left. Gareth could see undergrowth moving as Conte headed for the clearing.

Zigzagging quickly through branches and brambles, Gareth found a pathway and picked up speed. His shoes were rubbing his feet painfully, and he could feel the sweat running down his back.

Reaching the clearing at the top of the hill, he glanced around.

Shit! Lost him again.

Then came a metallic sound that he didn't recognise.

Following the direction where the noise had come from, Gareth jogged past the steep walls of damp, moss-covered slate, which were partly hidden by wild undergrowth. Then he saw an old brick archway, which was about twenty feet tall at its highest. Across the archway was a rusted metal-mesh gate. However, there was a small gap in the mesh at the far right-hand end which, if crawled through, would make the metallic sound that Gareth had just heard.

He knew where they were now. An abandoned nineteenth-century slate mine that he'd visited as a kid with his grandfather.

Fastened to the brickwork at the entrance to the mine was a yellow sign with a black triangle and black exclamation mark: PERYGL – ADEILEITH AMNIOGEL! DANGER – UNSAFE STRUCTURES! Then a less vague sign: CADWCH ALLAN! – KEEP OUT!

Gareth pushed through the gap in the gate and followed the path leading to the mine. The wide entrance soon narrowed as the pathway descended into darkness, and he navigated the narrow-gauge rail tracks that had once been used to ferry back the mine's slate by the tonne, but were now covered in orange rust.

Fifty yards down, the tracks disappeared under ankle-high water. The splashing of running footsteps echoed up the passageway and Gareth gave chase. He slowed as the mine became increasingly dark, and he flicked on his phone's torch.

Where am I?

It was getting impossible to see anything.

Up ahead the tunnel split into two sections. As the terrain rose again it revealed a huge, corroded iron turntable where the slate trucks could be turned.

Gareth peered into the darkness, his heart pounding. He was expecting Conte to jump him at any second.

'Anthony?' he called out, his voice reverberating around the yawning interior of the mine.

Holding his breath for a second, he listened intently.

Nothing but the drip of water against rock.

Silence.

Gareth raised his phone torch, and the bright beam caught a seam of metal ore within the green slate that glinted. The mine was cavernous, like a church, its roof thirty or forty feet high. As he moved slowly to take the tunnel to the left, the sound of the water that he was wading through echoed.

A figure appeared suddenly out of the darkness.

Jesus!

A fist hit Gareth in the face, stunning him.

Conte was on him in a flash, pushing him down towards the ground where there was nearly a foot of water.

Gareth struggled, threw a punch but missed.

Shit!

As he turned to move, Gareth lost his footing on the wet stone below. He landed on his knees in the icy water.

Putting him in a neck lock, Conte pushed and pulled Gareth down.

He's going to try and bloody drown me!

Grabbing the man's muscular forearm, Gareth pushed back but it was no use. Conte was too strong.

Suddenly, Gareth's face was under the freezing water.

He pushed back again but to no avail.

Conte's powerful fingers pushed hard against the back of his skull, holding his head under.

Gareth was running out of breath.

He struggled again but he was now dizzy. He was beginning to lose consciousness.

I'm not going to drown and die here!

Gareth abruptly pulled Conte, spinning him over his shoulder and into the water.

Gareth's head burst through the surface of the water and, gasping for breath, he grabbed Conte, punching him hard on the jaw.

Standing up, he pulled Conte upwards and smashed him back against the rocks and punched him again.

Conte swung his fist and knocked Gareth's phone flying.

The mine was plunged into complete darkness.

'Shit!' Gareth growled.

Then there was the sound of splashing water. Conte was clearly running further into the mine but Gareth couldn't see where.

How the hell does he know where he's going?

Moving forward, Gareth's knee cracked against rock.

'For fuck's sake!' he said loudly, his voice reverberating around the mine.

The sound of splashing water had stopped.

Conte had managed to escape.

HIM

It was dark by the time he drove along the roads of east Anglesey. It had been quite a day and he was exhausted. A hot shower, change of clothes and good drink of whisky had given him the boost he needed.

He wasn't quite sure where he was going. He just knew that he wanted to be out of the house, and driving around sometimes cleared his mind. Killing Zoey had only satisfied his desire for a few hours and it was starting to wear off already. Sometimes he could find temporary relief by going back to the pursuits of his teenage years and his twenties. Peeping and stalking. They were only light relief, though. He imagined it would be the same as an alcoholic being given a pint of shandy instead of the bottle of whisky that he truly craved.

Outside, the drizzle was intermittent. The roads and pavements were wet from an earlier downpour and the streetlights glistened on their surface with a cold, milky glow. The wind had died down a little but the smaller trees and branches still danced and jigged.

Glancing in the rear-view mirror, he caught a glimpse of the man looking back at him. How did he feel about that man?

He searched inside. He felt nothing. Neither love nor loathing. For a moment, he glimpsed his taid in his mind's eye. They shared the same forehead and hairline. Strong features and thick grey-black hair. His taid claimed they had Jewish heritage. But like every story that he'd ever heard as a child, it changed, became embellished or was disputed when he repeated it.

Out of the corner of his eye, he spotted someone walking towards the tiny rural bus stop. It was a young woman. As the drizzle turned to rain, he slowed the car and stared over at her. Realising that he recognised her, he buzzed down the window.

'Hayley?' he shouted.

Hayley, twenty-one years old, had pulled up the hood on her parka-style coat. She had olive skin and chestnut hair. Leaning down to the level of the open passenger-side window, she peered in at him.

'Hayley,' he said again. 'Which way are you going?'

For a moment, she clearly had no idea who he was. He was indignant.

Then the penny dropped.

'Oh, it's you,' she said. 'Don't worry. I can get the bus.'

'Come on,' he said with a smile. 'It's raining. Where are you heading?'

'Down to Pentraeth,' she explained, but she was clearly wary. He didn't blame her. There was a maniac killing young women out there!

'There you are then. I'm going to Beaumaris,' he said cheerily. 'I can drop you on the way.'

She shook her head. 'It's all right.'

Feeling a burst of grinding anger at her refusal, he took a breath to hide it.

Keep it calm. Nice and calm. Or you'll frighten her away.

'Listen, there's this bloke out there.' He gave her a serious look. 'It's dangerous. You shouldn't be travelling anywhere on your own at night.'

'I don't know . . .'

'Come on, Hayley. I'd never forgive myself if anything happened to you,' he said pleadingly. 'I used to be really fond of your mum and dad. Do you remember?' Looking at her sparkly skirt and heels, he remarked. 'Going to a party?'

Hayley nodded but didn't say anything.

He could feel the tension growing inside him. So close, yet so far. He could tell she was still toying with the idea of getting into the car. He knew that everyone had warned young women on the island not to get into cars with strangers.

'I told my mum I was going to get the bus,' Hayley said.

'In this weather? Tell you what,' he said with a winning smile. 'I've got to stop at that off-licence down there. They sell three bottles of wine for the price of two. I only need two so you can have the other one to take to your party. How does that sound?'

He'd pulled out all the stops. Every little manipulation he could think of. This wasn't his usual modus operandi. He had usually laid the groundwork for his killings with careful planning and attention to detail. But Hayley's appearance seemed too good an opportunity to pass up.

She blinked as she processed his proposition. Then she nodded and got into the car.

'There you go,' he said, his pulse racing with excitement. The adrenaline had kicked in. He just needed to mask how he was feeling. 'You don't want to arrive at a party like a drowned rat, do you?'

He didn't like to tell her that she wasn't going to arrive at the party at all.

CHAPTER 12

Laura and Gareth crept slowly towards Anthony Conte's house in the darkness. There had been a tip-off that there had been movement from inside. A neighbour from across the road claimed she had seen someone entering an hour ago. Another had seen a light on earlier. Laura wondered why Conte would be stupid enough to go back to his own home but she had encountered enough stupid criminals in her past not to rule it out.

Despite sending up the police helicopter and putting every unit on the island on alert for any sign of him, there had been no confirmed sightings of Conte since he vanished into the slate mine five hours earlier. Gareth had inspected some maps of the mine online and discovered that there were five other entrances spaced across that hilltop. Conte could have escaped from any of them.

Uniform units had also been deployed to the wooded area close to Benllech beach where Conte had been seen dumping the rubbish bag in the CCTV. So far, officers had drawn a blank in finding it or its contents.

The night air was cold and fresh. Laura glanced up and saw that the moon had sloped unnoticed behind a swollen grey cloud so that the area was now enveloped in darkness.

Gareth gave a signal to the AFOs. They were carrying Glock 9mm pistols and were dressed in their black Nomex boots, gloves, and Kevlar helmets over balaclavas as they moved purposefully to the low wall that bordered Conte's front garden. Their goggles and ballistic body armour gave them an eerie appearance.

They were taking no chances when it came to Conte. He was now their prime suspect in the murder of three women on the island, plus the disappearance of two more. He had attempted to kill Gareth in the mine so he was clearly both desperate and dangerous.

Laura watched as Gareth motioned silently for the CID officers and AFOs to head along the path to the front door. She felt the grip of anxiety in her stomach and the thudding of her heart. She adjusted her ballistic stab vest.

The AFOs took their positions by the front door in preparation for their forced entry. Gareth beckoned to one of the AFOs who then stepped forwards with a dark red steel battering ram that would break down the door in one hit.

The wind picked up and swirled noisily through the branches of a nearby tree. A dog barked somewhere in the distance.

A light from inside the house came on, illuminating the glass panels in the front door.

Bingo!

Someone was inside.

Gareth caught Laura's eye and nodded. It was time.

Laura clicked her Tetra radio and said very quietly, 'Gold Command from six-three. Officers in position at target location. Over.'

The radio crackled back. 'Six-three received. Gold Command order is GO.'

Laura's mind raced through the various dark scenarios they might find behind that door. She prayed that Conte was in there and they could get him off the streets before he killed anyone else.

Gareth gave another signal to the AFOs. He then glanced at Laura. 'Ready to go?' he whispered.

She nodded.

SMASH!

The front door swung open with an almighty thud.

The AFOs moved in, their weapons trained in front of them.

'Armed police! Show yourself,' they bellowed as they stormed into the house. 'Armed police!'

Laura followed, the adrenaline pumping through her veins.

The house was neat, tidy and tastefully furnished. The air was thick was the smell of cooking – garlic, onion.

Moving slowly down the hallway, Laura could hear the AFOs going from room to room, shouting 'Armed police!' and then confirming 'Clear!' as they went.

'Armed police!' an officer cried from a room further along the hall. It was followed by the piercing sound of a scream.

Who is that?

Laura rushed into the living room expecting to see Conte cowering on the floor.

Instead, the AFO had his gun trained on a woman in her thirties. She was terrified and had her hands up. She had black hair and olive skin.

'*Non sparare! Non sparare!*' she shouted as she stared in horror at the officer.

Sounds Italian, Laura thought.

'Get down on the floor, now!' the AFO yelled.

The woman glanced at Laura as if to say *Help*.

'It's okay.' Laura moved forwards, looking at the woman, trying to establish eye-contact and signalling to the AFO to put his gun down.

'*Non sparare*,' the woman cried, shaking like a leaf.

'Do you speak English?' Laura asked gently as she motioned for the woman to put her hands down now.

The woman frowned and then nodded her head to signal she understood. '*Si, un po.*'

Laura assumed this meant that she spoke a little.

'My name is Laura. I'm a police officer,' she said in a well-rehearsed and gentle tone. 'What's your name?

The woman stared up at Laura.

'Amara,' she replied.

'Amara. Okay. We're looking for Anthony,' Laura explained.

'Anthony? *Si,*' Amara said with a frown

'Is he here? Is Anthony in this house?'

Amara shook her head. 'No.'

'He's not here,' Laura said, gesturing to the rest of the house.

'No, no,' Amara replied, blinking nervously. Then Amara pointed to herself. '*Cugina*. Erm, cousin.'

'You're Anthony's cousin, yes?' Laura said to clarify.

'Si, yes, cousin.'

'Have you seen Anthony today?' Laura asked.

'Today?' Amara said with a frown. ' No . . . *Ieri* . . . You say, yesterday.'

Laura gave Amara an encouraging nod. 'You saw Anthony yesterday but not today?'

'Yes. Yes.'

Gareth came into the room and Laura looked at him.

'There's no sign of him anywhere,' he said.

'Shit,' Laura mumbled with disappointment.

Gareth glanced at Amara and gave Laura a quizzical look.

'This is Amara. She's Conte's cousin. She's Italian so she doesn't speak much English but says she hasn't seen him today. The last time she saw him was yesterday.'

'Okay,' Gareth said. 'Given what we've just found, we're going to need to take her for interview and find a translator.'

Laura frowned at him. 'What have you found?'

Gareth signalled for her to follow him. They went back into the hallway, turned left and Laura saw a door that had clearly been kicked down by an AFO.

Inside was what appeared to be a small study – desk, office chair, shelves.

Above the desk was a board that was covered in photographs of women who had been bound and gagged. In some, a man in a leather mask was having sex with them. Some of the women in the images were no more than teenagers.

'Jesus,' Laura said under her breath.

Gareth grabbed an evidence bag and held it up to show her. 'We also found this in a drawer over there.' Inside the clear evidence bag were five or six pairs of women's underwear.

Laura shook her head. Did those knickers belong to the murdered women?

'Plus this,' Gareth said, showing her another evidence bag. Inside there were hair clips, bobbles and a hair band, plus strands of human hair.

Laura felt her stomach tighten. 'You think these are trophies?'

'Yes.' Gareth gave her a dark look but there was also a glimmer of relief in his expression. 'I think we've got him, Laura.'

HIM

'This isn't the way to the off-licence,' Hayley said curtly. 'It's that way.'

'Is it?' he said with a frown. 'Are you sure?'

She glared at him and huffed. 'Yes.'

'Oh right,' he laughed. 'God, I'm such an idiot. No sense of direction. Tell you what, there's a twenty-four-hour petrol station just before we get to Pentraeth. We can stop there.'

Hayley gave him a very suspicious look.

'What wine do you like?' he asked her.

She shrugged.

'Mine is Barolo,' he said. 'King of Italian red wines. I like most Italian wines if I'm honest.'

'Right,' she said quietly.

'How have you been?' he asked.

Hayley was still agitated as she peered out of the car window. 'Yeah, fine,' she mumbled.

Inside he could feel that his indignation at her ingratitude and surly mood was turning to fury. Part of the thrill was his interaction with the young women. Getting them to like him. Charming them or making them laugh. Even flirting. The attack on Zoey had been perfect. She had been expecting a romantic walk along the beach so the look on her face had been quite wonderful. Hayley was proving to be a great disappointment. He would teach her a lesson about manners.

It was only a couple of miles down to Pentraeth and shouldn't take more than six or seven minutes. He would drive them to the beach on some kind of pretence and attack her there. That would be perfect. The beach was isolated with no main roads and virtually no houses.

Leaning over, he put on the radio. 'Under Pressure' by Queen and David Bowie was playing.

'Ah, brilliant,' he said as he turned up the volume. 'This is great. Do you like Queen?'

Hayley narrowed her eyes. 'I've never even heard of Queen.'

'What?' he laughed. 'Freddie Mercury?'

'No.' She shook her head.

'This bit is David Bowie,' he explained.

'Oh, yeah, I've heard of him,' Hayley said in a withering tone. 'My dad likes him.'

He sang along under his breath for a moment. '*Watching some good friends screaming, Let me out!*'

Wrapping her arms around herself, Hayley gazed out of the passenger-side window.

He turned down the music. 'Are you cold? I can turn the heater up?'

'No, it's fine.' She didn't turn but instead just muttered, sounding annoyed.

He took a breath but a red mist had already descended.

'What the fuck is the matter with you?' he snapped angrily. It was all he could do to stop himself from lashing out and hitting her in the face. Her arrogance. Her rudeness. How dare she!

Spinning to look at him, she appeared terrified. 'Stop the car.'

'Sorry.' He held up a conciliatory hand. 'I'm really sorry. Let me drop you off. It's only a few minutes and . . .'

'Stop the car! I'm getting out!' she shouted.

'Come on, Hayley,' he said gently. 'It's raining and you'll get soaked.'

'LET ME OUT!' she shrieked.

'I said I'm sorry,' he babbled. 'It's just that I've tried my best to—'

'Oh my God!' she thundered and held up her mobile phone. 'I swear, if you don't let me out of the car right now I'm calling the police.'

He was in a panic. His mind raced. Up ahead, traffic lights went to red.

Their eyes locked.

He was going to have to stop the car.

As he slowed the car, he spotted her hand go for the door handle.

Her eyes were still on his. Waiting for him to make a move.

It was like a Mexican stand-off.

In a flash, he grabbed at her coat and with his other hand went to hit the central locking. He was going to try and strangle her right there in the car.

CRACK!

Her fist smashed into his face, stunning him for a moment.

By the time, he had recovered and reached again for the central locking button, the passenger door was open and Hayley had made her escape.

Leaping from the car, he raced onto the roadside to follow her.

Hayley was sprinting away.

'Help! Help!' she screamed. 'Somebody help me!'

Breaking into a sprint, he went after her.

'Help me!'

Up ahead, there was a turning into rural business park. Signs advertised CARAVANS FOR SALE, SELF-STORAGE AND EXHAUSTS AND MOTS.

Hayley ducked left and disappeared out of sight.

He had fancied his chances of catching her along a country road but a rural business park was a different matter.

The rain was getting heavier and noisier. He jogged into the business park but it was difficult to see anything. Wiping water from his face, he blinked as his eyes roamed left and right.

Where the hell is she?

He jogged further into the site and to his utter frustration, saw that the road split in two different directions to various industrial units and warehouses.

Jesus! She could be anywhere.

Headlights appeared from the right, as a large Bedford van pulled out of a garage and headed his way.

Shielding his eyes from the lights, he squinted as the van slowed, stopped and wound down its window.

'You all right, mate?' the driver asked in a deep voice. 'You look lost.'

He gave the driver an ironic smile. 'I parked up here this morning and now I can't remember where.'

'Oh Christ,' the driver laughed, pointing to the torrential rain. 'Not a good night for it, is it?'

'No,' he replied with a shrug. 'You didn't happen to see anyone on your way down that road did you?'

'No,' the driver replied with a frown. 'Why? You looking for someone?'

'Not really,' he said. 'Just one of my work colleagues parked up here too. Bit of a long shot really.'

'Ah, well, good luck with finding that car,' the driver said with a grin as he drove away.

Glancing up, he saw that there were CCTV cameras mounted on a nearby warehouse. They covered the whole road.

Gritting his teeth, he took one last look at the buildings around him. He'd already been spotted by the van driver. There was CCTV everywhere. And Hayley could be anywhere.

FUCK! FUCK!

He'd left his car on the kerbside and the passenger door was still open. It wouldn't be long before it aroused suspicion and the police were called.

He needed to get back.

Clenching his fists, he stamped his foot like a petulant child.

CHAPTER 13

Laura walked from the kitchen to the living room with a glass of red wine and a cold beer for Gareth. Rosie was engrossed in her phone at the end of the sofa while a game show played quietly on the television. Jake was upstairs playing loudly on his X-box. Elvis lay flat on the carpet snoozing with a low, dull snore.

Flopping down into the chair, Laura let out an audible sigh. She put the beer down and took a long swig of wine.

That's better, she thought to herself.

Stretching out her toes, she pulled her foot back to take out some of the tension of the day. Conte was still out there somewhere and it was a frightening thought. Uniformed patrols had all been issued with Conte's photo, plus the registration number of his Audi. Gareth, who was upstairs in the shower, had set up a skeleton CID team to work overnight on tracking down Conte until the bulk of the team arrived back at six a.m. She would have this wine and try and get some sleep.

Laura took another swig and brushed her hair from her face. It was dry and full of split ends. Another wonderful advantage of the ageing process and her declining levels of oestrogen, she thought wearily.

As Laura looked over, she saw that Rosie was clearly distressed at something.

'You okay, darling?' Laura asked her.

Rosie shook her head – she had tears in her eyes.

Getting up, Laura went over, sat next to her and put a comforting hand on her shoulder. 'What's wrong.'

'I think Daniel is cheating on me,' Rosie said with a sniff as she wiped a tear from her face.

Laura frowned. 'Why do you think that?'

Rosie looked at her. 'Just a few comments at school. There was that house party at Felix Thomas's that I didn't go to. Gaby told me that Daniel and Katie Nelson were on the sofa together.'

'Okay,' Laura said gently. 'Are they friends?'

'Katie Nelson is a slag,' Rosie growled. 'I know she wants to get with Daniel. She's all over him in the sixth form common room.'

'Have you talked to Daniel?' Laura asked.

'Yeah,' Rosie said. 'He said nothing happened.'

'Do you believe him?'

'No,' Rosie admitted. 'He's been weird with me all week. I know something happened.'

Laura gave an empathetic look and then a hug. 'I'm sorry.'

'Why are boys and men such twats?' Rosie groaned.

Laura looked, brushed a strand of hair from her face and reassured her, 'They're not all twats. Honestly.'

'You mean Dad?' Rosie asked.

Laura nodded. 'Yeah, your dad and . . .' Before she could say anything else, Gareth appeared in the doorway. 'Hey . . .' He was fresh from his shower and wearing a robe and pyjamas. Gareth then said in a sing-song voice, *'Did you happen to see the most beautiful girl in the world . . .'*

'Cringe,' Rosie said under her breath, bristling.

'Be nice,' Laura whispered as she got up and went over

103

to Gareth. 'You seem very chipper,' she said, handing him his beer as he came past and plonked himself down in the armchair.

'Yeah, well, God knows why,' he admitted dryly. 'But I will give you ten points if you can tell me who sang that song.'

Laura frowned. 'I want to say Tom Jones, but I know that's wrong.'

'Charlie Rich,' Gareth said and then swigged his beer.

'Never heard of him,' Laura admitted. 'But I do know the next lyrics are, "*Who walked out on me. . .*" Which is why I'm guessing you stopped there.'

'Exactly,' Gareth said with a grin as he picked up the remote. 'Mind if I pop on the news?'

'Help yourself,' Laura said.

'Really?' Rosie huffed, got up and left the room.

Laura exchanged a look with Gareth and got up. 'Excuse me for a second,' she muttered angrily.

Rosie was stomping down the hallway.

'What's wrong?' Laura called after her.

'I was watching the television and *he* just turned it over,' Rosie growled.

'No, you weren't,' Laura said calmly, aware that Rosie was feeling emotionally vulnerable but not wanting to indulge her. 'You were on your phone and you weren't paying any attention to what was on the television.'

'How do you know?' Rosie snapped. 'You hardly register my or Jake's existence these days. Especially when he's here.'

'Gareth,' Laura said. 'His name is Gareth.'

'Okay.' Rosie shrugged with a deliberately uninterested look as she turned and headed for the stairs.

Laura knew that Rosie was upset by what was going on with Daniel and possibly taking it out on everyone else. It was best to leave it for now.

'Laura?' Gareth called calmly from the living room. 'You might want to come and see this.'

Laura came back to the living room only to see a photo of Butterfield on the television.

Jesus Christ! What the hell is he doing on the news?

The news anchor looked at the camera and said, '*Police in Lancashire are continuing their search for Superintendent Ian Butterfield, who went missing yesterday morning while walking in the area of Pendle Hill. Mr Butterfield of the Manchester Metropolitan Police set off on his own early yesterday morning from this car park, but hasn't been seen since. Lancashire Police have been using helicopters with thermal imaging equipment and dog search teams. Police have also appealed to anyone who might have seen Mr Butterfield in that area to contact them on a helpline.*'

Gareth frowned at Laura. 'Do you know him?'

She nodded slowly. 'We were in the same station. He was my boss.'

Having kept her quest to find out the exact details of what had happened to Sam and why, and who was responsible for his death, a secret from Gareth, she couldn't say any more. She could hardly start to explain that Ian Butterfield had turned up one night, six months ago, looking distressed. He had gone on to reveal his and Louise McDonald's connections to the Fallowfield Hill Gang and that he feared for his life. He had also made it clear that the OCG's use of intimidation, manipulation and bribery had permeated various police stations and the highest ranks of the GMP. Laura and Pete had spent the last six months digging around to see if they could corroborate anything that Butterfield had said but had got nowhere.

And now Butterfield had gone missing.

'I hope he's all right,' she said, feeling guilty for keeping all this from Gareth. Maybe she should just come clean and tell him? Her decision had been based on her feeling that their burgeoning relationship would never last if he knew that she was spending time looking into the death of her late husband. It was just too emotive and complicated.

Getting up from the armchair, Gareth muttered, 'I need another beer.' As he approached, he frowned at her. 'You okay?'

She nodded. 'Yeah. It was just strange to see him up there on the screen.'

Gareth gently took Laura's hand and led her out of the living room and into the hallway. He put his arms around her and looked into her eyes.

She gave him a quizzical smile. 'Oh, hello, what are you up to?'

He didn't reply but instead leaned in and gave her a long, soft kiss.

'I've spent all day with you, but I haven't *seen* you all day, if you know what I mean?' Gareth said quietly.

'Yeah, well, trying to catch a serial killer is kind of getting in the way of that,' she replied darkly.

He nodded. 'I know.'

They kissed again, passionately, as he pulled her into his body. She loved the feeling of his strong, protective arms around her.

CHAPTER 14

It was 6.30 a.m. as Gareth made his way out of his office for the morning briefing. He'd had two strong cups of coffee, and the intel that there had been a sighting of Conte camping out in some farm buildings was just the news he needed right now. It wasn't too much to expect that they could have their prime suspect in custody by lunchtime.

'Right, guys, listen up,' he said as he marched over to the front of the office. 'Declan, what have we got on this sighting?'

Declan stood up, went over to the map of Anglesey on the wall and pointed. 'There's a farm three miles east of Llangefni. Farmer spotted someone over by some feed sheds last night. The farmer called us this morning as he was worried. Uniform patrol checked twenty minutes ago and a navy-blue Audi with Conte's registration had been parked around the back.'

'Okay,' Gareth said brightly. 'Sounds like he's there.'

'I've stationed a uniform patrol on this track here,' Declan said, pointing to the map again. 'If he tries to leave, then they can stop him. Authorised Firearms Officers are meeting us down there at seven thirty a.m.'

'Great work, Declan,' Gareth said. 'Anything come back from his house?'

Laura glanced over. 'Digital Forensics found some pretty hard pornography on his laptop. Mainly bondage and rape fantasy. I don't think it's illegal but it certainly fits in with our killer's MO.'

'Boss,' Ben said. 'Forensics said that they might be able to trace the DNA on those hair clips and strands of hair by the end of the day.'

'Great,' Gareth said. 'Okay, so we also have a march this morning in Beaumaris. What do we know?'

Andrea signalled that she had a flyer. 'It says, *Our march is in memory of the three women on this island who have been so brutally taken from us and in solidarity with the two who are still missing. It is also a protest to highlight a culture of violence against women, which must stop. The Isle of Anglesey must be a safe place for all women. The march starts at 9 a.m. by the castle and will travel down to the beach, where flowers will be laid in memory of the victims.*'

Rubbing his hand over his scalp, Gareth thought for a few seconds. 'Andrea and Ben, while we arrest Conte, I'd like you to go down to the march this morning. Keep a relatively low profile, but we need to show our solidarity with the families and the island as a whole.'

'Yes, boss,' Andrea said.

'And, Ben, can you swing by Forensics on the way back and give them a nudge? I want the DNA on those hair cuttings asap.'

Ben nodded as he got up from his desk. 'Will do, boss.'

CHAPTER 15

The sun was slowly moving over the horizon as Gareth, Laura and other officers from Beaumaris CID moved into positions overlooking the disused farm buildings that had been identified.

Laura immediately spotted the navy-coloured Audi parked to one side, and felt a leap of triumph in her stomach. The intel had been correct. It seemed very likely that Conte was somewhere inside the buildings, probably camping out for the night in an effort to hide. The early morning sky flared an incredible flamingo pink and the wind off the nearby fields was bitter on her face and ears. Nearby trees showed the first buds of spring. A large marsh harrier watched their arrival warily before flapping noisily up into the sky. Its distinctive black-tipped wings spread and were still as it glided along the air currents in search of prey.

As the CID team moved forwards, they were accompanied by AFOs, who moved purposefully behind some old, rusty farm machinery. Their movements were well rehearsed. AFO training was repetitive, thorough and precise.

Gareth motioned silently for the CID officers and the AFOs

to head for the farm buildings, guns trained on the weather-worn doors and broken windows.

Laura said under her breath into her radio, 'Six-three to Gold Command. Officers in position two at target location, over.'

The radio crackled back. 'Six-three received. Units to proceed to position one, over.'

After last night's disappointment, Laura hoped to God that this time they'd get their man.

Laura gave Gareth a nod. He then signalled to the officers, who moved quietly over the final few yards of grass and uneven gravel, which crunched quietly under their feet.

There were two large wooden doors at the front of the main building that had been padlocked closed. If Conte was in there, he had used another door.

Gareth motioned and four AFOs moved away from them, heading for the sides and back of the building.

'Six-three to Gold Command. All units are at position one,' Gareth said into his radio.

There was an anxious moment as they waited and then, 'Six-three received. Gold Command order is go.'

Laura nodded at the AFOs and moved back against the grey stone wall. It was cold and hard, even with the vest on. Where was Conte? Was he lying in wait or was he oblivious to their presence at the farm?

CRASH!

Two AFOs used a steel battering ram to smash open the wooden doors, and a split second later the other AFOs moved in swiftly, weapons trained in front of them as they went.

'Armed police!' they bellowed as they stormed into the building. 'Armed police! Show yourself!'

Laura followed, her heart pounding in her chest. She scanned left and right into the darkness of the building. Were they going to have to play a tense game of hide and seek to smoke Conte out?

The building smelled damp and musty, and the floor was covered with straw and dry mud. As the wind picked up outside, the roof timbers creaked with an eerie groan. Laura continued moving, heart thumping, eyes searching left and right for any movement. CID officers and AFOs had fanned out throughout the building, clearing the stalls.

'Armed police!' the AFOs bellowed as they moved on through. 'Show yourself!'

Laura's heart started to sink. There was nothing.

Declan appeared and looked at Laura and Gareth shook his head. 'Nothing here, boss.'

'Bollocks!' Laura muttered to herself.

Suddenly, there was shouting from outside. 'Armed police, get down on the floor, now!'

Laura, Gareth and Declan raced out of the building to see Conte on his knees with a machine gun trained on him.

Thank God!

Gareth marched over, took out his handcuffs and in one movement cuffed Conte's hands behind him.

'Anthony Conte,' Gareth said, 'I'm arresting you on suspicion of murder.'

CHAPTER 16

Placards were being held quietly and unfolded banners carried in virtual silence as the crowd of protestors walked slowly onto Beaumaris beach to begin a solemn minute of reflection in memory of the women who had been murdered or had gone missing in recent months. A long homemade banner read 'STOP MEN FROM KILLING, RAPING, HARASSING AND ABUSING US.' Half an hour earlier, as the march made its way down from Beaumaris Castle, the air had been full of noise. Chants of *We will not be afraid!* and *Make Anglesey Safe* had come from a very vocal group of women from Reclaim the Streets who had travelled over from various parts of the North West of England and from all over Wales to support the march.

Andrea and Ben watched from a respectful distance. There had been a phone call from Laura to say that Anthony Conte had been found, arrested and was now in custody. Clearly the news of a breakthrough in the case hadn't been released yet but Andrea felt relieved that they had their man. She had instinctively known there was something very strange about him when she had challenged him at Benllech beach the day before. Something dark and uneasy about his manner. Then she had seen where he lived and the stuff they had found in his flat. And the CCTV footage of Conte hiding a rubbish bag in the woods close to Benllech the night that Zoey Garland had been so horribly murdered.

Andrea prayed that Conte confessed to what he had done rather than put the families of the victims through the torturous prospect of a trial.

The chattering and noise began to subside in preparation for a minute's silence. The press were everywhere. Photographers and TV camera crews trying to get the best shots of what was going on.

The wind swirled in from the sea and a flood of low sunlight illuminated the crowd. Andrea watched two girls in their late teens, slight with pale delicate faces, and underdressed for March. They could be sisters. They stood sadly by the railings beside the beach, holding each other, sobbing, oblivious to passers-by, lost in their grief. Beside them stood a man in his early twenties wearing a bright cycle helmet, from under which sprang thick brown curls and a beard. His hand went up to his face and wiped a tear from his cheek. He placed a comforting hand on the young woman beside him, who seemed lost in thought, her face gazing blankly skywards, white in the sunshine. There were whole families. One had four children in various sizes of blue coats, clearly under instruction to hold hands in silence. And a group of greying ladies in their quilted anoraks and robust shoes.

A whistle blew loudly and ripped through the air. The whole beach plunged into silence. A couple in their twenties stood with their heads bowed. The girl let the bearded man put his arm around her shoulder and her head lolled against him. Behind them, a stringy woman in a tracksuit crouched down by a three-wheel all-terrain pushchair to make sure her toddler kept quiet.

The silence was powerful. Still and respectful.

Just the sound of the waves skidding up the sand in the distance and the wind fluttering against banners and placards. A collective display of grief, anger and fear.

Further away, the families of Ellie Gates, Shannon Jones, Zoey Garland, Gemma Ramsey and Caitlin Thomas all moved forward in their desperate, unbearable sorrow to lay wreaths of flowers. Bethan Garland let out a wail as she clutched her husband. They stood together, staring at the wreaths.

Andrea took a breath as a tear welled in her eye. She wiped it away. Ben reached over and put a hand on her arm. She might have been there in a professional capacity, but she was also a woman in her twenties who lived on the island. It could have been her or one of her friends.

She wanted to go and tell them that they had someone in custody. That the monster who had so cruelly taken their daughters from them had been found and justice would be served. She knew that it wasn't her place to tell them and they would have to wait, but it just didn't seem fair.

The shrill sound of the whistle signalled that the minute was over.

As the families turned and moved away, for a few seconds, there was an air of uncertainty. And then a few murmurs of low conversation. Backlit by the low spring sunshine, silhouetted figures began to slowly walk away.

Ben looked at Andrea. 'You okay?'

'Yeah.' Andrea nodded but she could feel that she was churned up inside. 'I'm fine.'

'We've got Conte,' Ben said and then gestured to the families on the beach. 'So I hope no one else has to go through what they're going through.'

'Let's bloody hope so,' Andrea agreed.

Ben pointed over to a side road. 'Right, I'm parked up there. I've got to go to Forensics. I'll see you back at the station.'

'Okay,' Andrea said as she turned and began to walk in the opposite direction. She had parked behind the castle.

'Andrea?' called a voice.

She stopped and searched the busy road to find who had called her name, but couldn't see anyone.

That's weird. Maybe a different Andrea?

Side-stepping someone coming the other way, she continued heading back to where she had parked.

'Andrea?' the man's voice called loudly again.

Peering over to the other side of the road, closest to the beach, she spotted Professor Henry Marsh waving at her.

How does he know my name? she wondered. Maybe it was when she had shown him her warrant card on his doorstep.

Marsh was wearing a dark jacket and scarf. He was standing with a group of teenage girls who were milling around with placards and banners from the march.

Okay, he is seriously good-looking for an older man.

Their eyes met for a second and he gave her a half-smile. She could hardly walk off, so she wandered across the road to where he was standing. Even though she had never been convinced that Marsh had been a viable suspect, they now had Anthony Conte in custody and she expected him to be charged within the day, so she felt doubly safe talking to him.

'Professor Marsh,' she said as she approached.

Marsh immediately pulled a face. 'Oh God, Henry, please.' Then he gestured to the girls he was standing with, who were all aged around seventeen or eighteen. 'These guys are from my Sixth Form College. Everyone, this is Detective Constable Andrea Jones.'

The girls nodded awkward hellos.

'Obviously it's a very emotive time at Llangefni College,' Marsh explained. 'I said I'd come with them this morning.'

'Of course,' Andrea said, admiring the support he was showing to young women.

'Henry's a total legend,' a girl with red hair and pierced eyebrow informed her with a serious expression.

'Is he?' Andrea said with a bemused smile at the informal use of his name.

'Oh, yeah, totally,' a girl with a dark green beanie hat agreed.

'Looks like you're a hit with your students,' Andrea said.

Marsh shrugged. 'I just talk to them like grown-ups. And I have a decent sense of humour.'

'He's hilarious,' the red-haired girl declared, shaking her head.

'Right.' Andrea nodded. 'Well, that's good to know.' She pointed across the road. 'I'd better get going.'

As she turned to go, Marsh came closer to her and said under his breath, 'Look, I know we didn't meet under particularly auspicious circumstances. But, for what it's worth, I think you're the most attractive police officer I've ever seen. So, if you ever fancy meeting up for a coffee or a drink, just let me know.'

Andrea looked at his twinkly eyes, thought for a second and then said quietly, 'You know, I might just do that.'

'Good,' Marsh whispered with a laugh.

With an extra spring in her step, Andrea crossed the road and headed back to her car.

CHAPTER 17

'Interview conducted with Anthony Conte, Sunday, twenty-seventh March, eleven twenty p.m., Beaumaris Police Station. Present are Anthony Conte, Detective Inspector Gareth Williams, Duty Solicitor Patrick Clifford and myself, Detective Inspector Laura Hart.'

Laura glanced over. 'Anthony, do you understand you are still under caution?'

Conte blinked at her in utter confusion.

'Anthony?' Laura said gently.

Conte's confusion changed as he met her eyes with an icy glare that was more than unsettling.

'Do you understand you are still under caution?' Laura asked again slowly.

Clifford, the duty solicitor, leaned in and whispered something in his ear.

'Yes, of course.' Conte nodded. 'But this is utterly ridiculous. I haven't done anything.'

'Okay.' Laura moved the files so that they were in front of her. 'I would like to confirm that you are Anthony Giuseppe Conte?'

'Yes, that's correct,' he said, his eyes still glued to hers.

'Why are you asking me this? Why isn't he?' he asked, pointing to Gareth.

Laura wondered if he meant because she was a woman, the implication being that Gareth was a man and therefore senior – which he was, but not because of his gender.

'I'm a police officer, Anthony,' Laura explained. 'We're both detectives in Beaumaris CID.'

Conte gave her a withering look. 'Well, I want that officer to ask me questions, not you,' he snapped.

Clifford leaned in and whispered something to Conte, probably pointing out that this wasn't the best way to start an interview.

'I don't care,' Conte growled. 'I'm only answering questions from him.'

Gareth shot a look at Laura and sat forward. 'Can you tell us where you were last Friday evening, which was the twenty-fifth of March?'

Conte shrugged with a sneer. 'I was at home?'

'Can anyone verify that?' Gareth asked.

'No.' Conte shook his head condescendingly. 'I live on my own.'

'I thought your cousin Amara lived with you?' Laura asked with a frown.

Conte shrugged. 'I don't think she was in.'

Gareth ran his hand over his scalp and said, 'Did you speak to anyone? A neighbour or someone on the phone?'

'No, no one,' Conte replied. 'I wasn't feeling well so I went to bed early that night.'

'Can you tell us why you ran from us earlier today?' Laura asked.

Conte shrugged. 'I saw you outside my front door and I was scared.'

'Why were you scared?'

'I don't know,' Conte replied. 'I didn't know who you were.'

Gareth frowned. 'Do you normally run down your garden and over the fence every time someone you don't know comes to your front door?'

'No.'

'Would you agree that it's suspicious behaviour?'

'I don't know.'

Gareth waited for a few seconds, then took a photograph out of his folder and turned it to show him. 'For the purposes of the tape, I'm showing the suspect item reference 8DDE. As you can see, this image shows your car. You can see the registration plate, is that correct?'

Conte pulled the photograph angrily towards him and peered at it for a few seconds. 'Yes, that's my car.'

'Okay.' Gareth nodded. 'As you can see from the timecode and date stamp, that photograph was taken at 11.53 p.m. on Friday, the twenty-fifth of March. But you've told us that you were home all night and went to bed early because you were unwell. Is there anything you can tell us about that?'

'No,' Conte said with a shrug. 'It wasn't me.'

Laura raised an eyebrow. 'You mean someone else was driving your car?'

Gareth pulled out another photograph from the CCTV which showed the figure leaving the car with a black bin bag. 'For the purposes of the tape, I'm showing the suspect item reference 3FCV. As you can see, this person leaves the car and deposits this bag somewhere in these woods before returning.'

Conte snorted. 'Well, it wasn't me.'

'Does anyone else have access to your car, Anthony?' Gareth asked.

'Not that I'm aware of,' Conte replied.

'Does Amara use your car?' Laura asked.

Conte snorted. 'She can't drive.'

Gareth frowned. 'So, how do you account for the fact that

your car was at this location, at this time when you've just told us you were at home in bed.'

Conte tapped his fingers on the table and chewed his cheek. 'Friday, did you say?'

'Yes.'

Laura glanced over at him. She knew exactly what Conte was about to do. She'd seen that fake searching-through-the-memory expression before. It was hard to pull off and Conte's version of it was utterly woeful.

'Oh, Friday,' Conte said as he nodded slowly. 'I did go out Friday.'

Big surprise! You've suddenly remembered.

'You did go out now?' Gareth said with a hint of sarcasm. 'Can you tell us where you went and why?'

'I had a lot of recycling that I'd forgotten to put out,' Conte explained. 'I knew there were some big recycling bins down at Benllech beach. When I got down there, they were full. I'm ashamed to say that on the way home, I stopped and threw them away.'

Laura looked at Gareth with an expression that said that Conte was talking absolute bollocks.

'Come on, Conte,' Gareth huffed impatiently. 'You forgot that you went out just before midnight to go to recycling bins by the beach.'

'I work late sometimes. I get confused,' he protested.

Gareth reached into the folder and pulled out a photograph of women's underwear that had been found in Conte's flat. 'For the purposes of the tape, I'm showing the suspect item reference 9DJQ. Can you tell me what's in this photograph, please, Anthony?'

Conte gave an irritated sigh and moved the photograph to take a better look. Then he stared over at Laura for a second with the faintest hint of a smirk before focusing his attention on Gareth.

120

What the hell was that about? Laura wondered.

'Women's underwear,' Conte replied in a blasé tone.

'Why have you got a drawer full of women's knickers of varying sizes in your flat?' Gareth asked.

Conte shrugged. 'They're my girlfriend's.'

Gareth raised an eyebrow, pulled out a pen and went to hand it over to Conte. 'Okay. I want you to write down her name and address so we can go and ask her to confirm this.'

Conte went to take the pen and then stopped. He sat back for a moment and ran his hand over his chin. 'Okay, they're mine.'

'These belong to you?' Gareth asked with a frown. 'Do you wear them?'

Conte pulled an angry face. 'No, of course not!'

Laura frowned at him. 'What are they for?'

'For?' Conte shrugged.

'Why have you got women's underwear in a drawer in your home?' Gareth snapped.

Conte rubbed his nose as he thought for a moment. 'I buy them off the internet,' he explained as though it was no stranger than buying a book online.

'What do you mean?' Gareth asked with a confused expression.

'People sell their wives' and girlfriends' used knickers on sites. And I buy them sometimes,' Conte explained, rubbing his nose again. 'It's not illegal.'

Laura looked over at him. 'We will be checking your IP browser history and your bank accounts.'

Conte shrugged. 'That's fine by me.'

Gareth reached into the folder and pulled out photographs of the murdered and missing women. He laid them down carefully in front of Conte. 'Do you know or recognise any of these women, Anthony?'

121

'Of course,' he snorted. 'I read the papers and watch the news.'

'Have you ever met any of these women?'

'No, of course not,' Conte snapped. 'I only know who they are because I watch the news.'

Gareth narrowed his eyes. 'And none of these women have ever been in your flat or your car?'

Conte shook his head. 'No.'

'And, as far as you know, they've never been to your gym or one of your fitness classes and you've never had any of them as a client in your capacity as a personal trainer?'

Conte shifted awkwardly in his seat. 'No!'

'And if we check these knickers, your flat and your car for these women's DNA, we're not going to find any? Is that right?' Gareth asked.

Conte let out an audible sigh. 'You think that I killed these women? You must be mad.'

There was a knock at the door and Ben appeared. He looked over at Gareth in a way that suggested some sense of urgency. 'I need a word, boss.'

Gareth glanced at Laura and suggested under his breath, 'You okay to go?'

Laura nodded.

'For the purposes of the tape,' Gareth said as Laura got up from her seat, 'DI Hart is leaving the room.'

As she walked over to the door, she was aware that Conte was watching her intently and looking her up and down. She buttoned up her jacket, suddenly feeling self-conscious and uncomfortable.

'What's going on, Ben?' Laura asked as she went out into the corridor with him.

'A father and his nineteen-year-old daughter are downstairs, boss,' Ben explained. 'The daughter claims that she was abducted in a car last night but she managed to escape. She said her attacker chased her on foot, but she got away.'

CHAPTER 18

Andrea gazed down at the tyre on her car and groaned. The tyre was flat against the ground. She wondered if it had been done intentionally – or was that her just being paranoid?

Bollocks! You've got to be kidding me?

She was in a black, unmarked police BMW X2 and remembered someone telling her that many of the new police cars in the fleet didn't have spare tyres in the boot. They either had run flats or some kind of spray to pump into the tyre that would temporarily fix the problem. At the time she had nodded apathetically, never contemplating what she would actually do if she had a flat tyre.

Taking out her phone, she called Ben to see if she could grab a lift with him before he left the area. His phone rang out and went to voicemail. Then the first few drops of rain fell onto the skin on the back of her hand.

'Bugger!' she grumbled under her breath as she glanced up and saw the dark storm clouds overhead. 'Perfect.'

Lifting the BMW's boot, she began to rummage around and eventually managed to lift up the base. Underneath was an array of bits of equipment. She recognised the jack from when she'd helped an old boyfriend change the wheel on his car about a decade earlier.

As she let out a sigh of exasperation, there was a rumble of thunder in the distance and the intensity of the rain increased.

'Having problems?' said a voice.

She jumped, and moved from the boot to see who it was.

Henry Marsh stood there, underneath a dark green golfing umbrella, with a bemused smile.

'Oh hi,' Andrea replied and then pointed to the tyre on the car. 'Yes, slight problem here.'

Marsh walked around and inspected the tyre. 'Oh dear. You're not going anywhere on that, are you?'

'No,' Andrea said, rolling her eyes. 'And rather helpfully, these cars don't come with a spare.'

Marsh nodded and pointed to a new-looking BMW further down the road. 'Yeah, I've got one myself.' He gestured to the boot and gave a wry smile. 'I got a flat tyre a few months ago and did exactly that. I checked the boot and wondered what the hell half the stuff was. And as for pumping liquid into the tyre . . .'

Andrea laughed. 'Oh good, I'm glad it's not just me.'

'Not at all,' Marsh laughed.

Andrea grinned. 'I'm sure a uniform patrol can come and bail me out.'

Marsh frowned. 'I can drop you back to the station now, if you like? I'm literally driving past there on the way back to college.'

For a second, Andrea wondered if getting into the car with Marsh was a sensible thing to do. But Conte was in custody with a stack of evidence against him. The only thing that linked Marsh to some of the victims was that he'd taught at the college they'd attended – and the same would be true of all the teachers there.

'If you don't mind,' Andrea said gratefully.

'Of course not,' Marsh replied and gestured to the umbrella. 'Come on, you're getting wet.'

Andrea got a little fizz of excitement as she stepped under Marsh's umbrella with him.

They began to walk up the road to his car together.

He smiled at her. 'There is one condition though.'

'Go on,' she replied.

'You can buy me a coffee some time,' he said.

Andrea smiled. 'Deal.'

Marsh clicked the automatic locking system as they approached. The BMW bleeped and its indicators flashed.

Laura and Ben entered Interview Room 1, where the Duty Sergeant had asked the father and daughter to wait for officers from CID.

A man in his early forties, with short, dark hair, a fashionable beard and hooded eyes, sat at the table. Next to him was a girl in her late teens, presumably his daughter. She was pretty with dark eyelashes, olive skin and hair pulled into a ponytail. She was wearing a parka coat and blinking nervously.

'Hi there,' Laura said gently with a friendly expression as they sat down. 'I'm Detective Inspector Laura Hart. And this is Detective Constable Ben Corden.' Laura looked down at the notes she'd been given. 'If I can just confirm the details I've got here. It's David and Hayley Kent, is that right?'

'Yeah, that's right,' David replied.

Hayley just looked down at the floor, clearly feeling very anxious. Laura wondered if either of them had ever been inside a police station before.

'I understand that you were attacked last night, Hayley?' Laura asked very softly.

Hayley nodded but didn't look up at her.

'I'm so sorry to hear that,' Laura said. 'That must have been very frightening.'

There were a few seconds of silence, but it seemed that Hayley was too upset to talk.

David looked over at them. 'Hayley didn't really tell us what had happened last night until this morning. She said she was too scared.'

'Of course. That's understandable.' Laura leaned forward slowly and tried to make eye-contact with her. 'Hayley, do you think you could tell us exactly what happened last night?'

Hayley was jigging her leg nervously and she took a visible breath. 'I was waiting at the bus stop . . . and then it started to rain. And a car pulled up . . .' Hayley's hands began to shake and a couple of tears rolled down her face. 'Sorry . . .'

Laura gave her a compassionate look. 'Hey, you don't need to apologise. You're doing really well. So, just take your time.'

Hayley nodded and wiped the tears from her face. 'He asked if I wanted a lift.'

'Okay,' Laura said quietly.

Hayley looked at her. 'At first, I said no. You know, I've seen all the papers and the news.'

David pulled a face guiltily. 'We didn't know Hayley had gone out, otherwise I'd have given her a lift.'

'Okay,' Laura said and then waited for a moment. 'So, you said no. Then what happened?'

'He kept insisting,' Hayley explained, her voice quivering with emotion. 'He said I'd get soaked and he was going that way. He even offered to give me a bottle of wine . . . But then I got in and . . .'

There were a few seconds of silence. Laura could see how much Hayley was struggling and that no doubt she blamed herself for getting into the car with a stranger.

'I'm so stupid,' she sobbed.

'It's okay, Hayley,' Laura reassured her.

'But he could have killed me,' she whispered.

Laura gave her an empathic look to show there was no judgement on her part. Then she asked, 'Do you think you could describe the man who picked you up and then attacked you?'

Hayley blinked at her. 'I know who he is.'

What?

Laura narrowed her eyes. 'You know the man who attacked you?'

'Yeah, that's why I got into the car,' Hayley explained. 'He's a teacher at the Sixth Form College I used to go to. His name is Professor Marsh.'

CHAPTER 19

As Marsh's car stopped at the traffic lights in Beaumaris, Andrea glanced out of the car window at the castle. With its circular towers and turrets, and its moat, it looked just like a generic castle you would draw as a child, she thought.

'It's a strange tourist attraction when you think about it,' Marsh observed.

'Is it?' Andrea said. 'I really like it.'

'Don't get me wrong. Architecturally it's spectacular,' Marsh explained, gazing out at the long stone walls that now encircled a colourful children's playground.

Andrea took out her phone and began to type a message to Laura explaining where she was and why she had been delayed getting back.

Marsh continued, gesturing to the turrets. 'But it was built by the English as part of Edward I's attempts to conquer North Wales in the thirteenth century. Basically, it's a symbol of English oppression and imperialism.'

'And you think we should pull it down?' Andrea asked with a raised eyebrow as she finished her message, which read *Hi boss. Running late. Got a flat tyre! Henry Marsh is dropping me back at the station. See you in a bit. Andrea.*

'God, no,' Marsh said as he glanced back at her.

Andrea sent the text to Laura.

Marsh's eye quickly went down to Andrea's phone. For a second, he seemed agitated. Then he reached over and snatched it from her hand.

'What the hell are you doing?' Andrea snapped.

Suddenly, Marsh's fist shot out and hit her square in the face. For a second, all Andrea could see were stars as she was stunned by the punch. She could taste the metallic tang of blood in her mouth.

The lights changed and Marsh pulled away sharply.

Blinking, Andrea managed to focus her eyes, only to see Marsh buzz down the window and toss her phone out. 'You won't be needing that.'

'Stop the car now!' Andrea growled, desperately trying to rationalise what had just happened.

Marsh clicked the central locking system.

Andrea lunged across the car in an attempt to grab the steering wheel and pull it over to the side of the road. It was only then that she saw that Marsh now had a serrated hunting knife in his right hand. He slashed at her, cutting the palm of her hand.

'What the fuck are you doing?' she yelped, cradling her wound.

Marsh's expression had completely changed. His eyes were black and his face twisted in a look of utter hatred and disgust. 'Try something like that again, I'll slit your throat. Understand?'

With her head still ringing, Andrea's confusion turned into terror.

Then she glared at him. 'It's you, isn't it?' she hissed as she tried to stem the bleeding from the gash in her hand.

'Just shut up,' Marsh replied with contempt.

'Where are we going?' she snapped. The text she had

sent to Laura had informed her that she was with Marsh. But while Conte was their prime suspect, Beaumaris CID would have no reason to look for her. And by the time they did realise that she was missing, it might be too late. She needed to come up with a plan of how to escape without any further harm.

Marsh stamped the brakes hard, swung the car over to the side of the road and jumped out.

Andrea thought about running but Marsh looked like he took care of himself. If he caught up with her, he might stab her to death there and then.

Marsh opened the rear door and grabbed some things off the back seat, then hurried around to the passenger side. He jerked her door open and in a flash the serrated knife was up against her throat. She could feel it digging into and then piercing her skin. For a second, she thought he was going to slice her throat. She started to shake.

Instead, Marsh held out the plastic tie he had taken from the back of the car.

'Put your hands behind your back!' he barked.

'What?'

He grabbed her hair. 'Just do it!'

She obeyed him. She had no choice.

He looped the tie over her wrists with one hand, then yanked it until it cut into her skin. Grabbing the black gaffer tape, he moved the knife from her throat and covered her mouth with a long strip.

'We're going for a nice trip down to the beach,' Marsh informed her, stroking her hair gently.

He jumped back into the car and they sped away, heading along the coastline to the east.

* * *

Conte's interview had been frustrating to say the least, and Gareth had decided to give him a break in the hope that a few hours of sitting in a custody cell might get to him. When they'd left the interview room, Gareth immediately headed upstairs to talk to Warlow and give him an update.

'How long do you think before we can charge him?' Warlow asked, clearly trying not to show how much external pressure he was under.

'We're in continual contact with the CPS,' Gareth explained. 'But without something like a DNA match, we're not going to reach the threshold to charge him yet.'

Warlow peered over. 'And you think this is our man?'

'He does have a string of offences that fit the profile. He's a loner. There's photographic evidence that he has stalked women on the island. He had a spurious explanation of why there were women's underwear and hair clips in his possession. His computer is full of submissive-type pornography and he has regularly communicated on Incel websites. They're all red flags, sir.'

Incel stood for 'Intentionally Celibate' and was an online subculture of men who could be characterised by misogyny, hatred and the endorsement of violence against women.

There was a knock at the door and before Warlow could respond, Laura had burst in.

'Laura?' Gareth said with a cautionary frown. It wasn't professional to come unannounced into a meeting like this unless something was incredibly urgent.

'Sorry for barging in like this,' she explained, sounding a little out of breath and concerned. 'We've had a significant development in the investigation. Henry Marsh tried to abduct a teenage girl last night in his car. He attacked her and told her he was taking her, to the beach. She somehow escaped, and though he chased her, she managed to hide.'

Gareth stared at her, open-mouthed.

131

'Something else,' Laura said darkly. 'DC Andrea Jones had a flat tyre. Marsh offered to give her a lift and she's in his car. But she's not answering her phone.'

Gareth and Warlow got up from the table.

'You'd better see to this,' Warlow said to Gareth, the blood draining from his face.

Gareth and Laura headed out to the corridor and jogged along the corridor towards the stairs.

'When did all this happen?' Gareth asked.

'A few minutes ago,' Laura said. 'We've got Marsh's car make and registration. I've got every unit on the island looking for it. I've also got the helicopter heading down from Holyhead.'

'Good,' Gareth said as they thundered down the stairs. 'What about tracking her phone?'

'Digital forensics are doing that now,' Laura replied as they hurried down the corridor and into the CID office.

Ben approached immediately. 'We've located Andrea's phone just outside Beaumaris. But it's been stationary for nearly ten minutes.'

'Marsh has got rid of it, then,' Laura concluded.

Declan jogged over. 'Boss, helicopter has got a visual on Marsh's car.'

'Where?' Gareth asked as they headed over to the map on the wall.

'Just outside Moelfre,' Declan said, pointing to a small village on the east coast of the island.

Gareth looked at Laura. 'Go with Ben.'

CHAPTER 20

Marsh stepped on the accelerator and the BMW engine roared as they thundered through the village of Llanallgo, a mile to the west of Moelfre. It was a small seaside town with a harbour and lifeboat station. To the north there was a rocky headland and a large sandy beach at Lligwy Bay, which is where Andrea assumed they were heading given Marsh's previous MO.

The muscles in her shoulders and upper back were now in agony from having her hands secured behind her back and sitting awkwardly in the passenger seat. Having to breathe only through her nostrils was making her feel claustrophobic and adding to her growing anxiety. The only thing that calmed her a little was the distant sound of a helicopter. However, she told herself not to get her hopes up. No one in Beaumaris CID thought she was missing. And while they had Conte at the station under caution, Marsh wasn't a suspect.

Looking down at her legs, she wondered if she could roll to the side and kick out at Marsh and somehow knock them off the road. She might be killed in the ensuing crash but that had to be better than being dragged out to a beach by Marsh and strangled, raped and buried. Anything would be better than that. The very thought of what might happen to her was making her feel physically sick. And if that happened, she might very well drown on her vomit.

She played it through in her mind. If she dropped her left shoulder towards the floor and twisted, she might have enough room to kick out her right foot and hit Marsh. With less than a mile to Lligwy Bay, it had to be worth a try.

Suddenly, there was a loud noise from overhead. A deep, thundering sound. Rhythmic and vibrating.

Andrea glanced over at Marsh, who was looking nervously up into the darkening sky. Then his jaw dropped.

A second later, she saw exactly what was going on. A black-and-yellow police helicopter was hovering about three hundred feet above them. She felt almost dizzy with relief.

Thank God! They've spotted us.

Marsh glanced up again, then glared at her and shouted, 'Don't worry, you're not getting away!'

A bright light flicked on, and it dazzled over them as they drove. It was a high intensity discharge searchlight from the helicopter.

'This is the North Wales Police. Pull your vehicle over to the side of the road,' boomed a voice from the helicopter's sky shout public address system.

'Fuck off!' Marsh growled.

'This is the North Wales Police. Pull your vehicle over to the side of the road and stop.'

Someone somewhere had realised that if she was in Marsh's car, Andrea was in danger. Maybe they had used the GPS tracking system in his BMW to locate them?

Andrea glanced out of the window and saw the helicopter fly overhead and then circle back. She took a deep breath in through her nostrils.

'Don't get your hopes up,' Marsh hissed. 'I'm not stopping for anyone.'

134

Marsh turned onto the road towards the beach. He stamped on the accelerator and the 3.0-litre, six-cylinder engine roared as they hit 70 mph.

Andrea had a painful, nervous knot in her stomach. How was she going to get out of this?

She saw a very tight right-hand turn coming up and felt a jolt of fear. Without braking, Marsh turned the steering wheel sharply. The back tyres screeched and he completely lost the back end of the BMW.

Spinning the steering wheel back, he tried to regain control.

This is it! Andrea thought as she watched Marsh gripping the steering wheel, fully concentrating on controlling the car.

Dropping her shoulder and head hard towards the floor, she twisted, bringing up her right knee. Her boot cleared the footwell by about an inch.

She kicked out at Marsh with everything she had, catching his left shoulder and then his jaw.

Stunned for a second, Marsh blinked.

She kicked his head again as hard as she could.

The car juddered off the road, skidding left and right.

A second later, they hit a dry-stone wall.

CRASH!

There was the thunderous sound of metal and glass collapsing.

The airbags deployed with a loud hiss.

Andrea felt her whole body being thrown forward and then back. Her head cracked against the passenger door. And then a searing pain shot right up her spine.

The car came to a rest and for a few seconds there was an eerie silence.

She sat upright in the seat and glanced anxiously over at Marsh.

His bloodied face rested against the deflated airbag and the steering wheel. There was a deep gash on his temple. He was unconscious, but she could see he was breathing.

Andrea's head swam and for a moment she had double vision.

In the corner of her eye, she spotted the black-and-yellow police helicopter hovering and then touching down on a nearby field.

Thank God, I'm safe.

Then everything went black.

CHAPTER 21

'Interview conducted with Henry Marsh, Sunday, the twenty-seventh March, 3.30 p.m., Beaumaris Police Station. Present are Henry Marsh, Detective Inspector Gareth Williams, Duty Solicitor Patrick Clifford and myself, Detective Inspector Laura Hart.'

Marsh was now dressed in a grey sweatshirt and bottoms. His clothes had been taken for extensive DNA analysis. His mouth had been swabbed for a DNA sample and his nails clipped. The gash on his face had been stitched by the Force Medical Examiner – FME – the doctor who was attached to Beaumaris nick. The FME had also confirmed that Marsh might be suffering from mild concussion but was fit to be interviewed. That would be reviewed in two hours' time.

Marsh gave Laura an icy stare and then leaned in to talk to Clifford and whispered something in his ear.

Laura raised her eyebrow. 'Henry, do you understand that you are still under caution?'

Marsh nodded, his eyes quick and sharp. He then peered over at Laura with the faintest hint of a smirk. 'No comment.'

Are you kidding me? Laura thought with frustration.

Gareth shifted forward in his seat. 'Henry, I'd like to advise you that opting for a "no comment" interview isn't in your best interests here. The evidence against you is overwhelming and so some explanation is going to be needed.'

Marsh scratched at his beard and then gave Gareth a bemused shrug. 'No comment.'

Gareth shot an irritated look at Laura and then pulled some documents out of a folder. 'Henry, can you tell us what happened this afternoon?'

'No comment.'

'Detective Constable Andrea Jones was abducted by you in your car this afternoon. She was bound and gagged. Is there anything you can tell us about that, Henry?'

Marsh took a deep, audible breath and let it out slowly. 'No comment.'

'We also have a witness statement here from a Hayley Kent,' Laura said, pointing to a document in front of her. 'Can you tell us if you know Hayley Kent?'

'No comment.'

'Hayley says that you do know her, as she was a student at Llangefni Sixth Form College eighteen months ago,' Laura said. 'Which coincides with the time you have been teaching at the college, doesn't it?'

'No comment.' Marsh's nostrils flared for a second as if he was hiding his anger.

'Hayley told us that you picked her up last night and offered to give her a lift to a party that she was planning to attend. Is that correct?'

Marsh sat back with his legs wide apart, wearing a self-satisfied expression. 'No comment.'

'Hayley also told us that when you refused to let her out of the car, she ran and you pursued her,' Laura said. 'Is there anything you'd like to say about that?'

'No comment.'

Laura raised an eyebrow at Gareth – they weren't getting

anywhere. Even though she was frustrated, she didn't want Marsh to see that. She knew that they would continue asking questions for another ten minutes before calling it a day and letting Marsh sit in a holding cell overnight.

Then there would be the wait for the forensic evidence and DNA samples from the items that had been found in Marsh's boot. If Marsh wanted to play silly buggers, that was his call. Laura was confident that the testimonies of a serving police officer and Hayley Kent and the evidence from the car meant that however Marsh pleaded the following morning, he was going to prison for the rest of his life.

Blinking slowly, Andrea tried to focus on what was around her. Everything was blurred. As her hearing started to return, she could make out a rhythmic electronic beep. Then some chattering and laughter from outside.

Where the hell am I?

Her head was pounding like the worst hangover that she'd ever had. As she took in a short breath, she could feel her whole ribcage aching.

Wow, that really hurts.

Looking around, she started to piece together what she could see. She was propped up in a hospital bed in a single room with various drips and an ECG attached to her.

And then it came flooding back to her. Getting into Henry Marsh's car. His attempt to abduct her, the punch in her face and the crash. She felt her pulse and heart start to race just thinking about it. The dark, inhuman, malevolent look on his face.

She took a nervous gulp as she realised that she was lucky to be alive.

The door opened slowly and Laura's face appeared. 'Hey,' she whispered with a benign smile.

'Hi,' Andrea replied. Her throat was dry and she started to cough.

'Okay if I come in?' Laura asked with a tentative expression.

'Of course,' Andrea croaked. Her throat felt like it had been rubbed with sandpaper.

Laura headed across the room to the bedside cabinet and took out a plastic cup, poured some water into it and handed it to Andrea. 'Here you go.'

Andrea took a few gulps, then tried to move herself up on the bed. Her whole body felt like it had been run over by a steamroller.

'Thanks.'

'How are you feeling?' Laura asked as she sat down next to the bed on a grey plastic chair.

'Even my hair hurts,' Andrea admitted with a pained expression. Then she looked urgently at Laura. 'Tell me you've got Marsh in custody.'

'Yes.' Laura nodded reassuringly. 'Don't worry. He's in a holding cell at Beaumaris nick.'

'Thank God,' Andrea rasped and then drank some more water. Her breath was still catching on her dry throat. She coughed again.

'How the hell did I get here?' Andrea asked. She just couldn't remember a thing.

'Helicopter brought you over,' Laura explained.

Andrea took this in for a second and raised an eyebrow. 'Looks like I missed all the excitement. Shame, I've never been in a helicopter before.'

'I'm just glad you're okay,' Laura admitted.

'Except for feeling like Anthony Joshua has beaten the shit out of me.'

'Could have been a lot worse,' Laura said quietly.

Andrea looked at her. 'I know.'

Laura's face brightened. 'I was going to bring you some grapes.'

Andrea pulled a face. 'Yeah, I don't do grapes.'

'I'm going to go to the shop in a bit, so what do you want?' Laura asked.

'It's fine, boss,' Andrea said. She felt guilty that Laura was spending her valuable time at the hospital.

Laura smiled at her. 'Well, I'm not taking no for answer.'

'In that case, jelly babies,' Andrea admitted with a grin.

Laura laughed. 'I assume you bite the heads off first?'

'Obviously.' Andrea then shook her head. 'God, I feel like such a bloody idiot!'

Laura shook her head and leaned forward. 'You don't need to. We already had Conte in custody. There were lots of distracting red flags with him. Marsh wasn't on our radar anymore.'

'I know,' Andrea said with a shrug. 'But I'm never going to live down being that DC that got a lift with a serial killer.'

'Seriously, everyone just wants to make sure you're okay,' Laura reassured her.

Andrea nodded and tried to shift her legs. For some reason, she couldn't seem to move them. *That feels weird.*

'Can you remember why Marsh crashed into that wall?' Laura asked.

'I kicked him in the head,' Andrea replied.

'You were bound and gagged when you were rescued!' Laura exclaimed, her eyes widened with astonishment. 'How the hell did you do that?'

'I'll have to draw you a diagram,' Andrea explained with a forced smile. 'It wasn't easy. In fact, kicking him in the head is pretty much the last thing I do remember.'

'When I got your text, I'd just interviewed a girl who told me that Marsh had tried to abduct her and then chased her the night before. Then you told me you were in the car with him. I felt sick.'

'Have you interviewed him yet?' Andrea asked.

'Yes.'

'How did it go?'

Laura gave a frustrated expression. 'He's gone for "no comment".'

'Jesus,' Andrea groaned.

'SOCOs pulled a mallet and gloves from the boot of Marsh's car,' Laura explained. 'They're pretty sure it's the murder weapon as it's got blood and hair on it.'

'I'd like to see how he's going to explain that,' Andrea said and then shook her head. 'I'd always hoped that if we caught someone, they might cooperate and tell us where Ellie Gates and Shannon Jones were. I can't imagine how their families will cope if we charge someone but they refuse to tell us.'

Laura nodded and pushed her hair from her face. 'We're trying to see if there are others elsewhere. Marsh taught all over the country. He even taught over in Abu Dhabi and Dubai at an international school.'

'What about his wife?' Andrea asked, now wondering if Marsh had told them the truth.

'He lied about that. She's still alive,' Laura replied. 'She left him four years ago and filed for divorce. She cited violence and controlling behaviour.'

'Where is she now?'

'Cornwall,' Laura said. 'Looks like she wanted to get as far away from Marsh as she could.'

'Did they have kids?'

'No.'

'Well, that's one good thing,' Andrea said. 'Do you think he's going to confess?'

'I really don't,' Laura admitted, shaking her head sadly. 'I think Marsh is an egotistical, narcissistic psychopath who wants all the publicity and attention of a big trial.'

'Wouldn't surprise me,' Andrea said.

Before they could continue, the door opened and a very

142

young, blond-haired doctor came in with a folder and some notes.

'Andrea?' he said in a matter-of-fact way.

'Yes,' she replied as he approached the bed. While talking to Laura, she had tried to move her legs and wiggle her toes but she couldn't feel anything.

The doctor reached down and slowly pulled the bedsheet back to reveal Andrea's legs. 'Are you able to move your legs or your toes, Andrea?'

With a growing sense of unease, Andrea realised that however hard she tried, she couldn't.

Oh God.

'No,' she admitted as her pulse started to quicken. 'What's wrong?'

The doctor took out a pen and, ignoring her question, pushed it gently into her thigh, just above her knee. 'Can you feel that?'

Andrea shook her head but her heart was now thumping and her stomach tense with anxiety. She shot a look over at Laura, who looked concerned.

The doctor pushed the pen lid into her shin. 'This?'

She shook her head.

'This?' he asked as he tested her feet.

Shaking her head, she was beginning to be overcome with panic. *Oh my God, am I paralysed?*

The doctor moved up her body. She frowned at him, trying to read his facial expression, but he wasn't giving anything away.

Finally, he pressed the pen into her skin just above her hip bone. 'What about this?'

'Yes.' She nodded. 'I can feel that. What's going on?'

The doctor looked at her. 'At the moment, we're not sure. So, we're going to run some tests. You're going to need an X-ray straight away, and an MRI.'

'Am I paralysed?' Andrea asked in a virtual whisper.

'We really don't know at this stage,' the doctor admitted. 'I think you have some kind of spinal cord injury from the accident you were in.'

'If I can't move my legs now, does that mean it's permanent?' Andrea asked, hardly daring to listen to the doctor's answer.

'Not always,' the doctor replied. 'I don't really want to say anything until we've done the tests.'

'I think Andrea needs to know if this type of injury and paralysis is *always* permanent?' Laura said.

Andrea's heart was now thudding away in her chest and her breathing was shallow.

'No, not always,' the doctor replied, shaking his head. 'In an accident, sometimes you'll get something called transverse myelitis. Basically, your spinal cord is very inflamed, which causes temporary paralysis. But I don't want to get your hopes up until we do the tests. I'll pop back and see you in a bit.'

The doctor left and Laura leaned over and placed a comforting hand on Andrea's shoulder.

It was all too much for her. Tears welled in her eyes as she took a deep breath and then pursed her lips.

'Sorry . . .' she sobbed.

'Hey.' Laura comforted her by taking her hand. 'It's going to be fine.'

Andrea looked at her as she sniffed and wiped her face. 'What the hell am I going to do if I can't walk again?'

CHAPTER 22

The holding cell at Beaumaris nick was cold. Marsh blinked as he stirred and pulled the thin blanket over his shoulders. The rain pattered quietly against the small window that was high up above him and made from smoked, reinforced glass. He stretched out his legs, feeling the ache in his hamstring.

For a moment he lay back on his bunk and gazed up at the ceiling. He could feel the two sides of his mind fighting each other, as they had done for a long time. On the one hand, he felt an immense sense of relief. He had finally been caught. It was the only way he was ever going to stop killing. The desire had been too great. Too overwhelming and all consuming. And that had become increasingly exhausting. So, he was glad that he was now going to be locked up. The choice of when, how and if he would kill again had been taken away from him – and that was a release. However, the desire to kill again was growing. The compulsive side of his head was starting the chatter away with questions. Was he really ready to give up the very thing that made him tick? Now that he knew what it was to have it, who would he be without it? Think of the immense thrill and excitement that the planning and execution of a killing gave him.

He satisfied himself that if he didn't manage to escape, he would have the chance to tell his story. Like those who had gone before him. Bundy, Dahmer, Sutcliffe and Nilsen. He was going to join the pantheon of notorious serial killers. He ran through the books, the interviews, the television documentaries and the movies. And he would have a starring role in all of them.

He imagined sitting in one of the meeting rooms in the prison. A camera crew setting up, lights and sound equipment. The interviewer asking probing questions and hanging on his every word.

How did I choose my victims? That's a very good question. I was essentially killing the same person every time. It gave me a sense of possession, control and revenge.

Marsh smiled to himself at the thought of it. Academics, journalists and psychologists poring over every detail of his childhood. That was the key to his behaviour. How could it not be? He'd read that Ted Bundy had been brought up in a kind, loving home with two wonderful parents. He had insisted that right up to the very moment of his execution. Marsh knew that was nonsense. No one with that kind of environment would go on to rape, murder and mutilate dozens of women. Bundy had gone to the electric chair never able to reveal the darkness of his past. Marsh didn't understand that. He wouldn't make that mistake. He wanted a behavioural psychologist to study him and his life.

Why did I kill so many women? I suppose the more interesting question is: why not? If one didn't satisfy the obsessive, overwhelming need to take a life, why should two, or three, or four?

Maybe he would feature in the Netflix series *Confessions of a Killer – The Henry Marsh Tapes*. Yes, he'd like that. A chance to tell his story.

He played out another imaginary question in his head.

What drove your violent urge to kill? the imaginary interviewer asked.

Who knows what drives them to do anything? At first, I had no idea. The urge to scare and then commit violence towards women felt like an instinct, like breathing. It took years for me to sit down and really examine why. I think that many killers go to their grave never really understanding that. But I can tell you exactly why I acted the way I did.

Would you mind explaining it to our viewers?

Marsh took a few seconds as though he was in an actual interview. He mimicked an expression of deep thought.

Then he replied, *Wouldn't you like to know?*

And soon, they would.

CHAPTER 23

It was early evening and Laura and Pete were sitting out on the patio with blankets, a small outdoor heater, a bottle of wine and a cold beer. The moon above them was honey coloured and cast its glow over the yellow privet hedge that she had planted the previous year. It was a huge improvement on the dank, creosoted fence that had been there before. To the right, there had been an old decrepit rose garden she had paid someone to remove and pave. Now there were sprawling rosemary bushes that swept across the paving with their bluish branches. She could smell the rosemary on the gentle breeze. It was redolent of Sunday lunches, thick gravy and heavy red wine.

'When are you back on?' she asked as she sipped her wine, aware that it had now dulled her head nicely.

'Not until Wednesday,' Pete replied. After working in Manchester CID for the past twelve days straight, he now had a few days off.

Pete made the hundred-mile trip over from Manchester every couple of months. Not only was he godfather to both Rosie and Jake, he had been Sam's best friend.

'You guys must be relieved,' Pete said. 'Nothing like the

glare of the national media to make the job a thousand times more difficult.'

'Yeah, it was beginning to feel like a nightmare that was never going to end.'

Pete took a cigarette from a packet on the garden table, lit it and then blew out the smoke in a long plume. 'You interviewed him tonight?'

Laura rolled her eyes. 'He went "no comment".'

'Prick,' Pete groaned. 'Maybe a night in the cells will give him a different perspective?'

'He's intelligent and, at a guess, very controlling,' Laura said. 'I think he'll decide when and if he tells us anything.'

'Gareth must be pleased at getting a result,' Pete stated.

'Yeah.' Laura nodded. 'He's in the pub with the rest of the team.'

Pete raised an eyebrow. 'You two okay?'

Laura and Pete went back over twenty years. He was the closest thing she had to a brother.

'Yeah, we're fine. More than fine,' Laura admitted and then gestured to the house. 'Except madam in there has decided she can't stand him. And she's not hiding it.'

'Oh dear.' Pete pulled a face. 'Do you want me to have a word?'

Rosie had always looked up to 'Uncle Pete', especially since Sam's death.

'That's not a bad idea,' Laura conceded.

Pete leaned forward to tap his ash into the ashtray. Then he grabbed his beer and took a sip.

'Do we think that Carmichael and Watkins were just on a fishing trip?' he asked quietly.

Laura had already fed back to Pete the details of her interview with the detectives on the phone the day before. They were both concerned at the implication that they were somehow mixed up in Louise McDonald's murder. And, of

149

course, they were both now worried that they might be under some kind of surveillance.

'I just don't know,' Laura stated with a frown. 'I couldn't work them out.'

'The weird thing is that I've asked around and no one seems to know them,' Pete explained. 'You know the Manchester Police. It's rare not to know or at least have heard of CID officers in the Met.'

'If they're in the counter-corruption unit, that might explain it?' Laura suggested.

'True,' Pete admitted. 'And Butterfield is still missing.'

'After what he told me,' Laura said, 'it seems like an extraordinary coincidence that he went walking and has vanished.'

'That's what I thought.' Pete looked at her. 'Butterfield never gave you any names, though, did he?'

'No.' Laura shook her head. 'Just implied that there was an OCG in Manchester that had some very high-ranking coppers in their pocket. Every time I made any attempt to contact Butterfield after that night, he never responded. My guess is that he regretted ever contacting me.'

'Jesus,' Pete sighed and shook his head. 'I'd hoped the whole Paul Massey thing would be the last of it.'

Paul Massey ran several security firms in Manchester in the 1990s. It effectively allowed him to control the doors, and therefore the drugs, in many of Manchester's nightclubs. By 2000, Massey had established himself as a feared crime boss, with a gang known as The A Team. Massey was referred to as Mr Big by both criminals and police in Manchester. In 2015, Massey was gunned down and killed by a hitman from a rival gang. The assassination resulted in a gang war that led to nineteen shootings in Salford that year.

Before he was murdered, there had been growing allegations that Massey had Manchester police officers on his payroll.

When the Titan North West Regional Organised Crime Unit brought money laundering charges against Massey's associates, the case was dropped. It was rumoured that the defence were going to use the allegations of corruption at trial. The Crown Prosecution Service backed out of the trial, claiming that there were *disclosure issues* that affected their ability to charge. Many saw this as the Greater Manchester Police sweeping the allegations under the carpet.

Laura's phone buzzed with a text. It was from Gareth.

Sorry to ruin your evening but I've just seen that they've found the body of that police officer you used to work with at the GMP. Butterfield? Thought you'd want to know. See you in an hour or so. G xx

Laura frowned at Pete. 'You're not going to believe this.'

'What?'

Getting up from her chair, Laura gestured to the door inside. 'They've found Butterfield's body.'

Hurrying through the house, Laura came into the living room, clicked on the television and immediately switched it to the BBC News channel.

On the screen was an aerial shot of countryside and what looked like some kind of rescue team in hi-vis jackets.

'*The body of the missing police officer, Ian Butterfield, was found just after 1p.m. today at the bottom of a ravine close to Worsaw Hill in this idyllic part of Lancashire. Mr Butterfield, who was fifty-eight years old, had gone missing while walking in the area two days ago. Despite rescue services' desperate attempts, Mr Butterfield was pronounced dead at the scene . . .*'

Laura looked over at Pete, wondering if Butterfield's death was really 'accidental'.

CHAPTER 24

Marsh had been moved at dawn from the holding cell at Beaumaris Police Station over to HMP Rhosneigr, a small remand prison in the south-west of the island. He was now being interviewed in one of the ultra-modern rooms on the ground floor.

Laura pressed the red button on the recording machine and waited for the long electronic beep. She, Gareth, Duty Solicitor Patrick Clifford and Marsh were sitting in Interview Room 2.

Laura and Gareth were praying that Marsh would give them something but they were almost certain that he was going to go 'no comment' again.

As he had done yesterday, Marsh leaned in to talk to Clifford for a few seconds. They had a whispered and animated conversation.

Laura took out her A4 notepad and pen. She quickly wrote down the date, time and other details of the interview. Even though it was being recorded, she liked to get her own record of the major points.

Clifford then looked over at them. 'Against advice from counsel, my client has decided that he is willing to answer any questions that you have for him this morning.'

Thank God!

Gareth nodded. 'I'm very glad to hear that.'

'You have beautiful handwriting,' Marsh observed, gesturing to the notes that Laura was making. 'My mother had beautiful handwriting.'

Laura stopped writing and frowned at him. It was a strange observation but maybe this was a way in. 'What was she like? Your mother?'

For a few seconds, Marsh looked at Laura with narrowed eyes. She couldn't tell if she had hit a nerve or upset him by asking the question.

'My mother?' Marsh eventually answered as if amused by the question. 'Oh, she was a wonderful person. Kind, nurturing, warm. Wonderful.'

'Right,' Laura said, sensing his ironic tone.

There were a few more seconds of awkward silence.

Marsh laughed. 'I'm guessing you've sensed from my tone that she wasn't.'

He stared over at her with blank eyes and said coldly and quietly, 'My mother was the woman who persuaded me to allow my grandfather to have sex with me as a boy. She stroked my hair while he was doing it and told me I was "a good boy". And you know sometimes I even got an erection when he was inside me, so I thought that meant that I must have wanted him to do it.' Marsh took a visible breath as though trying to control the emotion of what had happened to him. 'And I couldn't tell anyone. They were the only family I had. And my mother told me that if I told any of the teachers at school, she and my grandfather would go to prison and I would end up in a home.'

Laura gave a slight nod. Despite his crimes, it was uncomfortable to hear what Marsh had experienced growing up.

Marsh stroked at his beard as he considered what he was going to say next. Now that he'd agreed to talk to them, it seemed sensible to let him discuss or divulge whatever he wanted to start with.

Marsh frowned. 'And the strange thing is, I wanted to protect them. You would have thought that escaping that and being in a home or fostered would have been the best option for me. But I never even thought about telling anyone.' Marsh gave her a dark smile. 'And the stuff my grandfather did to me physically damaged me for the rest of my life. Because a sixty-year-old man isn't supposed to put himself inside a nine-year-old boy.'

Marsh took a few seconds and then snorted and pointed to his temple. 'Can you imagine what that did to my head? Of course, the studies would show that the amygdala and hippocampus in my brain would have been permanently damaged by the abuse. A profound inability to foster human relationships, a predilection for addiction, all combined with, in my case, a matricidal rage.'

Laura shifted in her chair. Marsh was a psychopath and had brutally murdered young women, causing horrendous pain and suffering to many people, and of course there was nothing on earth that could excuse that. But there was still a part of her that felt empathy for what he had experienced as a child.

'As a boy, when I lay with my grandfather behind me, inside me, I started to remove myself from the bed. Not physically. Mentally. I took myself off to a warm, safe place where nothing horrible was happening to me. Like I was in a lovely dream. And it got so easy for me to do, that sometimes I'd wake in the morning unable to remember if my grandfather had visited me the night before or not. Of course, now I know that's disassociation.' Marsh sniffed as if taking a short, sharp intake of breath. 'Once my grandfather had finished, I would lie in bed and listen to him and Mother in the bath laughing and chatting. And then I would hear them having sex in the next bedroom. At first, every night I imagined getting away. I planned my escape. I would get a train across to Wales or to Liverpool. Or I imagined what I would do to my mother and grandfather when I was older and stronger. How I would tie them up and torture them to get revenge for what they had done to me.'

Laura turned the page from where she had taken notes. It was clear, in her limited knowledge, that Marsh's upbringing was the virtual textbook environment in which sociopaths and psychopaths are created.

'What happened to them?' Laura asked. 'Your grandfather and mother?'

'My mother died a few years ago,' Marsh said quietly.

Gareth looked over. 'And your grandfather?'

Marsh narrowed his eyes as he thought for a second. 'Oh, I killed him with my bare hands.'

Gareth frowned. 'Really?'

'Of course.' Marsh shrugged. 'I came back from university. I drank too much. He flirted with my mother. We got into a row and I flipped. I wish I'd done it a decade before.'

'Did anyone know?' Laura asked.

'No. And I don't think anyone cared,' Marsh said in a matter-of-fact tone.

'What about your mother?' Gareth said.

'Oh, she was a bit hysterical.' Marsh shrugged. 'She soon calmed down once I'd raped her.'

Laura closed her eyes for a second.

'You raped your mother?'

'Yes, of course,' Marsh replied in a withering tone. 'Don't you know your Oedipus complex, Detective? Freud's *Interpretation of Dreams*, 1899. Basically every man wants to sleep with his mother and kill his father. I'd done part of that successfully.'

'Your grandfather,' Laura said.

'My grandfather was also my father,' Marsh explained. 'I'm pretty sure that's not good for genetics, but that was the hand I was dealt. Anyway, I bundled grandfather's dead body into their car. Then I drove up to the Bryn Celli Ddu burial chamber and buried him up at the top of the mound. I'm pretty sure he's still there . . . And if you look to the north-east, you can see the lights of Llandudno twinkling.' Marsh leaned forward and stared directly at them both. 'I'm not stupid. I know what I am. The strange thing is that I don't seem to feel any self-pity for what happened. I used to when I was younger. Terrible jealousy of other people's lives. But not anymore. It's been a long time since I asked *why me?* or bemoaned the horrendous abuse that I suffered. I don't feel anything now.' Marsh raised an eyebrow ironically. 'But I guess that's the point. I wouldn't be able to do what I did to those girls if I felt anything. If I had any empathy for them or their families. But I don't. I just don't care.' He pointed to his chest. 'It's not in there. No compassion, no guilt and no conscience . . . Classic psychopath.' He snorted and gave a dry laugh. 'And when I was first drawn to following, stalking and eventually attacking the women, I never analysed why. I just knew that it was an overwhelming compulsion. But then I thought about them. They were in their early twenties, dark hair, dark eyes and slim. And then it came to me. It was my mother. When she had first opened the bedroom door and ushered my grandfather in. That's what she looked like. Effectively, I was seeking out women who looked like my mother when I was young and then I was killing them out of some perverse sense of revenge.'

Laura reached over, took her glass of water and sipped from it, her hand shaking. It was so incredibly chilling and unsettling to be in the presence of someone so cold, evil but so aware of why he had killed.

156

Marsh had a strange expression, as if remembering something pleasurable. 'It's just so overwhelming, elusive and addictive. Each time I killed, I promised myself it would be the last time. Definitely the last time. It had to be. Never again. But that's the nature of any compulsive or addictive behaviour, isn't it? A solemn promise not to repeat the addictive behaviour ever again. A growing build-up of anger, frustration and desire that becomes so overwhelming that the only release is to repeat the behaviour again. It doesn't matter what your drug of choice is – alcohol, heroin, gambling or sex. My drug of choice happens to be killing. It's not something I could go into rehab or a support group for, is it?' He smiled in amusement. '*Hi, my name is Henry, and I'm a serial killer. It's only been ten hours since my last murder, but I'm glad to be at this meeting.*'

Marsh laughed, then took his glass of water and sipped it.

Gareth cleared his throat and asked quietly, 'Do you believe that somehow you're not responsible for what you've done?'

'Far from it.' Marsh shook his head. He leaned forward and then stared directly into Laura's eyes. She felt her body tense as she took an anxious breath. 'But I want to ask you. How would you have fared in life if you had experienced all that I had? Would you be sitting there? Would you have been able to have a normal relationship, get married or have children?'

'It does sound like you blame your mother and grandfather for what you ended up doing,' Laura stated – no element of judgement, just curiosity.

Marsh snorted again. 'No. I knew what I was doing.' He pulled a serious face and said calmly, 'There are plenty of people out there who suffer terrible abuse and don't go on to commit murder. So I accept full responsibility for what I've done. I'm not going to hide away in lies or deceit. Now you have caught me, I'll cooperate as much as I can.'

157

Gareth interlaced his fingers and placed them on the table. 'And you're able to take us to where you buried Ellie Gates and Shannon Jones?'

Marsh thought for a few seconds and then nodded slowly. 'If it can be done with dignity.' He took a few seconds. 'Then yes, I can take you to where they are.'

CHAPTER 25

Two hours later, Laura stood with Gareth in the visitors' car park at HMP Rhosneigr. Now that Marsh had confessed to his crimes, he was officially on remand until his court hearing. He had agreed to plead guilty and save everyone the hideous prospect of a trial. It was a huge relief to everyone at Beaumaris CID. They could endure the colossal workload of a criminal trial. However, what no one could bear was to watch the relatives of the victims sit in court and learn the graphic details of how their loved ones had died. It was an agonising experience.

Gareth had spoken to Warlow to set up taking Marsh out to the sites where he had buried Ellie Gates and Shannon Jones. Paperwork for a temporary release had to be approved by the Welsh secretary of state's office in Cardiff, such was the magnitude of the offences that Marsh was facing. The chief constable of North Wales Police and HMP Rhosneigr's governor had also signed the release forms.

Laura glanced around at the frost on the grass verges and the prison's Astroturf football pitches. Towering wire fences encircled the whole area, but the newly built cell blocks wouldn't have looked out of place in a new secondary school. On the other side, a prison officer patrolled with an enormous

German Shepherd, which gave a thunderous bark that reverberated around the prison site.

Nearby, a beech tree was starting to fill with leaves. As the wind picked up, its branches creaked like rusted machinery. A small private plane flew overhead, heading south towards the Welsh mainland.

The Dog Search Team van, with their specially trained cadaver dogs, arrived. A small white SOCO van followed and parked up alongside them. *God, it's going to be a grim, dismal day*, Laura thought. She just needed to remember that after four torturous months, finding the remains of Ellie and Shannon would allow their parents the peace of mind of knowing what had happened, where they were, and finally laying them to rest with dignity. It was so important for them to get that kind of emotional closure.

Laura glanced over at the other unmarked police BMW. Declan was sitting inside the car at the steering wheel, keeping out of the cold. In the passenger seat, Ben gazed out of the window. He had the unenviable task of being handcuffed to Marsh for the day. Gareth had already warned Ben to ignore everything Marsh said and not to enter into any conversation. He didn't want Marsh getting inside Ben's head.

Laura was feeling nervous. She could feel it in her stomach. Taking a killer out to locate their victims' remains was a big operation, and it wouldn't be long before the media caught on to what they were doing. Gareth had asked the North Wales Police's media office in St Asaph to try to appeal for a media blackout. They didn't want anything jeopardising Marsh's agreement to show them where the bodies were buried. However, the media could sometimes be a law unto themselves. And it would only take one photographer with a high-powered telephoto lens, or one over-ambitious news producer to send a helicopter with a camera crew into the sky, and that could unsettle Marsh.

Marsh had agreed to take them to the two sites where he had buried the bodies. At first, he was reluctant to tell them anything until he was in the car. Gareth had explained that Marsh would be going nowhere until they had the rough locations of where they were going so they could carry out a risk assessment.

Gareth was on his phone. He finished the call and looked over at Laura. 'Okay, we're on.'

Laura signalled to Ben that he was needed, and he got out of the car.

They walked over to a large red steel door marked RECEPTION – DERBYNFA. Mounted to the brick wall was a modern video entry phone, which Gareth buzzed and showed his warrant card to.

A minute later, a young male prison officer opened the heavy door and escorted them down to the holding cell where Marsh was. The booking area was clean and white, with plenty of light from the frosted skylights above.

Gareth signed the paperwork in triplicate. Marsh was brought over and gave them a cheery, overfamiliar smile as he was handcuffed to Ben. He seemed fidgety, like an excited schoolboy before a day trip.

They took him outside and headed for the car.

Marsh took a deep breath and gazed up to the sky. 'Good to be alive, isn't it?'

Laura had no idea if Marsh was being ironic given what they were about to do. Maybe he was just trying to wind them up.

'Get in the car, Marsh,' Gareth snapped as he opened the back door and ushered Ben and Marsh inside.

The severe frost had rendered the Anglesey landscape a patchy white. The trees that lined the road were dusted with white too.

'It reminds me of Christmas,' Marsh observed from the back of the car as he peered outside.

Laura ignored him. She wasn't about to enter into a conversation with him.

'I've got a heart-warming Christmas story for you,' Marsh said chirpily.

'We're not interested,' Ben snapped.

'You say that now, but wait until you hear it. What is it that they say . . . "contempt prior to investigation"?'

Laura knew that there was no way of stopping Marsh from speaking. Gagging him, though tempting, would be against all Marsh's human rights.

'I was seventeen, so that's 1995, I think,' Marsh explained. 'And Christmas Day wasn't really the warm, loving family affair in our house that it is for most people. By then, the abuse had stopped. I guessed that now I'd gone through puberty, I wasn't to my grandfather's taste anymore. And he was getting old and ill. My mother had pretty much ignored me since I was fifteen or sixteen. Anyway, none of that is the point of this story,' Marsh said and then shifted in his seat for a moment. 'So, it's Christmas Day. Late afternoon and it's getting dark. And I'm thinking that it's an opportunity to go for a walk, prowl around and watch others in their homes. Of course, what I'm looking for is young women. But I know that people are with their families and that spotting a young woman on her own, which is exactly what I'm looking for, is unlikely. But I'm also happy to root through people's bins in search of trophies. Although Christmas Day is never a good day for that. Bins are full of wrapping paper, cardboard, things from preparing Christmas dinner, stuff like that. It's harder to find what I'm looking for.'

Declan slowed the car at a set of traffic lights and Laura saw him look in the rear-view mirror at Marsh. 'You do know that no one is remotely interested in anything that you have to say, don't you?' he growled in his Irish accent.

Marsh frowned with a look of mock offence. 'But I do love a captive audience. That's why I became a teacher and lecturer. So, where was I? Yes, I'm going through the bins and this old woman comes out. I'm guessing that she's heard me or something. Except, she's blind. And she says, "Rhys? Is that you?" And I freeze where I am. She can't see me but she can sense my presence. And for some reason, I just say, "Yes, it's me." And the women smiles and says, "I knew you'd come and see me on Christmas Day. I knew you wouldn't forget me. Come in, come in. I've got a present for you in the sitting room." So, I follow her inside.

'We go in the sitting room, which is very warm. There's a fire in the log burner. And the television is on. I sit down. And then the woman hands me a present. I open it and it's a box of Quality Street. So, I thank her and she starts to ask me all these questions about how I'm doing at college, if I've got a girlfriend, that kind of thing. It turns out that Rhys is her grandson and he's about my age. But she hasn't seen him or heard from him for about two years. And I answer all the questions as best I can. But I can't tell if she knew that I wasn't her grandson and was just playing along because she didn't want to think that this Rhys would have forgotten to come and see his own grandmother. I'm wondering if we're just entering into some kind of game. I'm looking for a warm room and an escape from my home. She's hoping that her grandson hasn't forgotten her.

'So for the next few hours, we sit and we talk. We share my chocolates, drink some Baileys, watch the television and talk more. She admits to me that she is so horribly lonely. Her children live over on the Welsh mainland and never come to see her. She hasn't seen Huw, her son and Rhys's father, for over six months. Meryl, her only friend in the village, died a few months ago. She doesn't know anyone. I see her dab at her eyes as the thought of how alone she is has made her cry. But she tells me that my visit has made it her happiest Christmas in many years. She drinks more Baileys and eventually she drifts off to sleep in her armchair in front of the fire. And I watch her sleep. I'm thinking that she looks so peaceful.

'I get up from where I'm sitting and begin to search around for anything I can steal. I find some money in her purse which I take. I go to the front door to let myself out and then I have a thought. It seems cruel that this old woman is going to have to spend the end of her life lonely, sad and upset. She's sleeping so peacefully. So, I take a cushion from the sofa and I place it over her face. Of course, she wakes up and struggles for a few seconds. But she's got to be nearly eighty and she's drunk a lot of Baileys. After a few seconds, she stops, I put the cushion back on the sofa and I sit and watch her for a while. She looks exactly the same as before. Peaceful and happy. I've helped her.' Marsh let out a sigh, sounding almost as if it was a wonderful memory. 'Of course, I left the fire and television on and let myself out of the back door this time. I guess a neighbour or someone found her eventually and it would have appeared that she had died in her sleep.'

There was a long silence. Laura had no idea how to respond to what Marsh had told them. She took an anxious breath as she glanced uneasily at Gareth. What had started as a curious but touching Christmas story had taken such a sickening twist.

Suddenly leaning forward, Marsh pointed. 'Yes, if we can go up this track then we'll be in the right place.'

Declan indicated left and pulled off the road.

For the next few minutes, they all sat in silence as they drove slowly up the pot-holed track until Marsh told them where to stop.

* * *

The police convoy had parked beside a stony track. They had then climbed a small hill to the spot that Marsh had identified as containing Ellie Gates's remains, which overlooked Bull Bay. Its Welsh name, *Porth Llechog*, meant 'sheltered bay'. Just off the coast lay the island of East Mouse, which had been dated as being over five hundred million years old.

Laura watched at a distance as the SOCOs carefully dragged away fallen branches that covered the area Marsh had indicated. He claimed that, as with his other victims, he had left Ellie's head visible above the shallow grave that he'd dug. It looked like the fallen branches had obscured that from view, which is why she hadn't been found.

One of the SOCOs held her hand up to signal she had seen something. The expression on her face said it all. Even though Laura was too far away to see what had been found, she experienced a cold shudder at the thought of it.

For the next few minutes, SOCOs erected a white forensic tent over the remains. They then used trowels and small spades to carefully remove the earth. Marsh had told them that Ellie's body had been buried less than a foot under the earth's surface three months earlier. There was an eerie silence with just the metallic tapping of the trowels against the stony earth below the grass.

Marsh, who was handcuffed to Ben, stood looking on about fifty yards away. Laura remembered the first time she and Andrea had met Marsh, only a few days before. On the surface, a handsome, charming professor of psychology. That was the terrifying thing about someone like Marsh. To everyone around him, he was successful, intelligent and, most importantly, seemingly normal. Serial killers like Marsh blend into society unnoticed. They can be married, have children, hold down jobs and even be incredibly successful in society. Ted Bundy had worked on presidential campaigns and was appointed to the Seattle Crime Prevention Advisory Committee. Dennis Nilsen was a respected civil service union representative who had skilfully negotiated with job centre bosses. Their ability to go unnoticed meant that anyone could become one of their victims.

Turning away from the scene, she gazed out across Bull Bay. The sea was a thick grey under the darkened sky.

'We've found her,' said a voice quietly.

Laura turned to look at Gareth but didn't say anything for a few seconds. She felt a sadness sweep through her. Finally, she said, 'That's good, isn't it?'

'Yes, it is.' Gareth nodded. 'I remember the haunted look on Ellie's parents' faces when I went to see them. They were so scared and so incredibly lost. And however much they hoped that Ellie might turn up alive, on my last trip to see them, her father admitted that he knew she was almost certainly dead.'

The wind picked up and swirled noisily in the nearby undergrowth. Somewhere in the distance, the deep caw of crows. It was an ugly sound.

'Their lives came to a terrible stop the day she went missing,' Laura said, thinking aloud. 'And I don't suppose they've been able to do anything since that day. Just exist.'

They looked towards the SOCOs, who were carefully taking Ellie's remains from where she had been buried. Her parents would finally know what had happened to her, however horrific that might be. And they would get her back.

Her mind turned to Rosie. Even if she'd been more challenging than usual in recent months, Laura loved her with every ounce of her being. She would lay down her life for her daughter. That was the unconditional love of a parent. So unremittingly powerful and strong. She didn't know what she would do if anything ever happened to Rosie. And she knew that she would regret every cross word, threat or unkindness if something did happen to her.

A lump came into her throat. And before she knew it, a tear in her eye. She let out an audible breath and blinked.

'You okay?' Gareth asked. He had clearly noticed.

'Yeah,' she whispered. 'Poor, poor Ellie. All that life in front of her. She was so young. And it makes me think of Rosie.'

Gareth gave her a sympathetic look and surreptitiously reached out his hand. He took her hand gently. 'Of course it does.'

Looking out, Laura said quietly, 'We're going to have to wait until tomorrow before we look for Shannon.'

Gareth nodded but didn't say anything.

For a few seconds, they stood secretly holding hands and watching the slow excavation.

CHAPTER 26

Laura stood with her arms out, eyes closed, relishing the feeling of the cold morning wind that blew on her face from the Menai Strait. The sea was unusually calm, lapping at the shore with an inaudible stroke and the occasional curl of a diminutive wavelet. The early morning light gave the water a bottle-green tint. Where it lazed onto the shore lay a mottled line of dark purple seaweed. The growing light on the water's surface shadowed and dappled the sand below with faint bubbles like imperfections in glass.

She remembered the first time she had taken the plunge into the sea at Beaumaris after reading about the benefits of cold-water swimming in some Sunday supplement. Her mother had suffered from dementia in the last few years of her life and the article had claimed that 'wild swimming' could help ward off its onset.

No longer did Laura let out a stifled scream as she hit the icy water. She had grown accustomed to the vice-like feeling around her chest and the way her breath was blasted from her by the cold. Long, deep breaths. Her toes patted gently on the sandy bottom as she bobbed in the sea, smiling like a madwoman at the release of dopamine that had just seared through her body.

Lying back in the sea, Laura felt the effects of some kind of emotional hangover from the previous day. Finding Ellie's remains and her thoughts about Rosie had left their mark on her. She gazed up at the early morning sky. About three hundred feet above her, a falcon was soaring, circling and dipping in the air currents. For a moment, it almost felt as if they were looking at each other. She wondered what it could see from up there.

Beyond that, the lightening sky bore the faintest of specks as the stars of the previous night began to dissolve with the sunrise. Laura wondered what lay up there. Someone had recently told her that the earth could fit into the sun 1.3 million times. How was that possible? Or, at least, how was her tiny mind meant to comprehend what that looked like? She didn't believe in any kind of regular God. Certainly not the one of organised religion. However, she had an overwhelming feeling that there was something far bigger and more powerful than her that was beyond all human comprehension. A higher power. She also believed that it was benign. All human instincts pointed to that, didn't they? She didn't understand atheists whose challenge to those who believed in any form of a God was *prove it then*. For Laura, that just smacked of naive arrogance. *If you can't prove it to me to the satisfaction of my incredible intellect, then I can't possibly believe it to be true*. To Laura's mind, the human brain was small in terms of an infinite universe. It seemed highly likely that there were powers, dimensions and realities that were way beyond our ability to comprehend or experience.

Setting her feet on the sandy seabed, she stood and pushed her wet hair back off her face. Then her mind drifted to the concept of the human soul. Was there some kind of altered state or reality that our conscious being drifted into once we died? She hoped that the souls of the poor women that Marsh had so cruelly killed had found some peace somewhere in this universe.

'It must be a relief,' a voice said. 'Having him in custody.'

Sam.

She turned to look at him and smiled. 'It is. It's a huge relief. It was making me feel sick every time Rosie left the house.'

'Of course,' Sam said with a heartfelt expression.

'I don't think I realised until this morning how much it had been affecting me,' Laura admitted.

'Who is he?' Sam asked. 'Professor Henry Marsh.'

'A narcissistic psychopath,' Laura said. 'You know, I just don't want to talk about him. He was in my dreams last night. Once he's sentenced, I want to try and pretend that I never even met him.'

'Sounds like he's got to you?'

'Yeah, he has,' Laura admitted, her voice wobbling with emotion.

Before she knew it, Sam had walked through the water towards her and put his arms around her.

'Hey,' he said in a soft voice. 'It's okay. He's under lock and key now. You and the kids are safe.'

'Yeah, I know,' Laura said in virtual whisper. Then she looked up him. 'It's been quite a while since we did this.' Since Gareth had spent time at the family home, Sam had virtually disappeared.

'Yeah.' Sam nodded. 'I guess that's part of the process.'

'If I let you go,' Laura said quietly, 'then there are things that I'll forget about you.' She pointed. 'This fat brown mole on your neck.'

'Oh yeah.' Sam smiled. 'You remember when I first met your mum? She baked us that cake. And then she thought the mole was a smudge of chocolate so she came over with a napkin and tried to wipe it off.'

'Oh God! She was mortified when she realised.' Laura laughed.

'There you go. You're not going to forget my mole because of that story,' Sam said with a loving smile. 'And if you do forget stuff, that's okay too.'

'I don't want to,' Laura said, looking intently at his face. 'I want to remember everything about you.' She felt her eyes well with tears. 'It's been four years. I thought it would get easier.'

'I don't think it gets easier,' Sam said. 'I just think you grow accustomed to it.'

Laura wrapped her arms around him and held him tightly. 'It's not fair.'

'I know.'

'What about those fuckers who stay married for forty years,' Laura said with her head buried in his chest.

'Those "fuckers" are very lucky.' Sam laughed. 'And most of them don't realise it. But that's just the way it is.'

CHAPTER 27

The sense of relief inside the Beaumaris CID office was palpable. The chatter between detectives was louder, more upbeat and peppered with the odd boom of laughter. It didn't mean that the team weren't still horrified by the crimes that Marsh had committed, of course. However, they had spent four long months working to get the victims and their families justice by finding and charging the man responsible. That had been achieved. It meant that the pervading sense of fear that had gripped the island for so long was beginning to dissipate.

Gareth sat in his office, looking out at his team with a sense of pride. The number of hours his CID team had put in had been phenomenal. Laura appeared at the open door, knocked at it while looking at him with a half-smile. She was carrying two coffees.

'Did you speak to Andrea?' Laura asked him as she handed him a black Americano.

'Yes,' he replied. 'She's just waiting for the test results of her MRI and CAT scan. But she was relieved that Marsh had been charged, was going to plead guilty and that we'd found Ellie's remains.'

'A lot of that is down to her,' Laura said, sitting down on the chair opposite him.

Gareth nodded. 'I shudder to think what would have happened if she hadn't attacked Marsh and caused him to crash.'

Laura blinked, sipped her coffee and then said quietly, 'She might not be alive.'

Gareth looked at Laura for a few seconds.

'What?' she asked with a bemused smile.

'I don't think I've really seen you properly for weeks,' he admitted.

'Oh, thanks,' Laura laughed.

'You know what I mean,' he said defensively.

'I'm teasing you, you berk,' she joked.

'Berk?' Gareth grinned. 'I haven't heard that for a while.' He smiled at her. 'I just think my head has been in this investigation for so long that I haven't been able to take in anything else.'

The feeling of relief that it was over and they had their man was overwhelming. He had expended every ounce of energy and thought for such a long time. There had been moments of terrible self-doubt. There had also been times when he thought he might just crack under the pressure and strain of it all.

He put his coffee cup down on his desk, sat forward and reached out to take Laura's hands.

'Oh, right,' Laura laughed. 'We're doing this in front of the whole of CID, are we?'

Gareth shrugged. 'I'm not sure I really care anymore. And I get the feeling that Declan and Ben are onto us.' He gazed right into her eyes.

As Declan approached they let go of each other's hands. He arrived at the door, tapped at his watch and gestured to the room: it was time for the morning briefing. 'Boss?'

Laura gestured. 'I think you should get out there.'

Grabbing his files, Gareth got up and headed out into the CID office. 'Right, team.'

There was a ripple of applause from the detectives, as was customary when any investigation got a result, along with some shouts of 'Good work, boss.'

Gareth suppressed a smile. 'Settle down, settle down. Right, Henry Marsh is going to his first hearing at Llangefni Crown Court this morning for his plea and trial preparation hearing. Marsh has confirmed that he will be entering a "Guilty" plea to all charges.'

There was a purr of approving comments from the CID team.

'The CPS are still going to require all the evidence from us before sentencing,' Gareth explained. 'So, I want all witness statements typed up in full. Double-check all the forensics.' Gareth looked out at them. 'Marsh has also agreed to take us to where he buried Shannon Jones over near Ynys Llanddwyn Harbour, so we'll be doing that today. We will be keeping Shannon's parents updated as we go along.' Gareth rubbed his hand over his head. 'Listen, guys, you've done an incredible job on this case so far. I'm extremely proud of the work you've done. And by the end of play today, Marsh will be locked away.'

Gareth had made the ten-mile trip to Llangefni Crown Court, following the blacked-out prison van that was transporting Marsh to his plea hearing. Given the severity of Marsh's crimes, and the growing media storm surrounding his arrest, they had been accompanied by four police motorcycles and two uniform patrol cars. In all his years of policing, Gareth had never experienced anything like it.

Gareth and Laura now sat quietly in the public gallery, along with some of the relatives of Marsh's victims. Others had just found it too upsetting to attend.

Marsh, now dressed in a suit, was sitting behind a large Perspex screen. He was handcuffed and sitting next to a female prison officer. He looked out at the courtroom as if he didn't have a care in the world.

The judge, a woman in her sixties, wearing glasses and a blank expression, peered over at Marsh. 'Will the defendant please rise.'

Marsh and the prison officer stood.

'Mr Marsh, you are here today to enter a plea to the crimes with which you have been charged. Do you understand that?' the judge asked.

'Yes, your honour,' Marsh replied in a calm, clear voice.

'Can you confirm that you are Henry James Marsh?' the judge asked.

'Yes, I can confirm that,' Marsh said.

'Mr Marsh, you are charged with five counts of murder contrary to common law. How do you plead to these charges?' she asked him.

For a few anxious seconds, Marsh hesitated.

What's he waiting for?

Gareth swallowed nervously. Was Marsh going to do as he promised?

'Guilty, your honour,' Marsh said.

There were a few gasps and sobs from the relatives in the public gallery. Even though they had been informed that Marsh had been arrested, charged and had admitted to the crimes, it was very emotional to see the man responsible stand up in court and enter a plea of guilty.

Gareth shared a look with Laura. It was such a relief not to be faced with the torturous prospect of a criminal trial.

'You may sit down, Mr Marsh.' The judge looked over at the prosecution. 'I understand that the Chief Prosecutor has asked for the sentence hearing to be adjourned while awaiting a full psychological report of the defendant. Is that correct?'

The prosecutor nodded. 'It is, your honour.'

The judge peered at the duty defence solicitor. 'But I also understand there is no desire on the defendant's part to enter a diminished responsibility plea, whatever is in that psychological report?'

The defence solicitor nodded. 'That's correct, your honour.'

The judge peered down at some documents and wrote for a few seconds. She then looked out into the court. 'I will adjourn sentencing until the fifth of April. The defendant will be remanded in custody at HMP Rhosneigr.' She then peered over at where Marsh was sitting. 'Will the defendant please stand.'

Marsh stood up again.

'Mr Marsh, you have pleaded guilty to the five charges of murder for which the sentence is fixed by law. I shall sentence you on the agreed date of the fifth of April of this year. I can tell you now that the sentence will be of imprisonment for life. The only issue will be the minimum term I must impose pursuant to the Sentencing Act 2020. As already stated, you will be remanded in custody until that date. Please take the prisoner down.'

CHAPTER 28

Descending the stairs from the public gallery, Gareth could see that the top corridor of the courthouse was unusually busy. Something was going on. With a sinking heart, he spotted that a couple of press photographers had managed to get into the building. They had clearly tried to take shots of the grieving relatives of Marsh's victims as they left, which had led to a growing commotion.

'For fuck's sake,' Gareth growled to Laura as they headed towards the kerfuffle.

There were a few angry shouts and then some pushing as relatives confronted the photographers, who had no business being inside the courthouse.

How the hell did that happen? Gareth wondered, knowing that there were uniformed officers positioned outside to stop stuff like this happening.

He pointed to the photographers. 'I want you lot out now or I'm arresting you for breach of the peace.'

As the photographers backed away, the door at the far end of the corridor behind where Gareth and Laura were standing opened.

Marsh appeared. His hands were still cuffed in front of

him and he was flanked by two prison officers and a uniformed constable.

Shit! What the hell is going on?

'What the bloody hell is Marsh doing down there?' Laura thundered as she and Gareth turned and approached.

Defendants and prisoners were usually escorted from the holding cells in the basement of the building to the rear entrance to avoid any interaction between them and their victims or the relatives of their victims. This was not a good situation.

'What's going on?' Gareth growled as he approached and saw that Marsh was smirking at the disorganisation in his departure from the courthouse.

'A lorry has broken down across the rear entrance to the court,' the male prison officer explained, looking very flustered.

'We'll have to take him out of the front,' the female police officer said.

Laura glared at her. 'You're not taking him anywhere while there are relatives of his victims standing just down there.'

'Wait there!' Gareth snapped to the prison officers. He could feel his stomach squirm with anxiety.

Marsh smiled. 'Bit of a mix-up, DI Williams?'

Gareth went to snap at him, but was distracted by yet another commotion: a photographer and several of the relatives had spotted Marsh's appearance at the top of the corridor.

'What the fuck is that scum doing out here?' a man in his forties shouted as he began to approach. He was joined by a couple of other men, whom Gareth recognised as being relatives of the victims.

Shit! he thought. If they weren't careful, they were going to have a public lynching here.

A bald man in his fifties clenched his fist as he approached purposefully. 'If I get my hands on you, I'm going to fucking kill you!'

Gareth, Laura, the constable and the two prison officers turned to face the half-dozen men heading their way.

'Stay where you are, please, gentlemen,' Gareth said firmly to them, putting up his hand.

'Six-three to all units,' Laura said quietly into her radio. 'We have a situation on the first floor of Llangefni Courthouse and we require assistance, over.'

'Six-three, received,' said a voice of the radio.

Gareth glanced back at Marsh who was now also looking concerned.

The men were now about ten yards away.

'Stay there, please,' Gareth said loudly.

The bald man pointed to Marsh, who was being shielded behind them. 'That *thing* shouldn't be out here.'

'I understand that,' Laura said in a conciliatory tone. 'And we are attempting to rectify the situation.'

'Please, guys,' Gareth said, taking a step forward. 'Just make your way out of the building down there. I don't want to have to arrest anyone.'

'Arrest anyone?' The bald man virtually spat out the words. 'That fucking scumbag there murdered my niece. He needs to be hanged.' He made a sudden lunge towards Gareth, his teeth gritted and his fists clenched.

'Come on,' Gareth said, now physically restraining him. 'Don't do this.'

A couple of the other men came over and there was a general melee of pushing.

'Right, I need everyone to back away, please,' Gareth yelled.

Laura had an alarmed expression as she grabbed at his arm. 'Where's Marsh?'

Gareth spun to look.

For a second, his eyes roamed frantically around the corridor. Marsh had vanished.

Gareth's stomach lurched. 'Where the hell is he?'

179

'I don't know,' Laura replied, sounding perplexed.

A fire exit door over to the left was open by about six inches.

'Jesus!' Gareth shouted as he sprinted over to the door and heard footsteps below. 'You have got to be fucking joking!' he growled as he thundered down the fire exit stairs towards to the ground floor.

He heard the crash of doors opening and then noisily crashing closed again.

This cannot be happening.

Spotting the double fire exit doors, Gareth knew that's where Marsh had made his escape. He kicked them open and then squinted at the daylight – he was now outside the rear of the courthouse.

'He went down that way,' an elderly woman said, pointing to the road that led away towards the centre of Llangefni.

'Thanks,' Gareth gasped as he sprinted away in pursuit, his eyes roaming for any sight of Marsh.

Out of the corner of his eye, he spotted a man running.

Marsh.

Gareth went into a full sprint, pumping his arms with everything he had.

Running across a main road, he narrowly avoided a car, which beeped its horn angrily, before hurdling a bench.

Marsh was now in his sights and about a hundred yards ahead.

He must have heard Gareth, because Marsh spun round, saw that he was being chased and left the pavement. Even though he had a slight limp and was in handcuffs, Marsh was still running at a decent speed.

Up ahead was a huge building site.

Marsh ducked behind a huge cement mixer lorry and out of sight.

Shit!

Slowing, Gareth crept around the side of the lorry in case Marsh had decided to lie in wait and attack him. It would be difficult in handcuffs, but he wasn't taking any chances.

He ducked his head around the lorry, heart pounding. But there was no one there.

Where the hell has he got to?

Scanning the building site, Gareth saw a series of huge metal cylindrical tubes. Thinking that Marsh could be hiding in one of them, he jogged over and meticulously checked them all.

Nothing.

Gareth clicked his Tetra radio, 'Nine-three to Dispatch, over,' he gasped.

'Nine-three, this is Dispatch, received, over.'

'I am in pursuit of suspect Henry Marsh. Our current location is a building site five hundred yards east of Llangefni Courthouse. I have lost visual contact. Request backup and for all entrances at this site to be sealed off, over.'

'Nine-three, request received, stand by, over.'

There was movement over to the right, which caught Gareth's eye.

It was Marsh.

He was making his way casually through scaffold poles on the ground floor of a four-storey building that was under construction. He glanced around nervously but hadn't yet spotted Gareth.

Gareth jogged in his direction, trying to keep behind a concrete mixing lorry so as not to attract Marsh's attention.

Hugging an exterior wall, Gareth glanced down the side of the building and saw Marsh now walking at speed towards a large mesh fence and open gate.

Gareth followed.

Marsh was now fifty yards ahead and Gareth was gaining on him.

Marsh went through the mesh gate, out onto the main road and his walk turned into a run.

Shit!

As Gareth turned the corner, he exploded into a sprint. Marsh's running would be hampered by his inability to use his arms. And Gareth had been a rapid rugby winger back in the day.

Marsh turned at the clattering sound of Gareth's feet on the pavement. His eyes widened as he tried to pick up the pace.

Gareth was now only forty yards away and closing.

I'm taking you down, you fucker.

Thirty yards.

Gareth was pumping his arms as he hit full speed. His heart was hammering and he was sucking in air – but he didn't care. Marsh was his.

Ducking right, into a side street, Marsh disappeared momentarily out of sight.

Gareth slowed a little as he came hammering right behind him.

However, the side street was deserted.

Marsh seemed to have vanished into thin air.

What the . . .?

To the right was a car park for a primary school. Maybe Marsh was hiding behind one of the dozen or so vehicles.

Jogging over, Marsh went quickly to each car to check for Marsh's whereabouts.

Nothing.

Scanning left to right, all Gareth could see were hedges that backed onto a cul-de-sac. But he couldn't see anyone.

How the hell had Marsh managed to disappear?

A young woman pushing a pram was walking down from the far end of the street. Gareth approached, taking out his warrant card.

'Hi there. I'm wondering if you saw a man anywhere along this street when you were walking up here?' he asked. 'He was wearing a dark suit.'

The young woman looked puzzled and shook her head. 'Sorry, I haven't seen anyone.'

'Thanks,' Gareth muttered as he frantically glanced around again but the cul-de-sac was deserted.

He had no idea how they had lost Marsh, but it was a complete disaster.

CHAPTER 29

The CID office at Beaumaris was a hive of nervous energy. Laura sat at her desk feeling sick at the thought that Marsh had escaped and was now out there on the island somewhere.

Gareth paced the room, looking anxious as he ran his hand over his head and blew out his cheeks.

Declan approached. 'Boss, we've got Armed Response Units on both bridges off the island. Everyone has got a detailed description of Marsh and a photograph. They're checking every car from now.'

'Good,' Gareth said, nodding, but he looked stressed.

Laura stood up. 'I spoke to North Wales Police at Wrexham. They're sending over a helicopter with thermal imaging, which they usually use for searching Snowdonia. If Marsh is hiding out somewhere, we might get a hit.'

'Okay, thanks.' Gareth nodded. 'I'll put the Canine Unit on stand-by in case we need to flush Marsh out of hiding.'

The door opened. Warlow walked in slowly, looking around. He spotted Gareth and thundered over to him. 'What the bloody hell happened, Gareth?' he asked in a tone of utter disbelief. Marsh's escape was a disaster for everyone, especially a career-orientated copper like Warlow.

'Fucking shambles, sir,' Gareth growled under his breath. 'Broken-down lorry was blocking the rear exit. Prison guards tried to take him out through the main entrance but he escaped through the fire exit.'

'He's still handcuffed?' Warlow said.

'He was when I was chasing him, sir,' Gareth explained.

'The press office at St Asaph have asked us to do a press conference as damage limitation,' Warlow continued.

Gareth shrugged. 'Maybe it should be a spokesperson from the prison service doing the press conference?'

'I don't think we can use it as an excuse to throw the prison service under the bus,' Warlow said. 'Give it some thought, Gareth. It might be that you write and deliver a prepared statement and take no questions. If we say nothing, we look more culpable.'

Laura could feel herself getting angry. There was a very dangerous psychopath on the loose and all Warlow seemed worried about was how it impacted in terms of PR.

Gareth frowned. 'I thought you would want to talk to the press yourself, sir.'

'No. If CID are running the show, then I want you guys leading from the front,' Warlow explained, not meeting Gareth's eyes.

Laura knew exactly what Warlow was doing. He was distancing himself as much as he could from the Marsh investigation in an attempt to limit damage to his career. He certainly wasn't going to appear on the national news fielding awkward questions about it.

Laura gave Gareth a withering look. 'Quite apart from the PR, I think the point is that Marsh is smart. It won't be long before he works out a way of getting the cuffs off. And then we really do have a problem, sir.'

'Yes, quite,' Warlow said. 'You've spoken to Holyhead?'

'Yes, sir.' Laura nodded. 'Holyhead is on full alert for

anyone matching Marsh trying to board a ferry. And the bridges are being manned. Every car is being searched. As far as I can see, he can't get off the island undetected.'

'Very good,' Warlow said approvingly.

'My worry is that Marsh is now on the run. He's desperate. He's going to need money, food and shelter.' Gareth gave them a dark look. 'And I'm pretty sure he doesn't care how he gets any of that.'

Marsh had managed to get as far as the village of Lledwigan, to the south of Llangefni, without detection. He had stolen a newspaper from a bin and was using it to cover his hand-cuffs as best he could. What he needed was to find some way of getting the handcuffs off, as well as changing his clothes and appearance. And quickly. The cuffs were biting into his wrists and bruising his wrist bones. He could feel a pain in his ankle from the fall. The sweat in his socks was beginning to cool and his mouth was dry.

Turning left off the main road, Marsh spotted a white bungalow up on the left-hand side. It had a grey slate roof, neat, well-tended flowerbeds and there was washing hanging out on the line. On the left-hand side of the garden was a large shed.

That will do, Marsh thought to himself.

Glancing around to check no one had noticed him, he ducked through the gate, across the tidy lawn, and got to the shed door in a matter of seconds. He took the plastic handle, twisted and it opened. Closing the door behind him, Marsh went into the shed, which had a workbench and tools as well as a lawnmower and other gardening equipment. The air was full of the smell of wood and grass cuttings.

Approaching the workbench, he immediately spotted a small hacksaw. *Perfect*.

Taking the hacksaw in his right hand, he very carefully

began to saw at the metal handcuff on his left wrist. The blade was sharp and soon began to make a small cut in the metal. After a few minutes, he managed to break the metal cuff. He massaged his left wrist for a moment before going to work on the right-hand cuff. After another couple of minutes, the cuffs were finally off.

Rolling his arms and shoulders, Marsh stretched, marvelling at the feeling of being free.

That's so much better, he thought.

Now that he had full use of his hands and arms back, he pulled off his tie and jacket, which had felt so restrictive. He rolled up the sleeves of his shirt and caught his reflection in an old mirror that was propped up on some shelves.

He looked at himself for a moment with a feeling of pride. The police were idiots to have allowed him to escape. He then studied his reflected appearance, which he knew needed to radically change if he was going to avoid being caught.

He studied his smile for a few seconds. He remembered reading that certain facial muscle groups were not activated in someone if they were faking a smile. If they were lying. The smile of a deceiver was flawed and therefore detectable. These particular muscles only came into use with the expression of a genuine feeling. An authentic smile just couldn't be faked. He wondered about the smiling face that gazed back at him. Had those particular facial muscles been engaged? He searched his mind but he was unable to recognise any discernible feeling. He guessed that was the sign of a true psychopath.

Opening the door to the shed, he watched the bungalow from the doorway for a few seconds. An old man was in the kitchen and looked like he was washing up at the sink. Marsh guessed that he was in his eighties and wouldn't provide much resistance.

Returning to the shed, Marsh grabbed a hammer and a long screwdriver. He strode outside and headed across the lawn towards the back door. Two tall, feathery acacia trees stood to one side.

Turning the handle, he was pleased to find that, like the shed, it was unlocked.

He went quietly inside.

CHAPTER 30

Gareth looked out at the press conference with some trepidation. Journalists from around the entire country were clamouring over the Marsh case and the hunt for his whereabouts now he had escaped. The room was bustling with local and national newspapers, radio and television. Gareth could feel the nerves in his stomach. Online, the media had already had a field day with their headlines about the 'Anglesey Ripper's' escape and the ineptitude of the Anglesey police.

Behind Gareth was a banner on the wall: HEDDLU GOGLEDD CYMRU – NORTH WALES POLICE, GOGLEDD CYMRU DIOGELACH – A SAFER NORTH WALES. The irony of the slogan wasn't lost on him.

On the table in front of him was a jug of water and several small tape recorders and microphones that eager journalists had placed there. Sitting next to him was Kerry Mahoney, the Chief Corporate Communications Officer for North Wales Police, who had come up from the main press office in St Asaph. Gareth had met her before and found her to be a rather pompous woman.

'This is about as tricky as it gets,' Mahoney said under her breath. 'No offence, but I'm surprised Superintendent Warlow isn't sitting here given the severity of the crimes.'

'None taken.' Gareth shrugged. 'And so am I.' He wasn't about to make excuses for the man they called Partridge.

For a moment, they both looked out at the massed ranks of the British press.

'I guess the PCTD training you've done will stand you in good stead,' Mahoney said, gesturing to the cameras.

Gareth vaguely remembered that the PCTD stood for PolComm Training and Development and was the UK's centre of police media training. As a Detective Inspector, Gareth had never had any form of media training to date. He was also pretty certain that Mahoney knew that. It was her way of making sure that if he wasn't already nervous, he would be now.

Gareth smiled and nodded but didn't reply.

'Good luck,' Mahoney said in the same tone as a commanding officer might use to a soldier about to jump out of a plane on a suicide mission.

Let's just get on with this, shall we? he thought, taking a deep breath.

'Good morning, everyone, I'm Detective Inspector Gareth Williams of the Anglesey Police and I am the senior investigating officer on the Henry Marsh case. I want to update you on developments in the last twenty-four hours. Our primary concern at the moment is the safety of the public on Anglesey, as well as the North Wales region.' Gareth took a moment and sipped his water. Now he had started, his nerves were under control. 'Henry Marsh escaped from his escort while officers were taking him through Llangefni Courthouse this morning. All measures and precautions had been taken with regards to Henry Marsh's security. It was an extraordinary set of circumstances that led to his escape. Obviously, our thoughts are with the families of the victims of these horrific crimes at what must be an extremely difficult time.'

Gareth looked up to see Warlow enter at the back of the room and give him what was supposed to be a supportive nod. *Why don't you just fuck off?* thought Gareth.

Clearing his throat, Gareth continued. 'Anglesey Police are absolutely committed to finding Henry Marsh. We are using every resource available to us to bring our search to a conclusion as quickly as possible. There are currently a number of operations under way on the island. For obvious reasons, I am unable to explain where or what those operations are. And I want to reassure you that both the bridges and the port of Holyhead are being manned by armed police officers to make sure that Henry Marsh does not escape from Anglesey before he can be recaptured.'

For the next five minutes, Gareth continued to update the press on the full extent of the search for Marsh before opening up the conference to questions, which he was dreading.

A young female journalist at the front of the room indicated that she wanted to ask a question and Gareth nodded in her direction. 'Lucy Redman, *Daily Express*. Can you explain to our readers how someone as dangerous and violent as Henry Marsh was allowed to escape? I understand that there were officers from the Anglesey Police as well as the prison service with him? That seems incredibly negligent and has put the population of Anglesey in great danger.'

'I'm not at liberty to give any more details of Henry Marsh's escape this morning. However, the incident will be investigated thoroughly. We have also voluntarily referred this to the Independent Office for Police Conduct and we will fully cooperate with their independent investigation and any rulings.' Gareth knew this wasn't what the journalist was looking for, but no one was going to tell the press how Marsh had got away.

Gareth pointed to a middle-aged television journalist who was standing towards the back of the room. 'James Lawton,

BBC News. Can you tell us what resources you have available in your search for Henry Marsh and whether you believe they are adequate?'

Gareth nodded. 'We have over a hundred police officers working on this case at the moment. We have received resources, in terms of officers, vehicles and expertise, from North Wales, Merseyside, Greater Manchester, Cheshire and Shropshire police forces. I would like to thank my colleagues from across the country for their ongoing support.'

Gareth fielded a few more questions and then thanked the assembled media.

Mahoney glanced at him as he stood up and started to grab his folders, while the assembled media began to chat noisily as they made their way out of the conference room.

'Nicely handled,' Mahoney said in a patronising tone.

Gareth gave her a sarcastic smile. 'Thanks, Kerry. Not sure I could have done that without you. Have a safe journey back to the mainland.'

Gareth turned and walked away, not stopping to wait for her response.

CHAPTER 31

The elderly couple sat with terrified expressions on their faces. Marsh had bound and gagged them. A swift nose around the bungalow had revealed that they were Elis and Bronwen Barker. From the photos that had been carefully positioned on every windowsill and table, Marsh had deduced that they had four children and seven or eight grandchildren. A wedding photograph in the middle of the mantelpiece looked like it had been taken in the early 1960s.

For the past half-hour, Marsh had busied himself in the bungalow. He had rummaged through the wardrobe and found a navy sweatshirt and a pair of jeans that belonged to Elis. They fitted Marsh, even if they were a little short in the leg. Under the bed, he'd found a pair of size 8 brandless trainers. Marsh was a size 9 but he'd squeezed into them with relative ease.

Moving on to the kitchen, Marsh had grabbed some food from the fridge. He'd found a bottle of cheap whisky which he was drinking neat. It was smoothing out the frayed edges of his nerves and taking the edge off the pain from his ankle.

Marsh came into the living room and looked around. He went over to Elis, who had a gash to his temple from where he had tried to wrestle Marsh in the kitchen. A swift crack of the hammer to his head had convinced Elis to do as he was told.

Crouching down, Marsh looked at Elis. He was a small man with delicate features and a long, thin, curvy mouth, which was now trembling. He had a shock of white hair, a wrinkled face and milky blue eyes.

'Is there any money in the house, Elis?' Marsh asked in a friendly tone.

Elis shook his head but something in Bronwen's face suggested that her husband was lying.

Marsh raised a dubious eyebrow. 'You're not lying to me, are you, Elis?'

Elis shook his head adamantly.

A quick glance over to Bronwen revealed that she was staring over at an old-fashioned bureau in the corner of the room.

'Ah, the bureau, of course,' Marsh said cheerily as he stood up and wandered over. He tried the drawer but it was locked.

March grabbed the long screwdriver he'd taken from the shed and jammed it into the top of the drawer. It broke open. Inside was a cash box, passports and other legal documents.

'Bingo!' Marsh said as he opened the cash box and saw a stack of £20 notes. By a quick estimation, there were several hundred pounds there. He grabbed a couple of credit cards that had Elis's name on them. They were chip-and-pin, so he could use them at tills until they were cancelled.

'Looks like you were holding out on me, Elis,' Marsh said, holding up the money as he wandered back. Taking the hammer, he smashed it directly onto Elis's knee. Elis gave a shriek from behind the gaffer tape that was over his mouth. Bronwen's eyes filled with tears.

Checking his watch, Marsh saw that it was time for the BBC News. He strode over to the television and turned it on.

The screen was filled with aerial footage of the Anglesey countryside.

'*The search continues today on the island of Anglesey in North Wales for Henry Marsh, the man who has been dubbed "Britain's Most Wanted". Earlier today, Marsh, a teacher and lecturer, was charged and pleaded guilty to five murders on the island in the past three months. Marsh escaped this morning from this courthouse in Llangefni . . .*'

The footage now showed the area outside Llangefni Courthouse.

'*. . . A police spokesperson said that the manhunt for Marsh is the biggest in the UK for nearly a decade, with over a hundred officers mobilised from over five Welsh and English counties. Police have appealed to Marsh to give himself up and have warned members on the public not to approach him as he is considered extremely dangerous.*'

The footage continued and showed some of the police officers leaving the courthouse. Marsh watched with great interest. He spotted DI Laura Hart, who had first visited him a few days earlier. At a distance, she reminded him of his mother. Then he realised that DI Hart was the woman he had spotted coming out of the sea three mornings earlier.

Grabbing an old, cheap-looking laptop, Marsh looked over at Bronwen. 'Have you got the password for this computer?' he asked in an almost friendly way.

Still completely terrified, Bronwen nodded.

'Good,' Marsh said as the screen to the laptop burst into life. It was time to take a closer look at DI Laura Hart.

CHAPTER 32

Gareth peered at the map of Anglesey on the wall of the CID office in utter frustration. It had been five hours since Marsh had launched himself out of the first-floor window in Llangefni and fled. The fact that they'd had their killer in custody and allowed him to escape was a deeply disappointing and infuriating thing for the CID team to come to terms with.

He looked around at his team, who were hard at work. They were shell-shocked by what had happened. Gareth felt somehow that he'd let them down – he'd been present at Marsh's escape, after all. He believed he was responsible for not spotting that Marsh had an escape route, however unlikely. There was also the sickening realisation that if Marsh killed again, there would be blood on his hands.

'Hey,' said a voice next to him. It was Laura.

'Where is he?' Gareth said under his breath as he looked at the map again.

'It's too difficult to go cross-country up here,' Laura stated with her finger on the map. There were no roads to the north of Llangefni. 'If I was on the run, I would stick to the A4080 here. And that either goes this way towards Pencarnisiog, or south this way to the coast at Porth Trecastell.'

Gareth nodded. 'And this is a man on foot, dressed in a suit, wearing handcuffs. But no one seems to have seen him.'

Ben arrived with a print-out. 'Bad news, boss. If Marsh did get to Llangefni railway station, there was a train leaving at eleven o'clock.'

'Where does it go?' Laura asked.

Ben pulled a face. 'All the way over to Wrexham and then Chester.'

Gareth shook his head. 'Jesus.'

'If Marsh had managed to get across Llangefni to the railway station and boarded that train, then he could be in England by now.'

'I'm not sure I can even begin to think of telling Warlow that's a possibility,' Gareth groaned.

Twenty minutes later, Laura entered the CID office with a fresh coffee. Declan looked over as soon as she walked in. Something was up. He gestured to the phone in his hand and looked at Laura. 'Someone reckons they know exactly where Marsh is hiding out.'

'Great,' Gareth said with some urgency as he came over. 'Who is it?'

Declan gestured to Laura. 'They said they'll only speak to DI Hart, boss.'

Gareth shot her a look.

What the hell is that? Laura wondered as she put down her coffee, took the phone from Declan and put it to her ear. 'Detective Inspector Laura Hart speaking.'

There was a silence at the other end, but she could hear someone breathing.

'Hello?' she said.

'Laura?' the voice asked in a virtual whisper. It was man's voice, relatively well spoken. Something about it sounded familiar.

Who the hell is that?

'Hi,' Laura said gently. There was more silence.

Whoever was about to give them the information about Marsh's whereabouts was acting very strangely. Or maybe they were just scared about talking to the police.

'Hello, Laura,' the voice said in a far clearer and more friendly tone.

And then her stomach pitched.

It was Henry Marsh.

Her eyes immediately locked onto Gareth's as she gestured to the phone.

'Henry?' she asked, trying not to show her unease at having him calling her.

Gareth's eyes widened as he realised who she was talking to. He signalled to Laura to keep Marsh talking as long as possible. There was a possibility that they could triangulate the signal and find Marsh's location.

'How are you guys doing, Laura?' Marsh asked in an amused, pompous tone.

'We've been better,' Laura said, trying to sound unflustered. 'Obviously your escape hasn't exactly covered us in glory.'

'No, I don't suppose it has. You lot are taking a hammering on the news,' Marsh snorted. 'The UK's biggest manhunt since Raoul Moat. I think that was 2010, wasn't it?'

'I'm not sure,' Laura said, happy to keep Marsh on the line. 'Where are you, Henry?'

Marsh tutted down the phone. 'Oh dear, Laura. There we were getting to know each other and then you ask me a stupid question like that. I can't stay long on this call because my guess is that you're trying to track my location as we speak. Is that right?'

'Of course we are, Henry,' Laura replied, trying to sound light-hearted. 'It's just that I got the distinct feeling when we spoke to you the other day that it was a relief for us to have caught you.'

'Well, yes, it really was,' Marsh admitted with a laugh. 'But that's the problem with anyone who suffers from my condition. The inner conflict. Part of me is desperate to stop. Unfortunately, the other voice in my subconscious telling me to kill again is too overwhelming. I'm afraid I've given in again as I don't think I'm quite done,' Marsh said in a dark tone that sent a shiver down her spine.

'But you'll never be done, Henry. Nothing will ever be enough,' Laura said gently. 'That's why you need us to help you stop.'

'Yeah, but I figure I might as well do one or two more before I hang up my proverbial boots. Or maybe gloves is a better metaphor,' Marsh said slowly. 'I'm never going to get this opportunity again, am I?'

Laura could feel her heart beating faster. In all her years of training as a hostage negotiator, she had never had to converse with a serial killer. Most of the psychological techniques just wouldn't work on a pathological psychopath. Her training had taught her to listen and look for emotional tells or weaknesses. Marsh felt no empathy so it was impossible to appeal to any part of his human nature – he just didn't have one.

'But you fully understand why you've chosen to kill these women,' Laura said. 'You're acting out your matricidal rage.'

Marsh laughed. 'Logic and reason just don't come into it. The instinctive desire to commit these murders is just too overwhelming.'

'Then come in and we can put you somewhere where you can't act out.'

'Mmm, that is tempting but . . .'

There were a few seconds of silence.

Laura hoped that Marsh was considering what she had just suggested.

Marsh cleared his throat. Then he said in a chatty voice, 'It's such a shame what happened to Sam.'

His words went straight through her as if she had been punched in the stomach. With a sharp intake of breath, she tried to steady herself.

Gareth gave her a look as if to ask if she was okay.

Despite her shock, Laura knew she needed to keep Marsh on the line. 'It's been very difficult since his death.'

'That's very honest of you, Laura,' Marsh said.

'I thought we were being honest,' she stated.

'Are we? Is that what we're doing?' Marsh asked. 'What's the hardest part of not having Sam in your life?'

Laura hated the fact that she was being forced to talk to Marsh about her life. 'It's difficult to pinpoint one thing. Everything, I suppose.'

'Must have been hard on the kids?' Marsh asked.

'Yes, it was.'

A few more seconds of silence.

'I saw you the other morning, actually,' Marsh said.

'Did you?' Laura asked, her pulse racing. 'Where was that?'

'On Beaumaris beach,' Marsh said. 'You'd been swimming in the sea, which is either very brave or very stupid. And you have a huge dog. It was you, wasn't it?'

'Yes,' Laura admitted. 'It was. Wild swimming not your thing, Henry?'

'No . . .' Marsh gave a sigh. 'Listen, I can't stand around all day chatting, Laura. I've got things to do and places to go.'

'Going anywhere nice?' Laura asked, trying to keep him talking.

There was no reply.

'Henry?'

The line went dead.

'Shit!' Laura snapped, slamming the phone down.

'Well done,' Gareth said quietly.

'Tell me Digital Forensics have got something,' Laura sighed, sitting down and putting her head in her hands.

Ben looked over. 'He wasn't using a mobile phone. He was on a landline. We're just trying to trace the address registered to that number. Shouldn't be more than a couple of minutes.'

Laura nodded, relieved that they might have a lead.

CHAPTER 33

Marsh ran the electric trimmer over his head then shook the hair into the black bin bag on the floor by his feet. He looked up and gazed at his reflection in the bathroom mirror. He smiled and then glanced at his watch. It was ten minutes since he'd ended his phone call with DI Laura Hart. It wouldn't take them long to trace the landline. But that was part of the fun. Toying with the police and giving them the hope that they might catch him, only to find that he was always just one step ahead. They were idiots.

Marsh ran his hands over his head, which was now shaved to a very close crop. His beard was gone and his face now clean-shaven and smooth.

He was transformed.

'The makeover is complete,' he said triumphantly, feeling the excitement surge through his body. He put the hair trimmer with its electric cord into the bin bag, too.

Spotting a bottle of moisturiser, he opened it, put some on his palms and smoothed it over his freshly shaved face. He then took a pair of reading glasses that he'd found next to Elis in the living room. They had thick black rims in a retro Buddy Holly or Harry Palmer style. Popping them on, he peered again at his reflection.

'Well, Professor Henry Marsh, no one is going to recognise you out there, are they?' he said with a grin.

He picked up the black bin bag that contained all his hair and beard trimmings. It was vital that the police didn't know that he'd changed his appearance so he needed to take the evidence of that with him.

He came out of the bathroom and marched back into the living room where Elis and Bronwen were still sitting, bound and gagged, on the sofa.

'What do you think?' he asked them, pointing to his new appearance.

He instantly got the pungent smell of urine.

Going over to them, he saw that Elis was now sitting in a wet patch of his own urine.

'Oh dear, Elis,' Marsh chortled. 'That's the problem with us men as we grow old. The old bladder starts to play up, doesn't it? You know, I'm up at least twice a night and I'm not even fifty.' He looked into Elis's face, which was full of terror. 'What happened to those halcyon days when we used to sleep a full eight hours with *bladder intactus*, eh?'

Marsh glanced at the BBC news channel, which was on silently in the corner of the room. The story of the Anglesey manhunt seemed to be playing permanently. A large photo of his face, complete with long greying hair and beard, filled the screen for a moment.

He gave a little laugh as he looked at it. 'Brilliant.'

Going out to the hallway, Marsh grabbed the car keys to the old silver Honda CRV that sat on the drive. Now he had transport too. He needed to get to Menai Bridge, not more than a twenty-minute drive away. Marsh assumed that there would be police officers on the bridge but they would be looking for a long-haired, bearded man in his forties. Once he got over the bridge, Marsh would be into Wales. And from there, England. He knew he would need to change vehicles once he'd got far enough away. It might take the police time to realise that there had been a car at the bungalow and that Marsh had stolen it, but eventually they'd have the registration, make and model of the Honda.

'Right, have I got everything?' Marsh said out loud. He grabbed a green Barbour wax coat from a hook in the hallway and a dark tweed flat cap, which he placed on his head. It felt strange against his close-trimmed scalp.

Spotting some green wellies, Marsh took off the trainers he'd been wearing and put them on. His new country look was complete.

'What do you think now?' Marsh boomed as he strode into the living room and looked at Elis and Bronwen. 'Proper country bumpkin.' He then went over to Elis, who visibly flinched. Marsh smiled, enjoying the effect he had on Elis. 'It's okay, I'm not going to hit you. I just need to know if you've got petrol in your car?'

Elis nodded and made a noise.

'A lot of petrol. Like, nearly a full tank?' Marsh asked.

Elis nodded again.

'Great,' Marsh laughed. 'Elis, you strike me as the sort of man who doesn't let the petrol get too low in his car. Am I right?'

Elis blinked and nodded cautiously.

Marsh looked at his watch again. 'Time to go, I'm afraid, kids.'

Thinking for a moment, Marsh marched into the kitchen and took the largest kitchen knife from the wooden knife block. He liked the feel of the cold steel handle in his hand.

Coming back into the living room, Marsh saw Elis and Bronwen wince and then make a distressed noise at the sight of the knife he was wielding.

'Don't worry,' Marsh laughed and gestured to the knife. 'I've only got this to cut all that string I tied you up with.'

Marsh then waited for a few seconds to watch Elis and Bronwen relax a little. He wanted them to truly believe that he was going to untie them and then leave.

Of course, he wasn't.

He just wanted them to feel that their terrifying ordeal was nearly over. Which it was.

Marsh pulled a face. 'Actually, guys, I was lying. Sorry. You see, I've transformed myself. I look like a different person. And there are only two people in the world who actually know what I look like now. And, I'm afraid that's you two.'

Bronwen's eyes widened in horror as she picked up on where he was going with all this.

'The police are going to be here very soon. And then you're going to tell them that I've shaved my head and beard, and I'm wearing these clothes.'

In unison, Elis and Bronwen shook their heads with a desperate urgency. Bronwen widened her eyes and made a noise as if to say *no, no, no.*

'Ah, but you guys can promise not to tell the police any of that,' Marsh said and then shrugged. 'But how do I know if I can believe you? I mean, we hardly know each other.'

In a flash, Marsh was upon Bronwen. Grabbing her hair, he jerked her head back violently, put the blade to her exposed throat and slit it open all the way across. A surge of blood cascaded from the wound down over her chest and stomach.

Elis had his eyes closed as he thrashed around. In the same swift fashion, Marsh slit his throat too.

He stood back to look at what he'd done. They were both already unconscious. They'd be dead in seconds. Even though there was a certain excitement in killing them, it paled into insignificance in comparison to the buzz he'd got from killing young women. These were murders out of necessity, rather than to satisfy his compulsion.

205

Tossing the bloody knife to the floor, Marsh made for the front door and opened it. He decided to leave it open, as if welcoming the police inside to view his handiwork.

Opening the car, Marsh settled himself in the driver's seat and turned on the engine.

The fuel indicator rose less than a millimetre and the orange fuel light went on. Then *5 miles* appeared beside it.

'You sly bastard, Elis,' Marsh growled. He would now have to stop on the way to Menai Bridge, which definitely wasn't part of the plan.

CHAPTER 34

Laura moved into position outside the white bungalow, which they now knew belonged to an elderly couple, Elis and Bronwen Barker. The village of Lledwigan was quiet. Glancing down the road, Laura could see half a dozen AFOs in position. She wriggled her shoulders. The Kevlar stab vest she was wearing was uncomfortable and digging into her collarbone.

Gareth, who was crouched with her behind the hedgerow, glanced over and gave a signal that they were ready to go. The whole operation had been conducted so far in virtual silence. They had no idea whether Marsh was still inside the bungalow or if he had taken the Barkers hostage. She glanced down at her watch. It had been over thirty minutes since she had spoken to Marsh on the phone. He was smart so he would have known they'd be able to trace the address of the Barkers' landline number almost immediately. She wondered why he had taken the risk. What had he achieved by making that phone call except to play mind games with her and Beaumaris CID? Maybe that was the point . . .

'Gold Command to all units,' Gareth said very quietly into his radio. 'Proceed to target location one with caution, over.'

'Gold Command, received,' said a voice.

Rising slowly up, Laura looked over the hedgerow, scanning the garden in case Marsh made a dash for it out the back.

Following Gareth along the pavement towards the main garden path, Laura noticed something. The front door to the bungalow was open by about six inches. She tapped Gareth on the shoulder and pointed. He spotted what she was pointing at and nodded to confirm that he'd seen it too now.

Keeping low, the AFOs scurried towards the front of the bungalow and took up their positions by the porch.

Gareth and Laura got to the iron gate and stopped.

'Gold Command to all units, the order is go!' Gareth said into his radio.

Two of the AFOs approached the front door and pushed it open with gloved hands, training their Heckler and Koch G36C carbine guns in front of them.

As they entered very slowly, the other AFOs went to the door.

Suddenly, there was a thunderous shout of 'Armed police! Get down!' followed by another shout of 'Armed police! Show yourselves!'

The AFOs had all disappeared inside.

Laura braced herself for possible gunfire as she and Gareth moved cautiously to follow them inside.

There were more shouts of 'Clear!' as the AFOs secured the bungalow.

Laura knew that it was too much to hope that Marsh would still be there and for him to be recaptured. He was too clever for that. She just hoped that Elis and Bronwen Barker were all right.

The lead AFO, Sergeant Glover, appeared, moved the visor up on his helmet and gave them a dark look.

'Mr and Mrs Barker?' Laura asked. She knew that whatever Glover had seen inside, it wasn't good news.

'Sorry.' Barker shook his head and gestured solemnly to the living room on the right. 'They're in there.'

Laura knew what that meant.

Taking a step inside the hallway, she composed herself before going into the living room.

Despite over twenty years on the force, nothing could have prepared her for the bloodbath that awaited her on the sofa. It was like the scene from some terrible horror film. A nightmarish vision.

Elis and Bronwen Barker, their clothes, the sofa and carpet soaked in blood. Bronwen's eyes were still open.

'Jesus Christ!' Laura gasped, looking away for a second.

Gareth shook his head and put his hand to his face. 'Sick bastard,' he whispered angrily.

Laura took a deep breath. She needed to get her head back into DI mode, however difficult that was. Moving carefully to the side of the sofa, she touched the back of Bronwen's hand. Her skin was still warm.

'He can't have got far,' Laura said, her shock turning to anger at the senseless waste of life.

'I wonder if they had a car,' Gareth thought out loud. 'We are going to need to secure this now and get SOCOs down here. I'll get the chopper up and let's get as many units as we can over this way. I want every road blocked off.'

Laura was already looking around the living room, searching for the slightest clue as to where Marsh might be heading and how he was travelling. She spotted the broken drawer of the bureau and looked inside.

She took blue forensic gloves out of her pocket and snapped them on, then pulled a pen from a jacket pocket. She used it to rummage a little in the drawer and then spotted something. A grey car manual and log book. She took them out and saw that they belonged to a 2012 Honda CRV 2 litre, registration DK12 SED.

'Found something?' Gareth asked, looking over.

She held up the CRV owner's manual. 'They've got a silver Honda CRV. DK12 SED.'

'Which wasn't on the drive,' Gareth said. 'Is there a garage?'

'Not that I could see,' Laura replied. 'Marsh could have taken it.'

Gareth nodded as he came over to grab the manual with a sense of urgency. 'Let's get this circulated to all units now.'

Laura followed Gareth to the door, still feeling the horror of what was on the other side of the room. She imagined the sickening terror of the Barkers' final seconds of life as Marsh attacked them. It made her shudder to her very core.

As Gareth went back out of the front door to circulate the make and registration number of their car to all units, Laura spotted a couple of the AFOs sitting on the garden wall. They both looked in their late twenties and had taken off their helmets – but they weren't talking. Instead they just stared into space, blinking, still in shock from the horrifying scene they had just witnessed.

Laura knew she should really wait until the SOCOs had arrived so they could put down aluminium stepping plates and give her a forensic suit. However, time was of the essence and any clues Marsh had left behind were vital if they were to catch him before he disappeared again.

Heading into the kitchen, Laura had a quick look around. Some milk had been left open on a work surface along with biscuit crumbs. She left the kitchen and walked down the hallway, where she spotted that the bathroom door was wide open. There were water droplets inside the sink itself and the hot tap was still warm. It had been used recently.

The carpet was a chocolate brown but something caught her eye. Crouching down, she looked closer and used her pen to examine what appeared to be strands of hair caught in the carpet fibres. She took an evidence bag from her pocket, opened it and dropped the hairs in. She held up the bag up, turned on the bathroom light and peered closely at what she had found.

The hairs were long and a mixture of dark brown and grey. There were also a couple of clumps of shorter brown and grey hair that was more coarse and curly.

'Wondered where you'd got to,' said a voice.

It was Gareth.

Laura held up the evidence bag for him to look at. 'Marsh has shaved his head and his beard. Which means that every copper on Anglesey has the wrong description and photo of him.'

'Jesus.' Gareth shook his head.

Laura said with a growing sense of urgency, 'I'll talk to Digital Forensics now. They can take Marsh's photograph and create a new image with a shaved head and no beard. We need to get that to the media and all units asap.'

Gareth looked at her. 'Great work.'

CHAPTER 35

Marsh banged the steering wheel in utter frustration. Since leaving Lledwigan, he seemed to have got stuck behind every tractor on the island, which had slowed his journey down to a snail's pace. He knew that he needed to get to Menai Bridge as quickly as possible before the police realised he had stolen the Barkers' Honda and the officers on the bridge were given the car's details. He also needed to stop for petrol, which was a major risk in itself. He was beginning to regret calling the police and giving away his location.

Maybe he should steal another car? The only issue would be that the driver would immediately report their car as having been taken, so he would be back to square one. Unless he took the car and then killed the driver so it remained unreported?

The tractor in front of him slowed and indicated, before pulling into a field.

Marsh immediately put his foot down.

Glancing down at the fuel gauge, he saw that it was empty with *0 miles*. As he looked up, he saw the yellow sign of a petrol station up ahead. Taking his foot off the accelerator, he let the car coast for a bit as the revs died.

There was a sudden clanking noise as the car juddered. The car had run out of petrol and the station was another five hundred yards away.

'For God's sake!' Marsh growled, pulling the Honda over to the side of the road as the car ground to a complete stop. He would have to march down to the petrol station and buy a can of petrol. He just hoped that by breaking down, he wouldn't attract the attention of any passing police.

He jumped out of the car, grabbed a handful of earth, went to the rear number plate and smeared it as best he could so that it was difficult to read. Rubbing his hands together to get rid of the dirt, he could feel the frustration and anger boiling over inside.

Setting off at a march, Marsh allowed himself to fantasise about what he would do once he was over the bridge and over the English border. He would start a new life. A total reinvention. A clean slate. And a completely new hunting ground. How wonderful it would be to start again from scratch. Others might have been daunted by being on the run. Marsh just thought of it as an exciting adventure.

As a lorry went thundering past, Marsh felt the vibrations but he was unfazed. If he was to escape, then it was going to take sharp focus.

After another few minutes, he arrived at the petrol station. To one side, there was a small, second-hand car dealership with around ten cars marked up with prices. Next to that, an auto repairs and body shop. From somewhere, music was playing as a mechanic tinkered noisily with an engine. The air was thick with the smells of oil and petrol.

Marsh stopped in his tracks for a moment. Looking at the cars for sale, he had an idea. There was a gleaming silver BMW 5 series priced at £14,999. He strode over to the office of the second-hand dealership and spotted a skinny man in his early twenties, with tufty blond hair and googly eyes.

'Can I help, sir?' the young man asked. He was wearing a cheap grey suit and scuffed brown brogues.

'I'm interested in the BMW 5 series you've got over there,' Marsh said, gesturing.

The young man jumped up from where he was sitting with an eager smile. 'It's just come in.'

Marsh nodded. 'Well, it's exactly the sort of car I'm looking for.'

'Great,' the young man said as he went to the door. 'Let me show you around it.'

'Any chance of us taking it for a spin around the block?' Marsh asked.

'Of course.' The young man nodded. 'Let me just sign it out and grab the keys. I just need a name.'

'John Cannan,' Marsh said. 'That's -an at the end.'

'Right you are,' the young man said, tapping at the keyboard.

Marsh was playing his own little dark joke. John Cannan was a convicted rapist and serial killer in the 1980s. He was also the man who was suspected of killing estate agent Suzy Lamplugh in London in 1986.

The young man went to a key box on the wall and took the BMW keys from a small hook.

As they wandered towards the car, the young man handed Marsh the keys. 'Here you go, Mr Cannan.'

'It's John,' Marsh told him.

'John,' the young man said and then pointed. 'If we go left out of here, we can take it down to the roundabout and back.'

'Sounds good to me,' Marsh said as he clicked the automatic locking system, opened the driver's door and got in. It smelled freshly valeted.

'You live around here, John?' the young man asked as he settled into the passenger seat and put on his seatbelt.

'Not far. A couple of miles,' Marsh replied as he started the engine.

'Are you looking for part exchange?' the young man enquired.

'No, no,' Marsh said. 'Just straight-up cash.'

'Oh right,' the young man said, trying not to sound too eager. Marsh assumed he'd be on a decent bonus for selling the car.

Marsh pulled out onto the road and pushed down the accelerator, enjoying the feel of the 3-litre engine.

'She goes a bit,' Marsh remarked, trying to sound as if he knew something about cars.

'That's the V6 engine,' the young man said with a smile.

Marsh looked over at him. His vacant, stupid face and slightly wonky teeth. Even the knot of his tie was badly tied. What a horrible, uneventful and worthless little life he must lead. He pitied and hated him at the same time.

Marsh slowed at the roundabout.

'Yeah, if we loop round and head back,' the young man explained.

Instead, Marsh accelerated and headed straight on towards Menai Bridge.

The young man glanced back with a confused expression on his face. 'Erm, I think we wanted to go back that way towards the garage.'

Marsh didn't respond but instead gazed ahead, enjoying the young man's growing anxiety.

Shifting awkwardly in the seat, the young man looked over at him and blinked nervously. 'Sorry, it's just that we need to head back that way towards the roundabout.'

Marsh looked over at him with a frown. 'Oh God, sorry. My hearing is appalling. I thought you said, "Go straight on."'

Pulling the car over onto a lay-by, Marsh glanced across. 'Tell you what, I've got a good feel for driving this car. Okay if you drive us back so I can sit in the passenger side?'

'Yeah, of course. No problem.' The young man smiled with relief as he opened the passenger door.

Marsh got out, went round the back and then stopped beside the boot. He looked at the young man, who was now beside him. 'Okay if I have a quick look in here now? Save us a bit of time when we get back, eh?'

The young man shrugged. 'Erm, yeah, why not.'

Marsh opened the boot and peered inside. It was empty. 'Quite deceptive, isn't it?'

'How do you mean?' the young man asked innocently.

This poor wretch doesn't even understand the word 'deceptive'.

'It's bigger than I thought it was going to be,' Marsh said by way of an explanation.

'Oh right,' the young man chortled as though this was hilarious.

Fishing into his pocket, Marsh glanced around to check the road. It was clear both ways.

Pulling a kitchen knife from his wax jacket pocket, Marsh brandished it, grabbed the young man's tie and hauled him suddenly towards the open boot.

'Get in,' Marsh growled.

'What?' the young man cried as he staggered off balance and tried to pull back.

Putting the knife against the flesh of his stomach, Marsh hissed, 'Get in the boot or I'll kill you.'

'I'm not doing that,' the young man babbled anxiously.

In a flash, Marsh drew the knife back and plunged it into the young man's side.

The young man gave a groan as the blood drained from his face. Marsh twisted him by his jacket and threw him into the boot as if completing a well-rehearsed judo throw.

Slamming the boot shut, Marsh got back in the car, placed the knife in the glove compartment and sped away.

Next stop, Menai Bridge.

CHAPTER 36

Laura spotted Gareth coming out of his office and headed his way. 'I've just spoken to the hospital,' she explained. 'The nurse explained that Andrea's CAT scan was clear so there's no damage to her brain. But they still need to run more tests as the MRI was inconclusive as to the extent of the damage to her spine.'

'Right.' Gareth nodded soberly.

'I asked if I could speak to her,' Laura said quietly, 'but she's asleep.'

'Thanks for letting me know,' Gareth said and then looked at her. 'She's a tough cookie, isn't she?'

'Yeah,' Laura agreed. 'She really is.'

'Boss?' Declan called from across the office with a sense of urgency.

'What have we got?' Gareth asked as he and Laura made their way across the CID office to where Declan was standing beside the large map on the wall.

Declan pointed to an area towards the south-east of the island. 'Uniform found the Barkers' Honda CRV parked just here, boss. On the A5 going into Gaerwen. Apparently there's a petrol station a few hundred yards down the road.'

Gareth, Laura and the remaining CID team looked to where Declan had pointed.

'Given that he started in Lledwigan, it looks like he's heading for Menai Bridge,' Laura observed.

'Looks that way,' Gareth agreed and looked across to Ben, who was sitting at his desk. 'Ben, how are Digital Forensics getting on with the new image of Marsh's appearance?'

'Just got it,' Ben said as he clicked a button and the monitor on the wall burst into life. 'Here you go.'

Marsh's face appeared on the screen. With a shaved head and no beard, his appearance was instantly chilling. The long hair and beard had softened his sharp features. However, what really stood out were his eyes. They were big and intense.

'Right, great,' Gareth exclaimed. 'Let's get that out to all units. And then every media outlet as fast as possible. I want that image on every television news bulletin, website and newspaper.'

Laura turned back to the map. 'If Marsh stopped close to the petrol station, that would suggest that he needed to get petrol or had run out, doesn't it?'

'Or the car broke down there,' suggested Declan.

'If he abandoned the Honda there, how is he travelling now?' Gareth said, thinking out loud.

'Maybe he hijacked another car?' Declan suggested.

Gareth frowned. 'Any reports from uniform in that area?'

'No,' Declan replied. 'But he could have taken the driver hostage. Marsh must be feeling desperate at the moment and we've already seen that he's capable of anything.'

'Someone ring that petrol station right now,' Gareth demanded.

'What else is around that area?' Laura said as she went over to her computer and tapped the location into Google Maps.

Searching the map that appeared on her screen, she immediately spotted a building marked 'D&L Autos and Second-Hand cars'.

'There's a second-hand car place at that exact location,' Laura stated, suddenly certain that Marsh had managed to take a car from there.

Ben glanced over. 'I've spoken to the petrol station. Nothing suspicious to report. They're sending over the CCTV for the last two hours on file for us to look at.'

'Okay,' Gareth said deep in thought.

Laura called the number for D&L Second-Hand Cars.

'Hi, this is DI Hart from Beaumaris CID,' she explained to the woman who had answered the phone. 'I'm wondering if you've sold any cars or if any cars have been taken out in the last hour and half?'

'If you can just bear with me, I'll check for you,' the woman said. A second later she came back onto the line. 'Actually, one of our salesmen took a fella out for a quick drive about half an hour ago and they're still not back.'

'How long would a test drive usually last?' Laura asked.

'No more than ten, fifteen minutes,' the woman explained.

'Right,' Laura said. 'Did anyone get the man's name?'

'It says the customer's name is John Cannan,' she said.

Laura instantly knew the name from the past. Was it just a coincidence or was it Marsh, playing a little game? She assumed it was the latter.

'If I send over an image of the man we're looking for,' Laura said, 'could you ask the people in the office to take a look?'

'Yeah, of course,' the woman said. 'My mobile number is 07822 343212. If you can text me that now, I can show it around.'

Laura took her phone, went to her emails and downloaded the new image of Marsh that Ben had sent out. She attached it to a text and sent it straight over to the woman at D&L Second-Hand Cars.

'Right, I've just sent that to you,' Laura said.

'Yep, I've got it,' the woman said and then paused for a second. 'This isn't that bloke who killed all them women, is it?'

'I'm afraid I can't discuss that with you,' Laura replied politely.

'I bloody hope not,' the woman said anxiously. 'I don't want Callum going out with him . . . Hold on a second.'

Laura met Gareth's eyes as he waited to see if she was onto something.

'Oh God, yeah, it is him. The bloke in the photo is the one that went out with Callum,' the woman said, sounding frightened.

'Thank you,' Laura replied. 'We just need the car make and registration.'

'Oh yeah, of course,' the woman said flustered. 'It's a BMW 5 Series, silver, registration YF15 DJD.'

'Thanks, that's really helpful,' Laura said, scribbling down the information.

'Please get Callum back safely,' the woman said, sounding upset. 'He's only a baby really.'

'We'll do everything we can,' Laura assured her.

Declan, who was on another phone, frowned and looked at Laura. 'Those detectives from Manchester are downstairs again, boss.'

'You're joking, aren't you?' Laura growled. She didn't have the time for their bullshit. They were in the middle of a bloody manhunt.

CHAPTER 37

The groans and banging from the BMW's boot had finally stopped as Marsh sped along the A5. The young car salesman had either fallen unconscious or bled out and died. It reminded him of the opening scene of one of his favourite films, *Goodfellas*. The three central characters, Henry, Jimmy and Tommy, are driving when they hear a banging from the boot. They pull over and open the boot to reveal the bloody body of gangster Billy Batts, who they assumed was dead. Tommy plunges a kitchen knife several times into his body before Jimmy fires a couple of bullets into him for good measure. In a voice-over, Henry admits, *As far back as I can remember, I always wanted to be a gangster.* Marsh loved the sentiment. Rather than being repelled by the brutality of the violence and murder, Henry was excited, even aroused by it. Marsh knew exactly how that felt.

Marsh didn't care if the young man in his boot was now dead. In fact, he felt that he was doing the young man a favour. Saving him from a long, tedious, uncomfortable life where he would believe the unremitting bombardment of imagery from social media and television.

Looking over at a sign, Marsh saw that he was getting

close to the village of Llanfairpwllgwyngyllgogerychwyrndro-bwllllantysiliogogogoch. With 58 characters split into 18 syllables, it was the longest place name in Europe and the second longest in the world. For a second Marsh remembered that it was superseded by a Māori township on the north island of New Zealand.

When Marsh had taught abroad, he used to delight ex-pats by his rendition of Llanfairpwllgwyngyllgogerychwyrndro-bwllllantysiliogogogoch. Searching back in his memory, he wondered what the signs had been of his dark disease or compulsion. His stalking of random women had continued sporadically. The excitement of causing feelings of fear or helplessness in others was so compelling. However, sometimes he would and could go months, even a year, without exhib-iting deviant behaviours. Marsh assumed there were men out there who had stalked and even attacked women, but had somehow managed to stop themselves, never returning to that kind of behaviour ever again. There were others, like David Fuller, who murdered and then never repeated the offence for decades. Fuller sexually assaulted and murdered two women in Tunbridge Wells in 1987. He wasn't arrested until 2021. Marsh wondered how men like that managed to control themselves and their urge for so many years. His own experience was that the euphoria of killings was so powerful, so overwhelming, that he wanted to experience it over and over again. He certainly wouldn't have been able to stop and live a seemingly normal life with the knowledge that such exhilaration and pleasure were out there. Once it had been untapped, there was no going back. He assumed it was like an addict discovering crack cocaine for the first time. This was the battle inside his head. A desire to get caught so that he would never be able to indulge in his compulsive killing again. And in direct conflict, an overwhelming need to kill to satisfy the craving that consumed him. His brain seemed to switch between these two thoughts every few minutes – it was exhausting.

A quick glance at the fuel gauge showed that he had ten miles left. He wondered how long it would be before the young salesman and the car were reported missing. And how long before DI Laura Hart put two and two together and realised that he had taken the car and disappeared? It would be better to stop now and get petrol than on the other side of the Menai Bridge, when the car might be flagged as having been stolen. He would need to switch vehicles somewhere in North Wales.

A petrol station loomed into sight about half a mile ahead. He had the Barkers' money in his pocket so he could get petrol, food and maybe some alcohol, just to take the edge off. He certainly didn't need to worry about being pulled over for drink driving or losing his licence today, he thought with an ironic little laugh.

Clicking the indicator, Marsh slowed the car and pulled into the brightly lit petrol station. It was empty. He reached over to the back seat, grabbed the knife from the glove compartment, wiped the blood onto the fabric seat covering and then put it in the inside pocket of his wax jacket. He got out of the car and started to fill the BMW with unleaded. He watched the young woman standing behind the till inside. She was looking out at the forecourt while chatting and laughing on her phone. For a moment, he thought she was laughing at him. She had made some joke about him to the person she was talking to on the phone and they were having a right old laugh at his expense. He felt the anger swell inside. He'd show her not to laugh. Her hair was black with red highlights. She looked cheap. She wouldn't be laughing so much if she knew that he could go in there and end her life in a split second. That would give her and her friend some-thing to laugh about.

223

Looking at the pump, he stopped when the digits read £20. If he was going to switch cars, it didn't make sense to fill up the tank. The smell of petrol was thick in the air as he put the nozzle back and made his way towards the doors to pay.

He caught his reflection in the glass as he approached and hardly recognised himself. With the flat cap, shaved face, glasses, wax jacket and boots, he'd done an excellent job of completely changing his appearance. He looked a million miles from the person that the police would be looking for and it gave him an extra spring in his step as he went inside.

The woman behind the till had stopped talking on the phone but didn't acknowledge him as he scanned the shelves for food and drink. He needed to be quick. Grabbing some crisps and a pack of beers, he headed over to the till. A television was on with the volume turned down. A weather man was standing in front of a map of Britain.

'Is that everything?' the young woman asked with a forced smile.

Marsh looked at her and fixed her with a steely glare. He didn't say anything. He could feel the weight of the knife inside the pocket of his jacket. The desire to kill her beginning to swell inside him. It was possessing him.

'Are you okay?' she asked him with a frown.

His breathing was shallow with excitement. Pulse starting to quicken. A sexual stirring of blood lust. He would get out the knife, threaten her, push her to the floor and rape her. Then he would strangle her, looking into her eyes as she died as he had done before.

This is it. I'm going to do it. It's going to be incredible.

Out of the corner of his eye, he saw a white Transit van pull onto the forecourt. Inside were three young men in hi-vis jackets.

Pulling himself together, he smiled at her. 'Sorry, miles away,' he said as he reached into the jacket, pulled out the cash and handed it to her.

'Thank you,' she said as she opened the till and handed him his change.

Something caught his eye on the television screen. An aerial shot of Anglesey. It was a news report.

And then a computer-generated image of a face filled the screen.

It was his face – with a shaved head and no beard.

A caption read – *Latest police image of Henry Marsh as manhunt continues.*

For fuck's sake! he thought, full of fury as he headed away towards the doors.

It was a huge blow to his plans to escape. He knew that the police officers on both the Britannia and Menai bridges would now be looking for a man in his forties with a shaved head and no beard. If they asked him to remove his cap and glasses, then they would know it was him. And he couldn't take this risk.

'Have a nice day,' the young woman called as he got to the door.

You have no idea how lucky you are, he thought darkly as he barged open the door aggressively.

He had clearly underestimated DI Laura Hart.

He started to hatch a new plan to get off the island and suddenly he knew exactly what he needed to do.

CHAPTER 38

'We're a little bit busy at the moment,' Laura said, trying not to sound annoyed.

She had just arrived in the conference room on the ground floor of Beaumaris nick. Watkins and Carmichael were sitting on the other side of the table with a couple of folders in front of them.

'And you told me to have my federation rep present the next time you came to speak to me about Louise McDonald,' Laura added. She could feel the frustration bubbling away inside.

Watkins sat forward with an expressionless face. 'We're not here to talk to you about Louise McDonald, which is why we didn't contact you first.' As Watkins's words sank in, Laura started to feel uneasy.

She shrugged. 'Then what are you doing here?'

'Can you tell us what your relationship was to Superintendent Ian Butterfield?' Carmichael said calmly.

What the . . .?

Laura frowned and took a few seconds to compose herself. 'Ian Butterfield? Why are you asking me about him?'

She could feel her pulse starting to quicken. She knew that

Butterfield had been found dead in Lancashire yesterday. She'd seen it on the news.

Keep nice and calm, Laura.

Watkins peered over her glasses at her. 'Could you just answer the question, please?'

'I don't have any kind of relationship with Ian Butterfield. And I don't understand why you want to ask me about a police officer I worked with four or five years ago. I watch the news. I know he was found dead after a walking accident.' Laura started to get up from her seat. 'I've really got to get back to CID unless there's anything else.'

Carmichael fixed her with a dark look. 'Superintendent Ian Butterfield was murdered.'

Laura couldn't help but sit back down. 'Okay . . . Right. Well, I'm sorry to hear that.' She then looked over at them and narrowed her eyes. 'I still don't understand what this has to do with me.'

Laura's mind was now racing.

'Could you tell us the last time you saw Ian Butterfield?' Watkins asked in an innocuous tone.

Did they know about Butterfield's visit to her home last September? Were they fishing to see if she would lie about it? How was she meant to bloody answer the question?

Laura looked at them and then frowned. 'I think it was at Sam's funeral.'

'And you haven't seen him since then?'

'No,' Laura replied.

For a moment, Carmichael didn't reply but instead looked down at a document in front of him.

'And Ian Butterfield has never visited your home here on Anglesey?' Carmichael asked.

Laura knew that she had lied and just hoped that Watkins and Carmichael didn't then confront her with the truth about Butterfield's visit. Was Carmichael's subtle glance down at the document an attempt to trick her into thinking that they had intel when they didn't? She had used this technique in questioning many times.

Laura was going to call their bluff. 'No. Never. And I don't understand where you're going with all this.'

'Did you ever suspect that Ian Butterfield was involved with your husband's death?' Watkins asked.

'What?' Laura said innocently. 'Why would I have any reason to think that he was involved in Sam's death? He's a superintendent in the Greater Manchester Police.'

Watkins fixed her with a stare. 'You didn't answer my question, Laura.'

Laura sighed and replied, 'No, I didn't have any reason to believe that Ian Butterfield was involved in Sam's death.' Laura then looked at them both. 'But I'm guessing from your questions that you might have reason to believe that he was?'

Carmichael scratched his face as he sat back in his seat and then glanced over at Watkins. 'I'm afraid we can't discuss the details of our investigation with you.'

Watkins took a document from in front of her and peered at it for a few seconds. 'Can you tell us where you were between three and six on Saturday morning?' she asked without looking up.

'Are you kidding me?' Laura asked. Did they really think she was a suspect? She decided that the best form of defence now was attack. She was completely innocent and the best way to prove that was by being utterly indignant at their questioning.

'No,' Watkins replied calmly.

Laura let out a sigh of annoyance. 'Four years ago, I watched a building explode, knowing that my husband was inside and had died. He was killed in the line of duty. I have given over twenty years to the police force. So, given all that, I resent the implication that I've had anything to do with the murders of Louise McDonald or Ian Butterfield. This is utter bullshit, and you know it.'

Carmichael didn't react to what she'd said. 'If you can answer the question, please, Laura.'

'I was in bed between three and five thirty. At five thirty, I went down to Beaumaris beach, where I went for a swim.'

'Can anyone verify that?' Watkins asked.

'No. Are you trying to tell me that you think that I jumped in my car and travelled over to Lancashire where I murdered Ian Butterfield and then I drove back here?' Laura hissed, shaking her head in bewilderment. 'Check the ANPRs and see if my car is on them. Better still, check the GPR tracker on my car and you can see where my car has been.'

Carmichael gave her a knowing look. 'You know as well as I do that a GPR tracker on a car can be disabled quite easily.'

'Okay, I've had enough of this.' Laura gave a long sigh. They were getting nowhere. She got up from her chair. 'I tell you what. I'm going to make this really easy for you. If you want to talk to me again about Louise McDonald or Ian Butterfield, I want prior notice. I also want you to interview me under caution with a federation rep and my solicitor present.' Laura headed towards the door. 'Until then, I have a really important investigation to work on.'

CHAPTER 39

It was late afternoon when Andrea woke. Her mouth was dry from the painkillers she'd been prescribed. She'd been dreaming about a wedding in a great stately home. The guests, the decorations, even the band seemed as though they had come from a lavish American film. She had been flirting with someone at the dinner and during the speeches. A cute man with bushy eyebrows and a Scottish accent. After that, she'd danced the night away.

As she came back to consciousness, the bleak realisation came flooding back to her that she might never dance again. However much she willed her legs and feet to twitch even a millimetre, there was nothing. The results of the MRI scan hadn't come back but she feared the worst. It had been an uncomfortable and claustrophobic experience as she slid slowly into the X-ray tunnel. The operator had played *Simon & Garfunkel's Greatest Hits*. Normally she might have liked that, but she had found the music intensely annoying.

Pushing herself up with her arms, she managed to jiggle so that she was sitting more upright. She kept having flashes of her leaving hospital in a wheelchair. And then having to have her home completely adapted so that it was wheelchair friendly. Her breathing started to quicken and her eyes filled with tears. It was so hard to come to terms with the fact that this was now a possibility.

The door opened and Dr Youens, the consultant who had been to see her on several occasions since her arrival, came breezing in.

'Andrea,' he said while looking down at the notes that he was holding. 'How are you feeling?'

'Well, I'm not feeling anything in my legs, if that's what you mean?' she replied, half-joking.

'Yes,' he said with a frown. 'I mean in yourself.'

She shrugged. 'I'm just very worried.'

'Completely understandable,' he said, looking over at her. 'I've got the results of your MRI scan. The good news is that there is no long-lasting damage to your spinal cord.'

'Okay', she said cautiously and then asked, 'And the bad news?'

'You have a condition called transverse myelitis. Essentially the myelin sheath, which is the insulating layer around nerves and your spinal cord, has become damaged by the inflammation caused by the accident. The inflammation interrupts the signals that travel down the spinal cord, and it's that which is causing your paralysis,' he explained.

'Is that permanent?' she asked, terrified of what he might say next.

'I don't want to make you any promises,' he said. 'The majority of patients that I've treated with this have made a full or partial recovery.'

'Okay.' Andrea took a moment to process what he had told her. It sounded a lot better than what she'd had in her head for most of the day. However, she wanted something more concrete than 'the majority'. 'What percentage recover?'

'At a guess, 90 per cent,' he replied.

She nodded and then asked, 'So, I have a one in ten chance of total paralysis?'

'It's not quite as simple as that,' he said, nodding slowly. 'But, yes, roughly speaking.'

'Well, I would have taken those odds about an hour ago, so I need to cling onto that,' she admitted. It was hard to get her hopes up in case she was one of the unlucky 10 per cent.

'As the inflammation dies down around your spinal cord, you may find that you start to get an intense tingling in the muscles in your legs. Even a muscle spasm or two. That is quite normal. If that happens, you just need to let us know immediately,' he stated.

'How long am I going to be in here?' she enquired.

Youens frowned. 'Very hard to say. In some cases, it can take weeks for the inflammation to die down. In other cases, it reduces quickly and the movement is restored to the legs almost as if by magic. I've known it happen over a couple of hours.'

'So I could be dancing out of here in a few days?' Andrea joked, not quite managing to keep the hope out of her voice.

Youens gave her a wry smile. 'It's possible, but you do need to manage your expectations.'

'It's okay, I was joking.' She gave a shaky laugh.

'I might try to get you down to physiotherapy today,' he said. 'I'll see you on my rounds tomorrow morning.'

'Thank you,' Andrea said as Youens breezed out again.

For the next ten minutes or so, Andrea tried to process what Dr Youens had told her. Despite the high chance of recovery, it was hard not to worry about the slim chance of permanent paralysis.

Looking down at her phone, she saw that she had a text message from her old friend Melissa wishing her well and promising that she would visit in the next few days. Melissa lived down in Gloucester so it was a long journey.

For a few seconds, a terrible feeling of loneliness swept over her. Most people had a family or partner to visit them. She fought the temptation to feel sorry for herself but it was difficult.

The door opened and a hospital porter, who was wearing a blue Covid mask, came in pushing a wheelchair. Andrea had noticed that some of the nurses and hospital staff wore masks while others didn't. She guessed now that it wasn't mandatory but a matter of personal choice.

'That was quick,' she said light-heartedly.

'Sorry?' the porter mumbled through his mask as he brought the wheelchair over to the side of the bed.

'You taking me down to physiotherapy?' she asked.

'That's right,' the porter replied as he leaned over, put his arms under her and helped manoeuvre her into the wheelchair. The metal and fabric were cold on her arms and back in contrast to the warmth of the bed.

'Can you pass me that blanket please?' she asked, pointing to the light blue blanket that was draped over the back of a chair.

'Of course, here you go,' the porter said in a friendly tone as he tucked the blanket around her.

Opening the door, the porter wheeled her along the corridors and down towards the lifts. The air was thick with the smell of detergents and hospital food.

Spotting one of the wards to her right, Andrea was grateful that she had been assigned a single room to herself. Then it dawned on her that she was in a single room due to the severity of her injuries.

As they reached the lifts, the porter pressed the call button, which immediately turned orange.

Andrea's phone buzzed with a text. It was from Laura, asking if she was okay and saying that she and Gareth would be visiting later. The fact that they were thinking about her cheered her up.

The metallic doors to the lift opened with a slight clank.

The porter wheeled her slowly into the lift and turned her around.

The doors closed and then she felt the lift starting to descend to the floor below. As a kid, lifts used to scare her. It wasn't claustrophobia or the feeling of being trapped. It was just the thought and sensation of going up and down the lift shaft that gave her butterflies. It was strange to imagine that there was nothing above or below them except a lift shaft and some pulleys.

Spotting the physiotherapy department on the hospital floor map that was secured to the inside of the lift, Andrea wondered what it would entail. And then a wave of surreal fear at the thought of never being able to walk again. It was something that happened to other people.

The porter pulled his mask down from his face. She didn't blame him. She remembered how hot and uncomfortable they were to wear.

'Hello, Andrea,' the porter said, smiling down at her.

She searched his uncovered face, wondering where he recognised her from. Maybe from her work as a police officer?

There was something familiar about his eyes, nose and mouth.

'Sorry, I . . .' she said, still searching her memory for his name and how she knew him.

Then her stomach pitched and she felt sick.

The hair and beard were gone.

But she was looking at Henry Marsh.

He had a manic, twisted grin across his face.

As she went to scream, he plunged a needle into her left arm.

Everything went black.

CHAPTER 40

Gareth and Laura were standing by the roadside in the small village of Rhoscefnhir which was seven miles due east of Beaumaris. Fifteen minutes earlier, a uniform patrol had found the BMW 5 series that Marsh had taken for a test drive with Callum Peters, a twenty-one-year-old car salesman from D&L Second-Hand Cars. Neither of them had been seen since.

Given the serious nature of Marsh's crimes, the uniform patrol had waited for CID to arrive to search the vehicle. They didn't want to run the risk of destroying any of the forensic evidence that might be inside the car itself. There was no sign of Callum Peters anywhere.

'Right, let's have a look, shall we?' Gareth said as they approached the car.

Laura frowned. 'Something doesn't add up.'

'What's that?'

'Marsh was heading down the A5 towards Menai Bridge,' Laura said. 'In fact, the garage where he picked up this car is only five or six miles from the bridge, so why didn't he attempt to cross it? We've had no reports of anyone acting suspiciously.'

'What if he knew that we'd found evidence that he'd radically changed his appearance?' Gareth suggested. 'And that the officers on the bridge were aware that he'd shaved his head and beard.'

Laura shrugged dubiously. 'How would he know that?'

Gareth opened the driver's door of the BMW and looked inside. 'I don't know. But it's been all over the news.'

'Maybe,' Laura said with a shrug as she opened the passenger door. There was nothing obvious on the passenger side either.

They walked around to the boot.

Gareth clicked the button just above the numberplate and lifted the boot lid.

Expecting it to be empty, Laura flinched when she saw what was inside.

A young man's body curled up and covered in a huge amount of blood. The carpet around him was also saturated.

It was Callum Peters.

She reached inside and felt his neck for a pulse.

Nothing. He was dead.

'Oh Jesus,' she muttered under her breath.

She looked at Gareth and shook her head.

'For fuck's sake!' he growled.

Marsh's murder spree was completely out of control. She wished that they could find and shoot him before he killed anyone else.

Laura's phone buzzed and she answered it. 'DI Hart?'

'Laura?' the voice said.

The wind had picked up and she couldn't work out who it was calling. The phone hadn't recognised the number.

'Speaking,' she replied.

'You're outside,' the voice said. 'My guess is that you've found the BMW and that poor boy in the boot.'

It was Henry Marsh.

She immediately signalled to Gareth that it was Marsh on the phone.

'I'm finding it difficult to understand why you killed Callum,' Laura said.

'Callum? Was that his name?' Marsh said with no feeling. 'He got a little bit agitated at the prospect of me stealing his car. So, I had to put him in the boot.'

'Let's not dress this up,' Laura snapped. 'You murdered him in cold blood.' She immediately regretted showing Marsh that she was angry.

Marsh tutted down the phone. 'Oh dear, Laura. This all getting to you, is it?'

'Is that what you want?' she asked. 'To get to me?'

'I'm not remotely interested whether or not my actions impact on you,' Marsh said with amusement.

'Really?' Laura asked sceptically. 'Then why do you keep calling me?'

There were a few seconds of silence. It might have been a tiny victory, but she had called Marsh out and stopped him in his tracks for a second.

'Actually, you're right,' Marsh admitted. 'You do intrigue me, Laura. You have a certain quality.'

The idea of a serial killer taking an undue interest in her sent a shudder down her spine.

'I would have thought you'd be over the bridge and long gone by now,' she said, trying to probe why Marsh was still on the island. 'Something holding you up?'

'Ha, ha,' Marsh snorted. 'Very funny. I'm not sure how you know that I've changed my appearance, but I *am* impressed, Laura.'

'So, what's the plan now?' Laura asked. 'You're running out of options.'

'Am I?'

'My suggestion is that you hand yourself in,' Laura said, although she wasn't holding out much hope.

'No, I don't think I want to do that, Laura.'

'Come on, Henry,' Laura said. 'There is no way you're getting off this island. You've got nowhere to go. It's over.'

He laughed. 'I think you'd be surprised at how resourceful I can be.'

She had no idea what he was talking about, but felt a stirring of disquiet at his apparent confidence.

'Please, Henry. Let's just put a stop to all this.'

'Unfortunately, appealing to a psychopath on any humane or empathic level is totally pointless. But you know that,' he said mockingly. 'You know what? I think I'm going to have another go at driving over Britannia Bridge.'

'Okay,' Laura said, confused. 'And how do you think you're going to manage that?'

'Well, I have some very good news for you, Laura,' Marsh chuckled. 'I'm going to have some very precious cargo on board as I cross the bridge. So, you're going to have to let me through.'

'Precious cargo?' Laura asked, her stomach tightening. Her immediate assumption was that he was referring to a person.

'Yes. Oh, and by the way, if you're thinking of visiting poor Detective Constable Andrea Jones tonight, I wouldn't bother,' Marsh said. 'I've managed to get her discharged from hospital into my care. I'm sure she'll be just fine with me.'

Laura felt sick. 'What are you talking about?'

'I do have a little confession,' Marsh said. 'They didn't discharge her. I mean, the poor woman can't walk, can she? I just took her and now I'm going to use her for insurance purposes . . . Lovely little tattoo of a butterfly on her hip, by the way. So, I expect a safe and trouble-free passage across Britannia Bridge in about an hour. I don't want to see any police officers. And if you attempt to stop or follow my vehicle, your friend here won't be returning to duty ever again.'

The line went dead.

CHAPTER 41

The Conference Room in Beaumaris was busy with various members of CID, senior uniformed officers as well as the head of the Armed Response Unit. It had been half an hour since Marsh had told Laura that he had taken Andrea. The whole station was on high alert. Now that a police officer had been kidnapped, the operation to rescue her and capture Marsh was taking a more direct and aggressive approach.

Gareth walked purposefully to the front of the room. 'Okay everyone,' he said loudly. The room quietened down. Behind him on the wall there was a large monitor, which had been linked to Ben's laptop. 'As you know, DI Hart received a phone call from Henry Marsh thirty minutes ago informing her that he had kidnapped DC Andrea Jones from Llangefni General Hospital. I've spoken to the Ward Sister and the Hospital Security Team, who have confirmed that Andrea was taken from the hospital an hour ago.'

Gareth pointed to the screen, where CCTV footage from the hospital security cameras showed Marsh wheeling Andrea into the lift. 'Marsh was posing as a hospital porter and was able to leave the hospital with Andrea in this wheelchair without being challenged.' The CCTV then showed Marsh

239

wheeling Andrea across the car park. 'Marsh took Andrea to this dark blue Renault Scenic – he must have swapped cars again. We've looked at the footage and we believe that Marsh administered some kind of sedative to Andrea as it appears that she is unconscious when he carries and puts her into the passenger seat of the car.'

'Gareth, I assume you have some idea of where they are now, or we wouldn't be sitting here?' asked Warlow who was sitting close to the front.

'Yes.' Gareth nodded. 'This Renault is virtually new and is fitted with a GPS tracking device. Using the registration, we have managed to locate that device.'

Ben tapped at his laptop and a virtual map of Anglesey appeared up on monitor. A small red dot was flashing beside the village of Lledwigan.

'As you can see,' Gareth stated, pointing to the flashing dot, 'the vehicle is parked here just outside Lledwigan. We have a unit that has made visual contact with the target vehicle and they have confirmed that Marsh and Andrea are inside.' Gareth took a sip of water and then looked out at the room again. 'While the vehicle is stationary and Andrea is in there, we cannot make a move to capture Marsh. It's far too dangerous. The only way to make any attempt to rescue Andrea is while Marsh is occupied driving the car.'

Warlow raised his eyebrows. 'You want to rescue Andrea from a moving vehicle?'

Gareth gave Warlow a forced smile, wishing that he would stop interrupting.

'Not exactly, sir.' Gareth pointed to the map. 'Britannia Bridge is nine miles from Lledwigan along the North Wales Expressway. Our assumption is that Marsh is waiting for the light to fade so that he can use the cover of darkness as he travels through North Wales into England. He's told us that

240

he's going to use Britannia Bridge. He will drive down this way, with Andrea in the car, and make his way across the bridge. With a police officer as hostage, Marsh believes that he will not be prevented from doing that.'

Warlow frowned. 'And we're going to just let him do that?'

'No, sir,' Gareth said as he looked over to Inspector Jim Neville, the head of the Armed Response Unit. 'Jim?'

Neville came over and Ben put up a photograph of a road. 'This is the approach road to Britannia Bridge. As you can see, the ground to the right of the road is banked up high with excellent cover. We have now closed off this straight section of the expressway. As we speak, I have four trained marksmen from SCO19 finding the optimum place on this hillside to take a shot at the target vehicle.'

'And we have the authority to use lethal force?' Warlow asked.

'Yes, sir,' Neville said. 'I've spoken to the Chief Constable. Given the severity of Marsh's crimes and the fact that an officer's life is in serious danger, the use of lethal force is permitted.'

Gareth pointed to the photograph. 'As soon as we know Marsh is travelling, a traffic unit will be deployed with a stinger at this point in the road. In the darkness, Marsh will be unable to see it. The tyres will burst and the target vehicle will slow rapidly.' Gareth looked back at Neville.

Neville came back over to the monitor. 'Marsh will be completely distracted. One of our snipers will be able to get away a clean headshot from this area up here. The shot will be virtually head-on. Given the trajectory, if the bullet does exit Marsh, it will continue through the back of the car and will pose no threat to DC Jones.'

Warlow looked concerned. 'Obviously I'm concerned that we are firing at a moving vehicle, but I can't see an alternative. And Marsh cannot escape with DC Jones.'

'No, sir.' Gareth looked at his watch. 'Okay, it'll be dark in an hour's time. Beaumaris CID and I will be acting as Gold Command on this operation. I will see those of you who are involved down at Britannia Bridge as soon as possible.' Gareth looked out at the room. 'Let's get DC Jones back safely.'

CHAPTER 42

Marsh sat tapping his gloved fingers on the steering wheel. He was waiting for the light of day to finally disappear. Andrea was still unconscious from the injection of the sedative propenal, which was usually used as an anaesthetic. Her breathing was shallow, but not dangerously so. Not that that was any kind of issue. If she died, she died. No one would know as long as her body was sitting upright in the passenger seat.

He watched her for a while. The delicate flickering of her eyes under their lids as if she was dreaming. And then the tiniest of muscle spasms in her face and a low, almost imperceptible murmur. Maybe it was starting to wear off.

He looked into the rear-view mirror and into the eyes of the person looking back at him. Into his eyes. He tried to think about how he felt as he gazed at himself. Pride, love or loathing? He couldn't fathom it. He knew he felt something, but he just didn't have the tools to identify it. It felt like the lag you got when 'blind' tasting food or drink. There are a few seconds of delay as the neurons from the taste buds feed the information back to the brain before it uses memory to recall and identify what is being tasted.

Except that this delay was everlasting. Never-ending. An emotion would arise somewhere in his body but nothing in his being could recall or identify it.

Buzzing down the window, Marsh looked up at the darkening sky. The wind was biting cold. He didn't care. He enjoyed it against his face, so icy that it felt like it was cutting into his skin. The nearby trees and hedgerows rattled with a noise that was virtually orchestral. A low hum that fought against the higher octaves of whistling and the percussive jangle and clatter of branches and leaves. An eerie symphony.

As the last fragments of light began to evaporate, Marsh took it as a sign that it was time to head for Britannia Bridge. He started the engine, released the handbrake and pulled away. He wondered what kind of life he would lead once he was in England. He'd always fancied Oxford. Maybe he would settle there? And just think of that city. The architecture, the culture and the plethora of young women. It would be like shooting fish in a barrel. His spirits soared at the very thought of it. Then a nagging voice that challenged this. He'd promised himself that Zoey would be the very last. No more. Never again. What happened to that decision? He knew that the elation, excitement and pacification of his murderous urge would be temporary. But that was the problem. He was addicted to his own pattern of thinking which was invariably dualistic. To take two steps back and gain perspective was counterintuitive.

Of course, addiction was just the modern name for what the Bible had called 'sin'. The medieval term described these patterns of thought as 'passions' or 'attachments'. Even two thousand years ago, it was recognised that this delusional thinking needed serious measures to be cured. The New Testament called them 'exorcisms' – they knew they were dealing with non-rational 'demons' that sometimes bordered on the evil. Such madness was seen to be the work of the devil.

Marsh looked up and saw a sign that Britannia Bridge was now only three miles away. He noticed that there was no traffic coming the other way, so he assumed they had closed the road and bridge in preparation for his arrival.

All this for me. How marvellous, he thought with a growing sense of self-satisfaction. He got such a kick out of creating havoc.

To his right, the trees that bordered the empty lanes of the expressway rocked and swayed in the wind. Their leafless branches were skeletal. Thin twigs and stems like the gnarled knots of diseased, fused bone.

Now impatient, Marsh pushed his foot down on the accelerator and took the car up to 70 mph. He just wanted to be over the bridge and away to some kind of freedom. While he had DC Andrea Jones as his passenger, no one was going to stop him.

A sign for a FFERN FOEL – FARM PARK flew past in a blur.

Up ahead, he spotted a concrete bridge over the road. It had white, metallic railings across its top.

Out of the corner of his eye, Marsh spotted something move on the bridge. A dark outline.

What the hell was that? he thought as he slowed the car. Something about it unnerved him.

Another figure moved and then disappeared behind the railings.

Then the tiniest glint of red light from somewhere.

In an instant, Marsh knew what it was.

The laser sight from a gun.

The bastards are going to shoot me!

Slamming on the brakes, he pulled up the handbrake and spun the steering wheel. The car went into a terrifying sideways skid.

Marsh braced himself in case they hit something.

Frantically turning the wheel the other way, Marsh managed to get control of the car as it slowed to a stop, facing back the way he'd just come.

He was now a sitting duck.

Stamping his foot down on the accelerator, he sped back down the expressway with a growing sense of anger.

How dare they!

His brain clicked into action as he planned his next move.

He needed to ditch the car.

And he either needed to find another way of getting off the island, or raise the stakes even further so they had no choice but to let him leave.

His face brightened. He knew just the thing.

CHAPTER 43

Laura was hiding in trees high above the North Wales Expressway. She and the various members of Beaumaris CID were 500 yards south of the bridge from where the snipers were going to shoot Marsh once the stinger had been deployed.

Anxiety churned within her. Thirty seconds ago there had a been a message to say that Marsh's car had been spotted and was virtually at the bridge.

Gareth gave her a concerned look as if to say, *Where the hell are they?*

'Alpha three-seven to Gold Command, over,' said a voice on Gareth's Tetra radio.

Gareth clicked his radio. 'Alpha three-seven, this is Gold Command. Received, go ahead, over.'

'Target vehicle was not intercepted at location,' the voice said. 'Target vehicle has now left location, heading north on the North Wales Expressway. We have lost visual contact with target vehicle, over.'

'Shit!' Declan growled under his breath.

'How the hell has that happened?' Laura groaned in utter frustration. Knowing that Andrea was still in the car with Marsh, she felt sick with worry.

'Received, Alpha three-seven,' Gareth said in a dejected tone. 'Stand by.'

Laura looked at him. 'Any idea what's going on?'

Gareth shook his head and pointed to his mobile phone. 'I'm expecting a call any second now from DI Neville, but this is not good.'

As if on cue, Gareth's phone rang and he answered it on speaker so that the rest of the team could hear.

'Jim? What happened?'

'I don't know,' Neville admitted. 'Something spooked Marsh as he drove towards the bridge. He must have seen something he didn't like because he put the car into a skid, turned around and sped in the other direction.'

'Jesus Christ,' Gareth sighed.

'I'm sorry, Gareth,' Neville said. 'I'll find out what happened.'

'Okay, thanks,' Gareth said, then hung up and regarded the CID team. 'What the hell are we going to do now?'

The team began to reassemble, looking dejected.

As they turned to head back to where they had parked, Laura's phone buzzed.

'DI Hart?' she said as she continued walking along the footpath downhill.

The wind swirled noisily.

'Laura?' said a familiar voice.

It sounded like Pete, but it was hard to hear because of the strong wind.

'Speaking.'

'It's Henry,' he said as though he was an old friend.

'Henry,' Laura said, trying to work out the best approach. Marsh seemed to delight in hearing her rattled or upset. She needed to keep it light despite her utter loathing for him and her anxiety for Andrea's safety. She looked at Gareth to indicate that Marsh was on the phone again. 'Everything okay?'

'Not really,' he said in a calm placid voice. 'I'm a bit disappointed that you were going to shoot me from that bridge. But I guess that's part of the game, now, isn't it?'

His use of the word 'game' unsettled her.

'I'd like to speak to Andrea,' Laura said sternly.

'I'm afraid she's still out for the count,' Marsh explained. 'You've backed me into a bit of a corner, haven't you?'

'Have I?' Laura asked.

'Well, you've shown your hand,' Marsh said. 'It seems that despite having young Detective Constable Andrea Jones sitting here next to me, you're willing to shoot me in cold blood.'

'What did you expect, Henry?' Laura asked, trying to sound calm and chatty even though the thought of Andrea sitting within two feet of him made her sick with worry. 'You're a highly educated man. Did you think we were going to let the man who murdered eight innocent people on this island just drive away into the distance?'

'Now that you've put it like that, I don't suppose you were.' Marsh laughed. 'Fair point, Laura. Touché. It seems to me that having Andrea here just wasn't enough of an insurance policy. I guess she's served her purpose now.'

There were a few moments of sickening silence as Laura contemplated what Marsh meant by that.

'Let's not do anything stupid, Henry. Please,' Laura said quietly, unable to disguise her panic.

'Oh dear,' Henry said. 'You sound very scared all of a sudden, Laura.'

She knew he was getting a kick out of toying with her. From all her training as a hostage negotiator, she knew that the best policy in a situation was to allow the criminal to feel in charge and in control.

'I am scared, Henry,' she admitted. 'Andrea's my friend.'

'Aww, that's very touching,' Henry said, mocking her. 'I get the feeling that you're pandering to me in an attempt to work

249

some kind of reverse psychology on me, Laura. Is that what you're doing?' He then laughed. 'Because I warn you, I have a master's degree in psychology.'

Laura thought furiously about how she could pull the conversation around, but challenging him was never going to work.

'What's the plan now, Henry?' she asked, trying to move the conversation in a different direction.

'Well, let's see. I guess the first thing I have to do is get rid of my companion here,' Marsh said. 'Don't worry, Laura, she won't feel a thing. I promise. It will be . . . humane. And I'll give you a call to let you know where she is.'

'Wait . . .' Laura exclaimed.

Marsh ended the phone call.

CHAPTER 44

Andrea slowly became aware of the sounds around her. She had no idea where she was but her head felt like it was in a vice. As she drifted in and out of consciousness, she started to get flashbacks. The car accident with Henry Marsh. She had been in hospital, hadn't she? Then the sickening thought that she had been told she might never walk again. Putting that together, she tried to will herself back into full consciousness.

And then she was back again, standing on Beaumaris beach at the march and vigil. She could hear the harsh squawk of gulls. She couldn't work out if she was dreaming or not. Henry Marsh was standing across the road waving at her. And then, in her mind's eye, she got the flash of Marsh's face, shaved head and clean-shaven.

Oh my God, he took me from the hospital.

She could feel that she was sitting in some kind of seat. It was padded. Her hands were tied behind her back and her shoulders ached from where they were being held in an unnatural position.

Come on, Andrea, wake up.

Straining the muscles in her face, she managed to pull up her right eyelid.

She felt so drained, so tired and so unwell. There was a stiffness to her back and a dryness to her mouth and throat, as if she'd just swallowed sand. As she attempted to move her toes and then her legs, she realised that they were still paralysed.

Her vision gradually returned as everything slowly morphed from a blurry grey to full, sharp colour. She was sitting in the passenger seat of a car that she didn't recognise. It was cold and smelled of stale cigarettes.

Her head began to clear sluggishly as she glanced around the car. It was a large 4x4 and the word SAAB was embossed in the middle of the steering wheel. It seemed that Marsh had secured himself yet another car, although she had no idea how.

They had parked up somewhere and the driver's seat was empty. The road outside was lined by trees and hedges, with a couple of detached houses over to the left.

Where the hell are we?

She glanced over to her right. They were parked opposite a large house with a gable wall and a wide entrance lane running down its side.

And then she realised that she recognised it.

She knew exactly where they were.

They were parked outside Laura's house on the outskirts of Beaumaris.

What the hell are we doing here?

She shifted in the seat and leaned forward so that she could get a better look at the house.

As her eyes moved up the pathway to the front door, she saw a figure standing on the doorstep.

Henry Marsh.

He was now dressed in a smart suit and tie.

Andrea's stomach tightened and her pulse quickened.

And then to her horror, the front door opened and Rosie appeared.

'No, no, no,' Andrea croaked out loud as she watched Marsh talk to Rosie, who nodded.

Marsh then pointed over to the car and waved at her. Rosie peered over and gave a little wave too.

Oh God, that bastard has told Rosie that I'm waiting in the car.

Shaking her head, Andrea tried to catch Rosie's attention, praying that she would see her and realise that something was wrong. It was no use. The car was too far away for Rosie to see Andrea's panicked expression.

While Marsh waited on the doorstep, Rosie went inside, leaving the front door wide open.

Marsh looked over and must have seen Andrea and realised that she was now conscious. He gave another little wave and then a thumbs-up.

Bastard!

Rosie reappeared. She was now wearing a coat and scarf. She closed the door and followed Marsh down the garden path.

'No, Rosie!' Andrea rasped but her throat was too dry to make any real sound.

Andrea shook her head again vigorously, hoping that Rosie would spot her and refuse to follow Marsh.

As they walked across the road, Marsh was in deep conversation with Rosie, who just listened and nodded.

They arrived at the car. Rosie cocked her head to look inside and gave her a little wave.

Andrea mouthed *No*, shaking her head again with a panicked expression.

Suddenly, Rosie reacted, realising that something was very wrong.

But it was too late.

Marsh pulled out a knife, grabbed Rosie by the arm and dragged her towards the back of the car.

Rosie screamed and Marsh immediately held the knife to her throat as he opened the back door.

'Scream again and I'll slit your throat,' Marsh growled and he pushed Rosie into the back of the car.

'I'm so, so sorry, Rosie,' Andrea gasped, looking around at her.

Before Rosie could respond, Marsh had clamped a strip of gaffer tape across her mouth and then began to tie her hands behind her back.

He then glanced over at Andrea. 'I wondered when you'd wake up, sleepy head.'

'Fuck off,' Andrea snarled.

Marsh said nothing, finished tying Rosie's hands and then slammed the rear door of the car.

As Andrea turned around, the passenger door opened abruptly. Marsh loomed over her and secured a piece of gaffer tape across her mouth.

'There you go, potty mouth,' he said, then he closed the door, headed around the car, got in and settled himself in the driver's seat. 'Well, ladies, have I got an adventure planned for you. Very exciting. Obviously I can't tell you where we're going as it's a surprise.'

Andrea glared at him. He gave her a smile and started the engine.

He clicked on the car stereo and 'Virginia Plain' by Roxy Music started to play.

'Roxy Music,' Marsh said with a grin. 'Classic.'

Turning up the volume loud, Marsh put the car in gear and pulled away.

Laura paced the CID office nervously. It was at times like this that she wished she smoked. The atmosphere was tense and subdued. Marsh was out there somewhere with Andrea and he'd intimated that he planned to kill her. Unless they found him quickly, there was nothing they could do. They now had two helicopters and every available unit scouring the island.

Laura glanced over at Gareth, who was sitting at his desk in his office with the door wide open. With his tie loosened and his shirt sleeves rolled up, he looked shattered.

Ben spun round in his seat with a piece of paper in his hand and looked over. 'Boss, we've got a reported carjacking. It's definitely Marsh.'

'Where?' she asked, getting up from her desk with a sense of urgency.

'Llanddaniel,' Ben explained.

Laura walked over to the map on the wall. Llanddaniel was a small village about ten miles south-west of Beaumaris.

'Have we got details?' she asked as Gareth came out of his office.

'Victim was driving a Land Rover Discovery,' Ben replied. 'A man flagged her down. He then held a knife to her throat. He had two female passengers with him that were bound and gagged. While the man put them in the Land Rover, our victim managed to escape on foot.'

'Two passengers?' Laura asked, her heart freezing.

Ben nodded. 'That's what she told the uniform officer.'

'How long ago was this?' Gareth asked.

Ben checked the details. 'Fifteen minutes, boss.'

Gareth approached with his hands on his hips. 'Okay, let's get the make and registration of the car out to every patrol.' He went to the map. 'There are only two roads down from Llanddaniel to the bridges, so let's get patrols on both roads.'

'Why has he got another woman with him?' Ben asked no one in particular.

Laura looked over. 'If he thinks you're going to try and shoot him, the more people he has in the car, the less likely that is going to happen. He's probably counting on the fact that if he positions someone behind the driver's seat, it will be far too dangerous for anyone to take a shot.' Her phone buzzed and she looked at it – *Jake.*

She needed to answer it in case it was an emergency, even though the emergency was likely to be that they'd run out of crisps.

'Hello, darling?', she said, answering the call.

'Hi, Mum,' Jake said sounding perplexed. 'I can't find Rosie.'

'How do you mean?' Laura asked, aware that Jake could lose his school uniform even when it had been laid out on his bed for him.

'Daniel's mum dropped me home after rugby practice, but Rosie's not here,' Jake explained.

'Have you been upstairs?' she asked.

'No,' Jake replied. 'I just shouted upstairs that I was home.'

Laura smiled to herself. 'Yeah, if she's wearing headphones, she won't hear a thing.'

'Okay,' Jake said as he wandered up the stairs. 'No, she's not in her room.'

'Bathroom?' Laura asked, starting to feel a little uneasy.

There were a few seconds of silence.

'No, she's not in there,' Jake said. 'And she's not in your bedroom.'

'I don't understand,' Laura said, trying to work out why Rosie wasn't at home. If she had been going anywhere, she would have texted.

'What about downstairs?' Laura asked anxiously.

'No,' Jake said, sounding confused. 'I don't think she's in the house anywhere, Mum. She must have gone out some- where. Don't worry, I'm all right here on my own with Elvis.'

Laura heard the sound of the front door bell.

'Who's that?' Laura asked. 'Don't answer it until you know who it is, Jake.'

'Hang on,' Jake said as he went to the door. 'It's Veronica.'

Veronica was the lovely retired woman who lived next door.

'Can you open the door and see what she wants, darling?'

Laura heard the mumbles of conversation.

'Laura?' a voice said on the phone. It was Veronica.

'Hi, Veronica,' Laura said, wondering why she had decided to talk to her on Jake's phone. 'I don't suppose you've seen Rosie anywhere, have you?'

'Oh, that's why I popped round,' Veronica explained. 'I saw her crossing the road towards a car with a man about an hour ago. She seemed to know him. I just wanted to check she got back home all right with all that's going on.'

Oh my God.

The blood drained from Laura's face as she processed what Veronica had told her. A wave of panic swept through her and she felt herself begin to shake.

'Erm, it's okay,' Laura said, her voice trembling. 'Are you okay to sit with Jake for a bit?'

'Yes, of course,' Veronica said obliviously.

'Okay, tell Jake that I'll be back later,' Laura said as she ended the call.

In total panic, she rang Rosie's phone. It was turned off.

Then she looked at the number that Marsh had called her on earlier. She rang it. It was turned off.

Please God, no!

'You okay?' Gareth said as he came over looking concerned.

Laura could feel her eyes fill with tears. 'It's Rosie,' she said, her voice blank with fear. 'Marsh has got Rosie.'

CHAPTER 45

The haze of moonlight cast a vanilla hue on the hilltop that marked Anglesey's most famous prehistoric landmark, Bryn Celli Ddu. Translated it meant 'Mound in the Dark Grove'.

Marsh put the spade down to inspect his work. It was amazing to think that this place had been the site of a tomb in the early Neolithic age, five thousand years earlier. There was a chambered tomb underneath the mound itself with passageways and an octagonal chamber. It was here that in 1928 human bones, arrowheads and carved stones had been found.

Marsh looked at the freshly dug shallow grave at the mound's summit. It had taken him almost an hour to complete. He could feel the cold sweat on his brow and his back as he used a spade to pat the earth flat. The skin on his palms had been worn raw by the sheer effort.

He took a few steps back. Burying someone alive was a first for him. Underneath the earth lay Detective Inspector Laura Hart's teenage daughter Rosie. He had injected her with a little pethidine to make the whole process a lot easier. He had attached a plastic tube to her mouth, the top of which now poked above the earth by about three inches.

Squatting down on the earth, Marsh put his ear close to the top of the tube. At first, he thought that Rosie had stopped breathing. Then, as he strained his hearing, he could just make out the soft sound of air going in and out of the tube. She was still alive. How long she would last under the earth was a different matter.

The rhythmic hoot of an owl, somewhere in the distance, broke the silence. The wind picked up and scattered leaves across the patch of earth.

Marsh had come fully prepared with his own camouflage. A freshly dug patch of earth on the grassy hilltop would stand out to anyone. He had dragged a couple of long branches and large bag of leaves to the summit of the mount to disguise the grave. It might have been easier to lock Rosie away somewhere, but not only did he love the sheer theatre of her burial, he also thought of Bryn Celli Ddu as a place of significance to him.

He looked down towards the car and saw the top of Andrea's head. She was unconscious again from a pethidine injection. He had changed his mind about killing her once he had hatched his plan to bury Rosie. He was now armed with two pieces of insurance. DC Andrea Jones by his side in the car. And the knowledge of where Rosie Hart was buried.

Marsh crouched down and scattered the leaves and then carefully placed the branches over the small patch of earth. Although not perfect, it was suitably camouflaged for his purposes.

That should do it, he thought, taking pride in his handiwork. As he stood up, he glanced over to the shimmering lights in the distance. It was the seaside town of Llandudno over on the Welsh mainland, probably twenty miles away as the crow flies. He'd only ever visited once on a school trip and could barely remember anything about it.

Then his gaze went over to a patch of land about fifty

yards further along the top of the mound. It was where he had buried his grandfather on a warm summer's evening in 1996. Marsh had just turned twenty-one. Having left the family home when he was eighteen, he had managed to get a place at Essex University to study psychology. His drinking and behaviour there had become increasingly out of control. He knew that this was what behavioural psychologists would call *acting out*. It referred to the behavioural expression of emotions which served to relieve tension, stress or emotional pain. Self-medicating with alcohol was part of this. Marsh had also used his life as an undergraduate to refine and accelerate his stalking of young women. The all-female halls of residence at the university were perfect hunting grounds.

Having graduated in the summer of 1996, Marsh had returned to Anglesey. Despite the pain and torment she had caused him, he longed to see his mother. He wanted to tell her that he'd graduated with a first-class honours degree in psychology and that the university had accepted his application to stay on to do a master's. Having sat outside his childhood home for hours drinking, Marsh had summoned up the courage to knock on the door. His grandfather gave him an utterly uninterested look and ushered him inside as though he had merely stepped out of the house for five minutes – rather than three years at university doing a degree.

In his drunken state, Marsh had hoped that his mother would find some pride in what he had achieved. Instead, she asked what he wanted and told him that he wasn't welcome. Flying into a rage, Marsh had knocked her unconscious and raped her. He then turned on his grandfather whom he had strangled slowly with his bare hands. After sitting with the dead body until it was dark, Marsh had driven his grandfather's corpse up to Bryn Celli Ddu.

Marsh had remembered a myth about the tomb there. It was said that the souls of anyone buried on that mound would be trapped in eternal torment. However, the tomb had been designed so that on the summer solstice – so once a year – shafts of sunlight would shine directly down the tomb's underground passageway to illuminate the chamber within. Legend had it that Arawn, the Celtic God of Death in Welsh mythology, and ruler of the underworld (*Annwn*), would appear on the summer solstice. He would look into the souls of those that had been buried there and take those whose lives on earth had been well spent. Those whose souls were full of sin would be plunged into a burning pit of flames until the following solstice. This process would go on eternally. Marsh loved the idea of the evil soul of his grandfather being dragged out to be judged once a year, only to be tossed back into the fiery abyss once again.

Turning back, Marsh wandered down the grassy slope, wondering what the next forty-eight hours would bring.

CHAPTER 46

Laura sat at her desk staring at her mobile phone. She knew that Marsh would be calling her to tell her that he now had Rosie. Even though the CID office was bustling, she just couldn't think about anything else. How could she?

As predicted, her phone buzzed and rang on her desk.

Gareth, who was standing nearby, took it before she had a chance to answer. She knew he was trying to protect her but it was annoying.

'This is Detective Inspector Gareth Williams,' Gareth said, clicking the phone to speaker.

There were a few seconds of silence.

'Put Laura on,' Marsh said coldly.

'I'm the Senior Investigating Officer on this case and—'

'I don't care if you're the Pope,' Marsh interrupted angrily. 'Put Laura on the phone now or two more innocent people will die and it will be your fault.'

Gareth looked at Laura, who was feeling physically sick. She nodded and reached out her hand to take the phone.

'Where is she?' Laura asked in a virtual whisper as she tried to contain her feelings. The mixture of anger and fear was overwhelming.

'Where's who?' Marsh asked in a supercilious tone.

'If anything happens to Rosie—' Laura hissed.

'Just calm down, Laura,' Marsh said, interrupting her. 'If you can follow a few simple instructions then you will have your daughter back by midnight tonight. And I'll throw in your colleague for good measure.'

Trying to compose herself, Laura knew that it should be someone else dealing with Marsh. But if he wouldn't speak to anyone else, there was very little she could do.

'Okay,' she said, taking a breath, but her heart was pounding.

'I have some good news and some bad news for you,' Marsh said. 'Which one do you want first?'

'I don't care,' Laura growled in despair. Allowing Marsh to play games with her daughter's life was unbearable.

'Okay. Well, the bad news is that Rosie is buried alive in a shallow grave somewhere on the island,' Marsh said casually.

For a second, Laura couldn't process what he'd said. It was too much. Then her stomach lurched as the terror swept through her. 'What do you mean?' she stammered, aware that her voice was full of emotion but unable to do anything about it. All she could do was picture Rosie being petrified under the earth somewhere.

'Don't worry,' Marsh assured her. 'The good news is that she has a plastic pipe in her mouth so she can breathe. Well, at least for a while.'

Laura moved the phone away, put her hand to her mouth and gasped. With a sharp intake of breath, she tried to steady herself. *Come on, Laura. You need to stay strong for Rosie.*

'This is the deal. I want you to arrange a boat for me at Ynys Llanddwyn Harbour. Nothing fancy. Just a simple motor-boat,' Marsh explained. 'I will take that boat across the Menai Strait, with Andrea on board, and land at Caernarfon. There you will provide me with a car. I will drive across the border to England. You won't track me or follow me, because if I get one hint that you are, the deal will be off. And your daughter will never be found and she'll die. And I'll kill DC Jones. When I'm satisfied that I've gone far enough, I'll set Andrea free and let you know where Rosie is.'

The thought of all this struck panic into Laura. Rosie was buried somewhere and there was nothing they could do. She must be terrified.

'How do I know we can trust you?' she asked him, finding it hard to think straight.

'You don't have a choice,' Marsh said lightly. 'You can sit around and wait for your daughter to die, or you can do something about it.'

Laura looked at Gareth who nodded.

'Okay,' Laura said quietly. 'It's going to take us a while to get a boat.'

'Clock is ticking, Laura,' Marsh warned her. 'I don't know how long Rosie is going to last under there. I expect to hear from you very soon.'

It was thirty minutes since Marsh had called Laura, and Gareth's adrenaline was pumping. Every available police officer on Anglesey was now out scouring the island for Rosie. A helicopter had arrived from the mainland with a thermal imaging camera. Gareth had also liaised with the Canine Unit to be on standby should they get any clue as to where Rosie might be buried alive.

Running his hand anxiously over his scalp, he knew that even though Anglesey was only 260 square miles, finding someone buried in a shallow grave in the middle of nowhere in the dark was going to be virtually impossible. He was trying to hide those thoughts from Laura, though, who was veering between manic anxiety and shock.

Gareth had just arrived back in CID after speaking to Warlow, who had sanctioned getting a small motorboat delivered over to Ynys Llanddwyn Harbour. They were now working on sourcing a car for Marsh on the Welsh mainland at Caernarfon. He had also spoken to the North Wales Police media office in St Asaph and told them they needed a news blackout. The last thing anyone needed was journalists or news crews getting a sniff of what might be going on and spooking Marsh.

Gareth approached Laura, who was sitting at her desk lost in thought. 'Do you want to go home?' he said under his breath.

'No.' Laura looked at him with a frown. 'Thank you, but no. I want to be here. We've got to find Rosie. And I can't do that from home.'

'Of course,' Gareth said with an understanding expression. 'I can't imagine how you're feeling.'

'I just keep thinking of her out there all alone, thinking she's going to die,' Laura said, standing up and striding over to the map. 'Where the hell is she?'

'We really have got everyone out there looking for her,' Gareth reassured her.

'Yeah, but they can't cover the whole island, can they?' Laura put her head in her hands. 'I'm just wondering if there's a safe way of narrowing down the search area?'

It was a good point but the risk in that was that they could miss an area where Rosie had been buried.

They studied the map of Anglesey for a few seconds. The red pins marked the spots where the victims of Marsh's crimes had been found to date.

'We know Marsh was at your home in Beaumaris,' Gareth said, pointing to the south-east coast. 'And he's asked for a boat at Ynys Llanddwyn here,' he said, pointing to the south-west coast.

'Okay,' Laura said with a nod. 'I'm assuming that he hasn't taken a massive detour to the north of the island. In fact, can't we rule out this part of the island?'

Gareth looked at her and narrowed his eyes. 'It's a big risk, isn't it?'

'I think it's a bigger risk trying to cover this whole area with so few officers,' Laura pointed out. 'My understanding is that most serial killers have a very well-defined geographical sense. They have a small area that is a comfort zone they are familiar with. In fact, they rarely stray too far from where they live, despite that making them easier to catch.' Laura pointed to the pins. 'Marsh has killed and buried his victims solely on the beaches of the east and south coast of the island. He lives here, which means he has never strayed more than ten miles from his home. I would argue that you could draw a line diagonally across the island from Moelfre to Rhosneigr. Marsh doesn't travel to or operate in the part of the island north of this line. He's unlikely to have broken that pattern of behaviour today.'

Gareth was impressed by what Laura had said. 'Yeah, you're right. That's spot-on. Ben,' Gareth shouted across the office.

'Boss?' Ben replied.

'Talk to all units out on the island looking for Rosie,' Gareth said loudly. 'And talk to the helicopter pilot too. Tell them to concentrate their search on an area of the island south of a line that stretches from Moelfre to Rhosneigr. Tell them to ignore anything north of there for the time being.'

'I'm on it, boss,' Ben said, grabbing his phone.

Laura pointed to the map again. 'The quickest way between Beaumaris and Ynys Llanddwyn is the A4080 coastal road.'

Gareth nodded but was then distracted as Declan approached him.

'Boss, traffic are supplying an Astra that can be delivered close to the pier in Caernarfon,' Declan explained. 'They're going to place a small tracker under the chassis where no one is going to find it.'

'Good work, Declan,' Gareth said. They weren't about to let Marsh drive off with Andrea without knowing where they were heading. And whatever he said, Marsh wasn't going to find a tracker expertly hidden under the middle of the car.

Gareth looked up to see Neville, the head of the Armed Response Unit, coming through the doors of the CID office.

'Jim,' Gareth said as he came over.

'Jesus,' Neville said, shaking his head. 'I've been doing this for nearly thirty years, Gareth, and I've never come up against something like this.'

'What's the plan?' Gareth asked.

Neville pointed to the flat playing field that lay to one side of Beaumaris Police Station.

'Royal Navy Wildcat helicopter from 893 squadron is going to land over there in . . .' Neville checked his watch. 'Five minutes precisely. I have two snipers on board already. They're taking us down to Ynys Llanddwyn. They've got thermal imaging and radar on board plus enough lights to illuminate a football pitch. I suggest that we keep visual contact with the suspect for most of the journey across to the mainland.'

Gareth shook his head. 'He was pretty explicit that we weren't to follow him at any point.'

'Don't worry,' Neville said. 'The Wildcat can take us up to ten or even twelve thousand feet and the thermal imaging will still work. The suspect won't even know we're there.'

'Okay.' Gareth nodded. 'We'd better go then.'

Neville frowned. 'You're coming with us?'

'Yes,' Gareth replied. 'If I'm making any decisions, I need to be with you guys.'

'Hope you've got a strong stomach,' Neville said. 'There's a storm on its way.'

Gareth didn't like to admit he felt terribly sick the last time he went up in a helicopter. And that was on a calm, sunny day. But his colleague and his girlfriend's daughter were in mortal danger, and he had to do all he could to save them.

'Boss?' Declan called over.

Gareth pointed to the door. 'I've got to go, Declan.'

'Message from the unit down at Ynys Llanddwyn,' Declan explained. 'The boat is ready to go.'

'Good,' Gareth replied. 'Ring Marsh and tell him they're ready for him and Andrea. If he asks to speak to Laura, tell him that she's not available.'

'Will do, boss,' Declan said, grabbing his phone.

'Don't worry. I'm not going to be here anyway,' Laura said as she marched over to her desk and grabbed her car keys.

'Where are you going?' he asked.

'I can't sit here,' Laura explained. 'I'm going out there to help look for Rosie.'

'Okay,' Gareth said and gestured to his radio. 'I'll stay in touch.'

He turned and walked quickly out of the CID office and headed for the waiting helicopter.

CHAPTER 47

It started to rain, and Andrea huddled in the corner of the boat in Caernarfon Harbour. The water lapped against the hull as a dozen or so police officers watched. Marsh started the engine. The AFOs had their guns strapped across their chests, ready to use them. However, they needed Marsh alive, for Rosie's sake. Andrea wiped a wet strand of hair from her face, unable to believe that this was all happening to her. She had heard of the phrase *a living nightmare* before. Now she knew exactly what it meant. A terrifying, surreal nightmare.

Marsh pulled away from the long wooden jetty in the RYCK 280 motorboat provided by the police. The harbour had been cordoned off by three marked police cars who had their lights flashing silently in the eerie darkness.

Five minutes earlier, Marsh had plonked Andrea unceremoniously on the far side of the vessel. The cockpit was open. It had a low windscreen, which meant there was hardly any protection from the elements. As Marsh turned the boat in the water and headed for the Welsh coast, he spun towards her and yelled, 'Hang on to your seat, it's going to be a bumpy ride!' like a man possessed. It was unsettling to witness another human being so devoid of all feeling, empathy and rational thought.

They hit a small wave. The boat bobbed up and down so that the water in the bottom of the hull sloshed down towards her. The air was now thick with the salty smell of the sea and the diesel from the boat's engine.

Marsh had told Andrea what he'd done to Rosie, and Andrea thought of the poor girl now, stuck under the earth. She would be terrified. She had no idea why Marsh had committed his crimes. Frankly, she didn't care. The world would be a far better place without him and she imagined that even the most bleeding-hearted, *Guardian*-reading liberal would find it hard to justify his ongoing existence.

Lightning flashed a bright white on the horizon. It looked like a storm was heading their way. Andrea hoped they got to the other side of the strait before it hit. She squinted as the rain started to blow into her face.

A sudden swirl of wind made the boat lurch to one side. Then a deep rumble of thunder sounded from the direction in which they were heading. Andrea listened to the noise and realised that it wasn't thunder. It was the distant sound of a helicopter, high above them. They were being tracked. *Thank God.*

Marsh opened the throttle and the boat seemed to leap forward in the water. As she turned and looked back, the jetty and the blue flashing lights were slowly fading in the distance. The smoky moon was throwing an eerie inky blue light over the sea on both sides. She was glad the moon was out, otherwise they would have been in total darkness.

Andrea clutched the side of the boat as another wave slapped against the hull. Her heart was racing. Her stomach ached from the knotted anxiety. She tried to calm herself and find the rhythm of the waves so that she didn't lurch from side to side with every bump.

Glancing over at Marsh, she saw that he was staring ahead intently. The twinkling lights of the Welsh mainland were just about becoming visible. It was no more than two or three miles to Caernarfon. By her calculations, that would mean another fifteen to twenty minutes in the boat.

Her mind turned to what was in store for her on the other side. Even though Marsh had promised to release her and give Laura details of where he had buried Rosie once he was safely in England, she didn't trust him to stick to his word. She could see no reason why he should. He had nothing to gain from keeping his side of the bargain. He was a psychopath, so being responsible for the death of two more innocent people wouldn't register on his moral compass – he didn't have one.

As they hit another wave, Andrea felt herself lift off the bench seat. Her knee banged against the hull and she winced at the pain.

Ow, that hurt!

Something dropped from some netting from the seat beside her. It was a flare gun.

As she picked it up and placed it back, she realised that her knee was now throbbing.

Oh my God! I can feel pain in my knee.

With a little bit of effort, she managed to move her right foot. And then she slowly wiggled her toes.

Despite her dire circumstances and terrifying ordeal, she felt a grin flit across her face.

The sensation was slowly returning to her legs and feet.

CHAPTER 48

The noise of the Lynx helicopter's twin Rolls-Royce Gem turboshaft engines was deafening, even though Gareth was wearing headphones. He knew that with a top speed of 250 mph, it was the fastest helicopter on the planet.

Looking at the thermal imaging feed and the radar, Gareth could see Marsh's journey. A young radar operator sat next to him, explaining anything on the screens that Gareth didn't understand.

As far as he could see, Marsh was sticking to what he had told them and heading across the Menai Strait to Caernarfon. Declan had already told him that a car with a tracker would be waiting. They still had no idea whether Marsh meant to keep his promise.

The ongoing search for where Marsh had buried Rosie had so far been a frustrating series of false leads and dashed hopes.

Glancing back, Gareth nodded at Neville and the two police marksmen who were sitting in the back of the helicopter. At the moment, they needed Marsh alive for Andrea's safety and so that he could reveal where he had buried Rosie. However, if anything changed or Marsh did something that required him being stopped, Gareth wanted to be able to react in a second.

'Gold Command from Alpha Zero,' the pilot said over the radio that Gareth could hear in his headphones. 'We've got a weather system heading in from the west, sir. To avoid the turbulence, I suggest that we come down to two thousand feet, over.'

Gareth clicked his radio. 'Alpha Zero, received. Yes, I agree, let's do that, over.'

A second later, Gareth felt the helicopter dive and his stomach pitched a little.

Spotting a tiny dot in the channel, Gareth frowned and looked over to the radar operator. He was worried that it was another vessel in the strait.

'What's that?' Gareth asked, pointing to the luminous green dot. 'Is it another boat?'

'It's an island, sir,' the operator replied. 'It's one of the Saint Tudwal's islands.'

Gareth shrugged. 'Never heard of them.'

'One of the islands has a small lighthouse. Another one has a priory that's over a thousand years old,' he explained and then gestured. 'On this one, there's a neolithic burial chamber. It's not as extensive as the one over at Bryn Celli Ddu.'

Gareth processed what the operator had told him. Then he remembered something. Marsh had talked about how he had buried his grandfather in Bryn Celli Ddu!

Was that significant? It might be.

Grabbing his radio, Gareth hoped it had the range to reach Laura's Tetra radio. He knew she was now out helping the search for Rosie.

'Gold Command to six-three, are you receiving?' he asked.

Nothing but a static crackle.

Come on, Laura, come on.

'Gold Command to six-three, are you receiving?'

The crackle intensified and then there was a voice.

'Gold Command from six-three, I'm receiving you, over,' Laura said, even though her voice was faint.

'You need to get to the burial mound at Bryn Celli Ddu! It's where Marsh buried his grandfather. If he's dug a grave there before and knows the place, maybe that's where he took Rosie, over,' Gareth explained, praying that there was some kind of connection in Marsh's mind.

'Yes, that might make sense,' Laura said. 'I'm on my way, over and out.'

Twenty minutes later, Laura used a torch as she desperately scrambled her way up the grassy burial mound at Bryn Celli Ddu. The rain had started to pelt down. A white flash of lightning lit up the whole area for a second.

As Laura ran up the hill, she slipped on the wet ground and fell.

'Jesus,' she yelped as she got back to her feet and continued upwards.

Please God, let Rosie be here. Please.

Standing still for a moment, she wiped the water from her eyes. The rain was so hard, it was difficult to see anything. She shone her torch across the grass. Heart thumping like someone punching her chest. Breathing fast and shallow.

Come on, come on. Where are you?

Her eyes scanned left and right anxiously. Something, anything that would signal recent digging. As far as she could see, the turf was smooth and untouched.

Putting her hand to her head, she began to despair. What if Gareth was wrong? What if Rosie is lying somewhere else? What if she was already dead?

'Rosie?' Laura shouted wildly. 'Rosie?'

Then she spotted something on the level ground to the right-hand side of the stone entrance to the chamber. An uneven patch of grass and earth. Leaves and a branch had covered it slightly. Was that it? It had to be, didn't it?

Clambering down the wet hillside, she slipped and fell again. Tumbling over herself, she came to rest on the grass.

With the torch held high, she sprinted to the uneven ground. Dropping to her knees, she searched for the end of a plastic pipe that Marsh had mentioned.

Nothing.

She didn't care. This was the only sign of disturbance she had seen.

With her bare hands, she pulled and grabbed at the grass and soil feverishly.

'Please be here, please be here,' she mumbled hysterically.

The more she burrowed, the more she could see that there was nothing buried underneath.

'No, no,' she wailed. 'Come on.'

Her hands were now cut to bits by the rocks in the soil. Blood running down her fingers. She carried on regardless.

Scrabbling. Rummaging with her hands in the earth.

I can't give up. Please God, let me find her. Please!

It was too much to bear.

She stopped digging and sank to the wet ground, sobbing, trying to catch her breath.

CHAPTER 49

As the helicopter bumped on some turbulence, Gareth grabbed onto his seat. They were now in the middle of a storm. A crack of thunder sounded like it was on top of them.

He had calculated that if Laura found Rosie alive, then Marsh wouldn't have Rosie's whereabouts as a bargaining tool. And that meant if a police sniper shot him dead from the helicopter, Andrea could be rescued unharmed. Even though all this was a remote possibility, Gareth just prayed that his hunch about where Rosie had been buried was correct. Otherwise, she could be anywhere. He couldn't bear to think of her under the earth in this driving rain with a plastic pipe in her mouth. Marsh could have been lying. He didn't want to think about what else could have happened to Rosie.

A sudden flash of lightning. The helicopter rocked again.

Gareth peered at the thermal imaging monitor but the storm was playing havoc with the feed. He glanced at the radar. He could see the flashing green dot of Marsh's boat was getting close to the harbour at Caernarfon.

'How long before they get to the shore?' Gareth asked the operator.

'Ten minutes, sir. Maybe less,' the operator replied.

Gareth went to the window and cupped his hands to look outside. All he could see was cloud and rain.

He grabbed his radio. 'Alpha Zero from Gold Command, can we go in lower as they reach the shore? If we have the opportunity to shoot the suspect, then that seems to be the place to take it as they slow down, over.'

'Gold Command to Alpha Zero, received,' the pilot replied. 'I can take us under these clouds, sir, but we are going to alert the suspect and target boat of our presence. How low do you want me to take us, over?'

Gareth thought for a few seconds. He glanced back at Neville and beckoned him forward in the helicopter. Another bump of turbulence nearly knocked Gareth out of his seat.

'Jim,' he shouted over the noise of the engine and the storm outside.

'What's going on?' Neville yelled as he got closer.

'If we take this in low over the boat as it slows going into Caernarfon,' Gareth hollered, 'what are the chances of one of your men getting a decent shot away at the suspect and not hitting my DC?'

Neville pulled a face. 'Not the best of conditions for it. But they're accurate at five hundred feet. Anything over that, we're going to struggle.' Neville frowned. 'I thought we needed to keep the suspect alive.'

'Yeah, we do at the moment,' Gareth shouted. 'But if that changes, I want Marsh to be in our sights for a shot straight away.'

Neville frowned as the helicopter bounced again. 'We're not going to be able to hide from Marsh at five hundred feet, Gareth.'

'I know,' Gareth said. 'I'll take that risk.'

Neville glanced back and beckoned for one of the snipers

to come forward. He was holding an Ares army-issue L42A1 sniper rifle with night vision sights and laser scope.

Gareth looked over to the radar operator and pointed to the screen. 'How long now?'

'Five minutes or less now, sir,' he replied.

Gareth grabbed the radio. 'Gold Command to Alpha Zero, can you take us down slowly to five hundred feet, over?'

'Roger that, Gold Command,' the pilot replied as the Lynx helicopter descended below the storm clouds.

Neville moved over to a small sliding door, grabbed the handle, swung it back and opened the door.

Suddenly, the helicopter was filled with thunderous noise and swirling wind.

The sniper moved into position.

Gareth glanced out of the window and down at the sea.

At first, he couldn't see anything, then he saw the lights of Caernarfon Harbour up ahead.

As the helicopter lowered beneath the clouds over the black sea, the moonlight spilled across its surface.

Thank God we've got the moon tonight!

Between the helicopter and the harbour lights, it was now clear to see a small boat moving steadily through the water.

The sniper loaded his rifle, clicked the night vision sights, closed one eye and moved so that he was now aiming at the sea below.

Gareth looked at Neville, who was crouched by the sniper. The wind coming in through the open door thrashed around them.

'Let me know when you've got a clean shot,' Gareth shouted at the top of his voice.

Gareth's mind immediately switched for a moment back to the hunt for Rosie. He grabbed the radio again. He hadn't heard anything since suggesting to Laura that Rosie might be at Bryn Celli Ddu.

'Gold Command to six-three, over,' he yelled over the din. His radio crackled but there was no reply.

'Gold Command to six-three, over,' he yelled again.

A faint voice through the crackle. 'I can't find her, Gareth. I just can't find her. What am I going to do?' Laura sounded broken.

For a moment, Gareth closed his eyes. Maybe he'd been wrong about Marsh's need to go somewhere he'd been before. Rosie could be buried somewhere else.

Thinking back, he tried to remember exactly what Marsh had said.

Then it came to him.

'Laura, look out north-west. Can you see any lights on the coast in the distance?' Gareth shouted.

'What are you talking about?' Laura said, sounding utterly distraught.

'Marsh said that when he buried his grandfather, he could see the lights of Llandudno in the distance,' Gareth thundered as loudly as he could. 'If you can't see the lights you're in the wrong place.'

The radio crackled in his headphones.

'Laura? Can you hear me?' he yelled desperately.

All he could hear was the static of the radio.

'Laura?'

Nothing.

'Shit!' he hollered.

Neville came across and cupped his hands so he could be heard. 'We've got a clean shot of target one. What do you want to do?'

'We need to hold on, Jim,' he replied, shaking his head.

Neville gave him a serious look. 'I'm not sure how long we've got.'

Gareth gritted his teeth, praying that Laura had heard his message.

CHAPTER 50

Scrambling like a woman possessed, Laura sprinted up the steep side of the burial mound. She glanced out but all she could see were trees. Gareth had told her to look for the lights of Llandudno. Maybe she wasn't high enough.

Come on! Come on!

Using her hands to keep her balance, she continued upwards until she reached the top of the grass mound.

Pushing her soaking wet hair from her face, she turned.

The twinkling lights of Llandudno on the Welsh mainland were there in the distance.

'I'm in the right place,' she said to herself as she held the torch high to inspect the very summit of the burial mound.

Before she could see anything, everything went black.

Her torch had gone out.

She shook the torch and turned it on and off.

Nothing.

Despite the moonlight, it was virtually impossible to see anything.

She started to scramble around on her hands and knees, looking and feeling for the smallest sign that the grass and earth had been disturbed.

Then she had a thought.

Grabbing her phone from her pocket, she clicked on the torch and held it up. She didn't know why she hadn't thought of it immediately.

'Rosie?' she cried at the top of her voice.

Moving the torchlight around, she desperately searched the ground.

Nothing.

'I can't do this,' she started to sob.

Looking to her left, all she could see was flat turf and grass.

She's not here.

Laura shook her head.

Then out of the corner of her eye, she spotted a long branch resting close to the far edge of the hilltop.

What's that?

She sprinted over and pulled it away.

Hardly daring to believe her eyes, she saw that a rectangular patch of grass had been dug up.

Oh my God. This could be it.

Then she saw something sticking out of the ground.

Plastic tubing.

'Oh my God, Rosie,' Laura sobbed as she clawed furiously at the packed earth. Pulling out stones and earth, she dug and dug, jamming her fingers until she felt something.

A human limb.

'Please be alive,' she mumbled, sick with fear.

The limb moved slightly.

Scooping more and more earth away, she saw an arm and then a hand. They moved.

'Rosie, Rosie, it's me,' she shrieked. 'It's me, darling.'

Suddenly the earth began to move away.

Rosie was starting to gradually move to free herself.

Then her head and face appeared through the earth.

Laura scooped the earth away, put her hand under Rosie's shoulders and pulled her up with every ounce of energy that she had.

'Rosie, it's me,' Laura sobbed. 'You're safe.'

Now coughing and spluttering, Rosie managed to sit up, scraping the earth frantically from her face and eyes. Her blonde hair was matted with soil.

'Mum?' she croaked as she coughed.

'It's okay, darling,' Laura said. 'You're safe.'

'Mum,' Rosie cried as she put out her arms and spluttered again.

'Hey, it's okay,' Laura reassured her as she took her in her arms. 'I've got you.'

'Gold Command to six-three, over,' came a voice through the crackle on her radio.

Laura grabbed her radio. 'I've found her! I've found Rosie!'

'Can you repeat? You've got Rosie and she's safe?' Gareth asked through the static.

Laura reached out with her hand and took Rosie's. Her eyes were filled with tears. 'Yes. She's safe. Rosie is safe. I've got her.'

There was a second as they held each other.

Then the radio crackled again.

'Take the shot! Take the shot!' Gareth's voice screamed on the other end of the radio.

Then Laura heard what sounded like a gunshot.

CHAPTER 51

The sky and sea around the motorboat suddenly exploded in light. Andrea shielded her eyes as she gazed up at the naval helicopter that was hovering nearby. Its rotors and engine thundered overhead.

What the hell are they doing? she thought with a stab of terror.

Marsh's instructions had been clear. If he had one inkling that he was being tracked or followed, he'd kill her and not reveal where Rosie was buried. What were they thinking?

Marsh had stopped the boat and was now dashing around like a madman. He was furious. Even though the feeling had started to return to her legs, she wasn't going to be able to fight him off.

'What are you doing?' Marsh screamed up at the helicopter.

Then he glanced over at Andrea with a twisted sneer.

'I'll show you!' he yelled up into the sky as he manoeuvred along the side of the boat towards her with a large knife in his hand.

Andrea's heart was thumping. Marsh was coming to kill her, and there was nothing she could do about it.

CRACK!

A shot rang out across the sky.

Marsh stopped in his tracks and frowned at her.

He staggered, fell against the wooden railing and then tumbled into the sea.

Jesus Christ! They shot him!

Andrea didn't understand. What about Rosie?

She looked up at the helicopter as if to say, *What the hell is going on?*

Using her arms to support herself, she had an idea. She crawled over to the control panel and the boat's steering wheel.

To one side was the boat's VHF radio system. Peering closely, she saw that she could change the frequency channel which the radio was operating on. It had been switched to Channel 16. She turned the dial to Channel 99, which was the UK police emergency frequency, picked up the handset and clicked the talk button.

'Mayday, Mayday, this is DC Andrea Jones. This is an emergency,' she said, realising that they were only about a kilometre from Caernarfon Harbour. 'Mayday, Mayday, is anyone out there or receiving, over?'

The radio crackled. 'Andrea? It's DI Williams, over?'

Thank God.

'Boss,' she sighed with such relief. 'I don't understand. You shot Marsh.'

'We've found Rosie,' Gareth explained. 'Laura found her. She's safe and well.'

'Thank God for that,' Andrea said as she sat down on the chair beside the boat's wheel.

'Stupid question, but are you okay?' Gareth asked.

'Yeah, just about,' Andrea said overwhelmed by the sense of relief she was feeling. 'My legs and feet are starting to get feeling back.'

'That's incredible news,' Gareth said. 'Do you think you can get that boat into Caernarfon Harbour okay or do you want me to send someone out?'

'No, I'm fine,' Andrea replied. 'I've driven a boat like this once before.'

'Right, okay,' Gareth said. 'I'll see you in the harbour in a few minutes then?'

'Yes, boss,' Andrea said, still trying to take in all that had happened.

Moving the throttle up, she pressed the button and the boat's engine rumbled into life.

Taking the wheel in both hands, Andrea let the wind blow into her face. It had stopped raining.

'Andrea!' Gareth screamed at the other end of the radio breaking her thought.

What the hell's the matter? she wondered now, startled.

'Andrea! He's behind you!'

Suddenly, a soaking wet figure loomed over her and dragged her from the seat.

It was Marsh.

The bullet had gone through his shoulder, knocking him into the sea.

Pulling her by the hair, Marsh pinned her down and tried to strangle her. His eyes were narrow and black as he glared at her with rage.

Andrea was struggling to breathe. She gasped as she tried to tear his fingers away from her throat.

Her head was swimming as she tried to suck in air.

If I pass out, he's going to kill me!

With a sudden movement of her knee against Marsh's back, she knocked him off balance. She twisted, using her arms to throw him off.

Scrambling along the deck, she knew that the sniper in the helicopter wouldn't shoot at Marsh until he had a clean shot. At the moment, that was impossible.

The boat hit a wave and Andrea felt herself being thrown down the length of it. Marsh was now up. He grabbed a length of rope, wrapped it around his hands and headed down the boat towards her.

A shot rang out from the helicopter but Marsh didn't flinch.

This time they had missed.

Clambering towards the side of the boat, she cowered. Marsh was ten yards away.

Glancing right, she saw something nestled in the back of a seat.

The flare gun.

With every ounce of strength, she leaped towards it, grabbing it in her right hand as she landed on her back.

Marsh appeared over her.

It was now or never. She pulled the trigger of the flare gun. Nothing.

Oh God, no!

Suddenly a cloud of smoke and burning red nitrate and magnesium filled the space between them.

The distress flare hit Marsh square in the upper chest and exploded with a *bang*.

'FUCK YOU!' she screamed with utter rage.

As he staggered backwards, his chest and head were engulfed in red and orange flames.

He gave a horrific scream.

Ripping at his burning clothes, Marsh flailed around.

The air was thick with the smell of burning flesh.

Marsh dropped backwards onto the deck, his body still thrashing.

Then, after a few seconds, he was still as the flames continued to consume him.

Andrea held on to the side of the boat and managed to get to her feet.

She gazed down at Marsh's blackened form.

He was dead.

CHAPTER 52

Six hours later

Laura drove over the hill and saw Beaumaris stretching out before her. Rosie sat in the passenger seat beside her. She'd spent a couple of hours at the hospital being checked. She'd managed to have a shower and was now wearing clean clothes. The doctors had wanted her to stay but Rosie was insistent that unless there was a medical reason, she just wanted to go home with her mother.

Laura reached over, a lump in her throat, and took Rosie's hand. It felt like it was only yesterday that she had held her daughter's hand all the time when they were shopping, crossing the road or coming back from primary school.

The sky was full of the early light of dawn. Rosie buzzed down the window and the wind brought with it the soft sound of waves breaking in the distance. The mist was lifting to reveal the contours of the low hills that curved away above the shoreline to the east.

'We can stop at the shop if you want anything?' Laura said gently as they entered Beaumaris. Most of the shops were closed but she knew the Co-op opened at 6.30 a.m.

Rosie shook her head. 'I just want to go home, Mum.'

'Of course.' Laura nodded sympathetically. 'We've got plenty of stuff there.'

Rosie gazed out of the window. Laura glanced at her and wondered if she'd ever recover from the ordeal of the past ten hours. She gave Rosie's hand a squeeze and she squeezed it back. She would need lots of time and patience.

'You know, it was Gareth that worked out where you were,' Laura said quietly.

Laura turned to look at her. 'Really?' she said with a frown.

'Yes.' Laura nodded. 'I just thought you should know.'

'Yeah, of course.'

A moment later, they pulled up onto the driveway.

Rosie bit her lip as she gazed up at their house. 'I didn't know if I was ever going to come back here.'

Laura looked at her and put her hand to Rosie's face as a tear trickled down over her cheek.

'Hey,' Laura whispered as she started to feel tearful herself. 'You are here. And you're safe. Shall we go in?'

Rosie nodded as she opened the car door.

They walked across the drive arm in arm, opened the front door and went inside.

Elvis bounded over and jumped up at Rosie, his tail wagging furiously.

'Hello, mate,' Rosie said, as she crouched down and stroked him.

Jake came sprinting up the hallway, still in his Manchester United pyjamas.

'Hello, scruff,' Rosie said, going over and giving him a hug.

'Hello,' Jake replied with a slightly uncertain tone, clinging tightly to his big sister.

Laura gestured. 'Let's go through to the kitchen and I'll put the kettle on.'

As they all walked down the hall, Laura was momentarily overwhelmed but so grateful to have Rosie at home, safe and sound. She knew that sometimes she took stuff like that for granted. She promised herself that she never would again.

As they arrived in the kitchen, Gareth was at the sink filling the kettle with water.

'You must have read my mind,' Laura said, pointing to the kettle.

Gareth put down the kettle and looked over at Rosie. 'How are you doing?'

Rosie nodded and blinked tearfully. 'Yeah, okay,' she whispered.

Then she took two steps across the kitchen, wrapped her arms around him and sobbed.

'Hey,' Gareth said as he hugged her.

'I'm sorry,' Rosie said as she unwrapped her arms from him.

Gareth frowned. 'What are you sorry for?'

'For being a total bitch,' Rosie said as she wiped the tears from her face.

'I don't know what you're talking about,' Gareth said gently.

'It's okay,' Rosie said. 'I know how happy you make Mum. I think I was just jealous or angry that she was happy without Dad.'

'Of course you were.' Gareth gave her an understanding nod. 'I don't blame you for that.'

There were a few seconds as they looked at each other with a new understanding.

'I'll pop the kettle on, shall I?' Laura asked, taking a breath to try and hold back her own tears that threatened to come.

'Can I have something stronger?' Rosie asked.

'You can have anything you like, darling,' Laura replied with a fond smile.

Rosie thought a moment. 'Brandy, then.'

'Brandy?' Laura snorted as she looked up at the kitchen clock. It was 7 a.m. 'Sod it. I'll join you. Gareth?'

'Yeah.' He shrugged. 'Why not?'

As Rosie went over to where the glasses were, Jake looked up at her and said quietly, 'Make sure you get four glasses out.'

Laura smirked at him. 'Nice try, sunshine. You're not having brandy at seven o'clock in the morning.'

'Pepsi Max?' Jake asked hopefully.

'You can have a Pepsi Max.'

'Yes!' Jake clenched his fist.

Laura laughed and put her arms around him. Jake had been through a lot in the last twenty-four hours too.

'Do I have to go to school? I've hardly had any sleep,' Jake asked.

Laura squeezed him tightly to her and then gave a weary smile. 'No, you don't have to go to school today.'

Jake smiled. 'Nice one.'

CHAPTER 53

One week later

At the top of the graveyard, the thin grey spire of St Mary's, the parish church of Llanddyfnan, loomed ominously up into the pale sky. To the west, the roof of Llanddyfnan House, a stately home, was just visible beyond the slopes of the ancient oak trees that had been bent sideways by the strong sea winds.

Laura and Gareth stood a respectful distance from Zoey Garland's funeral. Her coffin had now been lowered into the grave and the local vicar was delivering his blessing and final prayers. Laura watched with the knowledge that she had been so very close to losing Rosie. She couldn't imagine how Zoey's parents were feeling at this moment. Their grief had to be unbearable.

It had been a week since Marsh's death off the coast of Caernarfon. The media storm since then had been intense. SOCOs and forensics teams had pulled Marsh's home to pieces. In a locked cupboard, they had found the trophies that Marsh had kept of all his victims. They had also found Marsh's detailed notes of his murders on a hidden memory stick.

Thankfully it had allowed them to finally locate the remains of Shannon Jones. Her parents would be able to lay her to rest at a funeral being held the following week.

From where Laura and Gareth stood in the graveyard, the whitish-grey monuments to their right tapered into invisibility in the over-abundant light. The church itself was sprinkled with small-leaved ivy. Beyond the shimmering forms of the graves, the afternoon sky was empty, a pale void. A pair of brimstone butterflies, playing together, passed flittering in front of them. Laura stretched out her hand towards the butterflies for a moment.

Gareth was looking down at his phone and reading something intently.

'Something wrong?' Laura asked.

He gave her a sardonic look. 'It doesn't really matter now, but someone found that rubbish bag that Anthony Conte buried in the woods down by Benllech beach.'

'Right.' Laura nodded.

'Some mountain bikers found it yesterday,' Gareth explained. 'Turns out it was full of boxes that had contained illegal anabolic steroids. Conte's been importing them and selling them.'

'No wonder he did a runner when we knocked on his door,' Laura said.

'Declan is taking some officers to raid his gym and fitness studio.'

Laura raised an eyebrow. 'If they can prove it, he'll serve time.'

'Given the stuff we found in his house, that's not a bad thing,' Gareth said.

Laura nodded and then her attention went back to the relatives and friends that were gathered around Zoey's grave.

As the clouds above them cleared, sunlight came through the gaps in the rounded hills and lit the pale rectangular façades of houses in the distance. Laura peered around at the graves that surrounded them. The draped urns and obelisks. The sublimely truncated columns. The obliquely leaning slabs inscribed with simple messages of love and loss. She thought how strange it was that that's where we all end up. Old, young, rich, poor, good, evil. That's how it ended for everyone. But maybe that was okay. Embracing her own mortality, rather than denying or avoiding it, meant she could concentrate on getting on with living every day with a sense that it was precious.

As the funeral ended, the mourners began to drift away.

Turning slowly, Laura and Gareth began to wander across the churchyard towards the car. They had already given their condolences to Zoey's parents in the church.

'That song was incredible,' Laura said. They had played Billie Eilish's 'Ocean Eyes' during the service as it had been one of Zoey's favourites.

Gareth looked at Laura. 'Have you got one?'

'A funeral song?'

'Yeah.'

'I'm not sure,' Laura admitted. 'Something by The Cranberries. Maybe 'Ode To My Family'. I love that whole album. What about you?'

'Rainy Days And Mondays' by The Carpenters,' Gareth said.

'Good choice,' Laura said.

'And I've got a very moving inscription that I want on my gravestone,' Gareth said as they arrived at the car. 'Just so you know.'

Laura raised her eyebrow. 'Oh yeah? What's that then?'

Gareth gave her a wry smile. '*Told you I was ill.*'

Laura laughed as she opened the passenger door and got in. 'Very good.'

Starting the car, Gareth turned on the radio.

BBC 5 Live news. Greater Manchester Police have confirmed that a man has been arrested in connection with the murder of Ian Butterfield, a serving police officer in the city, whose body was discovered at Worsaw Hill in Lancashire ten days ago. A police spokesperson said that a Peter Marsons, a detective chief inspector also with the Greater Manchester police force, was helping them with their inquiries.

CHAPTER 54

It was dawn the following morning and the sky over Beaumaris beach was a light, uniform dark blue. The sun had just started to tinge the horizon with an apricot light. The smooth surface of the sea was peppered with leisurely shifting patterns of blacks and dark greens. It was calm as a pond.

Laura, still energised from her swim, sat in the sand next to Elvis, who was panting after a long run down the flat, wet beach. His paws were matted with dark sand that had the look of sticky brown sugar.

She and Gareth had the day off work and they had decided to start the day with an early morning swim. Laura was now dressed in a snug hoodie, hat and trackie bottoms. She sipped the hot tea they had brought in an aluminium flask. Peering out to sea, she could see that Gareth was still swimming. He launched into a front crawl with perfect technique, arms cutting into the sea while his feet and legs powered him through the modest waves.

Look at him go, she thought. *He looks so powerful like that.*

Laura took a shell in her hand and blew the gritty sand from it. She was lost in thought. It had been hard for her to get the news about Pete's arrest out of her mind since she'd heard it. Despite her exhaustion after the Marsh case, she hadn't slept well. How could the GMP think that Pete, a DCI with a flawless record, was involved in Butterfield's murder? It didn't make any sense to her. After the frustrating conversations with Watkins and Carmichael, the only solution was that someone in the GMP was attempting to frame her and Pete. She didn't know whether it was some kind of warning for them to stop investigating Sam's death. Until she could speak directly to Pete and understand the events surrounding his arrest, she knew she was going to worry.

Laura looked down at the shell in her palm and saw that it was in fact a fossil. An almost perfect ammonite. The delicate, finely indented spiral of the shell was clearly marked on both sides. The sea had rounded the edges and blurred the pattern, but it was beautiful. She put it on her towel. She would show it to Jake later so he could add it to his extensive collection.

She watched Gareth leave the water and walk slowly up the sand towards her. His chest was defined and his arms sculpted. In the dark chaos of the last few days, she had all but forgotten how attractive he was. He looked like James Bond as he paced powerfully over to her and picked up his towel. Her James Bond.

'Looking good there, mister,' she said with a half-smile.

He looked down at her and draped the towel around his neck. 'I'm starting to feel human again.' Then he gave her a concerned expression. 'No offence, but you look a bit tired.'

'Charmed, I'm sure,' she joked.

'Worrying about Pete?' he asked as he pulled on a navy sweatshirt.

'Yeah.' Laura nodded. 'I'll see if I can speak to his solicitor later.'

Gareth sat down, snuggled next to her and poured himself some tea.

There were a few seconds of comfortable silence.

She looked at him for a second. 'What are we going to do on our day off?'

Gareth gave her a cheeky grin.

She gave him a playful hit on the arm. 'Apart from that.'

Gareth shrugged. 'I'm just happy to be hanging out with you.'

'Creep,' she joked.

Then she took his face in her hands and kissed him softly on the mouth. They looked at each other and smiled. Laura traced his face with her fingertip, lightly outlining his profile. His brow, his strong nose, full lips, prickly chin and over his eyebrows.

'We should get married,' Gareth said as if the thought had come to him in that moment.

Laura paused in her stroking of his face. She was going to make a joke about wanting a formal proposal of marriage rather than Gareth's unromantic suggestion.

Instead she gave him a beaming smile. 'We should.'

'Really?'

'Yes.'

Taking her in his arms, Gareth kissed her and then pulled her close.

As his powerful arms encircled her, she felt safe and protected. Over his shoulder, she gazed out at the sea with a growing sense of calm that everything was going to be okay.

On the surface in the distance, something seemed to appear from under the water. At first she thought it might be one of the seals that inhabited the Menai Strait. But then she got the overwhelming feeling that it was a person watching them from the sea. She could feel their gaze. And then, before she could focus her eyes properly, the shape had gone back under the water and disappeared.

CHAPTER 55

Four hours later, Laura and Gareth were in bed. They had made love, eaten breakfast and were now watching the movie *It's Complicated*. She was lying with her head on Gareth's chest, dressed in her huge white towelling robe. It was a perfect morning as far as Laura was concerned. She had made a concerted effort to put all her worries to one side and enjoy their day off.

'So, where shall we get married?' Gareth asked as he sipped his coffee.

'Bloody hell!' Laura snorted. 'We've only been engaged for a whole four hours, you loon.'

'Hey.' Gareth shrugged defensively. 'Just some ideas. I guess Vegas is out?'

'Yes.' Laura laughed. 'And if we have any conversations about the colour of table decorations then it's not happening.'

'Balloon drop?' Gareth suggested with a wry smile.

'How many people do you think are coming?' she asked with a mock look of surprise.

'I'm joking,' he reassured her. 'I'm guessing it would be me and you—'

'That is traditional,' she quipped, interrupting him.

'And the kids?'

'Yes. That sounds good to me. No stress and no fuss.'

'Somewhere local to here?' Gareth suggested.

'Tell you what,' she said with a mild sense of amusement. 'Why don't I grab my laptop and we can look for a place now.'

'Really?' he asked, with a raised eyebrow.

'Really.' She nodded. 'I get the feeling you won't settle until we do.'

Gareth shrugged. 'I can't help but be excited,' he admitted.

Laura got to her feet, adjusted her robe and smiled at him. 'I think it's cute.'

'Do you?'

'Needy, but cute,' she teased him.

He gave her a pained look. 'Uncalled for.'

Walking away, she padded down the stairs, into the living room and over to where her laptop sat open on a table.

As she touched it, the screen burst into life and she saw there was an email that had been sent to her at 4 a.m. She would have completely ignored it but for the sender's address – *GMPLanceurD'Alert@gmail.com*.

For some reason, she knew *lanceur d'alert* was French for *whistle-blower*.

Greater Manchester Police Whistle-blower? she thought with a growing sense of unease. *What the hell is that about?*

Opening the email, she saw there were two MPEGs attached.

Laura, I'm an investigative journalist. At this stage, I'm not going to give you my name or the newspaper that I work for. I have sent you two clips of CCTV that I want you to watch. I think it's important that you see them. You should know that this CCTV footage was requested as part of a murder investigation by Manchester Police's Major Incident Team. The footage was examined

299

but considered not to be of any use in terms of evidence to the murder investigation itself.

Once you've watched them, maybe you'd like to call me. My number is 07803 456388. Clearly this is highly sensitive but I can assure you that what I'm showing you has not yet come to the attention of anyone at the Greater Manchester Police outside of the MIT. I look forward to hearing your response.

Laura was frightened, but also intrigued. Her heart pounded as the thought occurred to her that the CCTV she was about to watch could have something to do with Sam's murder. Maybe it would give her and Pete a clue as to who was responsible.

Clicking the first file, she saw that the CCTV that played was marked: *National Trust Car Park – Worsaw Hill, Lancs 24th March 2022 06.23a.m.*

The screen was from a camera mounted high above a car park. On the far side, a black Audi A3 was parked. A man got out of the Audi and wandered over to where there was a wooden notice board and map. The man was wearing a baseball cap that covered his face. He wore walking gear – waterproof jacket, trousers and boots.

A minute later, a Range Rover pulled up and parked next to the Audi and a man got out. As soon as he walked away from the car, Laura recognised him

Superintendent Ian Butterfield.

Butterfield shook the man's hand. After a quick discussion, they made their way over to what looked like the beginning of one of the walks that started up Worsaw Hill. It appeared that they had met up to go for a day's walking.

Laura's mind was already whirring. She knew that Butterfield had never made it back. He had been murdered at that location on that day.

Clicking the second MPEG, she saw that the CCTV was from the same camera. *National Trust Car Park – Worsaw Hill, Lancs 24th March 2022 07.55a.m.* The footage was from ninety minutes after Butterfield had left the car park with the unknown figure. Both cars were still parked where they had been before.

On the left-hand side of the screen, the man with the baseball cap came back into view. He marched swiftly back towards the Audi. He went to the boot where he took off a pair of gloves and the baseball cap and tossed them inside.

He closed the boot and went round to the driver's door.

As he turned, she immediately recognised him.

Her stomach lurched as she tried to comprehend what and who she could see.

Detective Chief Inspector Peter Marsons.

AUTHOR NOTE

This book is very much a work of fiction. It's nothing more than a story that is the product of my imagination. It is set in Anglesey, a beautiful island off North Wales that is steeped in history and folklore spanning over two thousand years. It is therefore worth mentioning that I have made liberal use of artistic licence. Some names, places and even myths have been changed or adapted to enhance the pace and substance of the story. There are roads, pubs, garages and other amenities that don't necessarily exist on the real island of Anglesey.

It's important for me to convey how warm, friendly and helpful the inhabitants of Anglesey have always been on my numerous research visits. The island itself is stunning and I hope that my descriptions of its landscape and geography have done it some justice.

Acknowledgements

Thank you to everyone who has worked so hard to make this book happen. The incredible team at Avon who are an absolute dream to work with. Thorne Ryan and Helen Huthwaite for their patience, guidance and superb notes. The other lovely people at Avon – Elisha Lundin, Gabriella Drinkald and Maddy Dunne-Kirby, as well as Toby James in the art team, who produced such a fantastic cover; Sammy Luton in the sales team; and Emily Chan in production, without whom this book wouldn't exist.

To my superb agent, Millie Hoskins, at United Agents. Emma and Emma, my fantastic publicists at EDPR. Dave Gaughran and Nick Erick for their ongoing advice and working their magic behind the scenes.

Finally, my mum, Pam, and dad, Dave, for their over-whelming enthusiasm. And, of course, my stronger, better half, Nicola, whose initial reaction and notes on my work I trust implicitly.

If you loved *Blood on the Shore*,
why not go back to the beginning of
the Anglesey series?

Will there be blood in the water?

The first book in Simon McCleave's gripping,
atmospheric crime thriller series.

Available in all good bookshops now.

Some secrets should stay buried for ever. . .

The second book in Simon McCleave's pulse-pounding crime thriller series.

Available in all good bookshops now.

Your <u>FREE</u> book is waiting for you now!

Get your FREE copy of the prequel
to the DI Ruth Hunter Series NOW!

Visit:
http://www.simonmccleave.com/vip-email-club
and join Simon's VIP Email Club